P9-DMZ-218

P.S. I LIKE YOU

ALSO BY KASIE WEST

PIVOT POINT

SPLIT SECOND

THE DISTANCE BETWEEN US

ON THE FENCE

THE FILL-IN BOYFRIEND

BY YOUR SIDE

LUCKY IN LOVE

P.S. I LIKE YOU

KASIE WEST

Point

AGAIN AND FOREVER TO JARED

If you purchased this book without a cover, you should be aware that this book is stolen property. It was reported as "unsold and destroyed" to the publisher, and neither the author nor the publisher has received any payment for this "stripped book."

Copyright © 2016 by Kasie West

This book was originally published in hardcover by Point in 2016.

All rights reserved. Published by Point, an imprint of Scholastic Inc., *Publishers since 1920*. SCHOLASTIC, POINT, and associated logos are trademarks and/or registered trademarks of Scholastic Inc.

The publisher does not have any control over and does not assume any responsibility for author or third-party websites or their content.

No part of this publication may be reproduced, stored in a retrieval system, or transmitted in any form or by any means, electronic, mechanical, photocopying, recording, or otherwise, without written permission of the publisher. For information regarding permission, write to Scholastic Inc., Attention: Permissions Department, 557 Broadway, New York, NY 10012.

This book is a work of fiction. Names, characters, places, and incidents are either the product of the author's imagination or are used fictitiously, and any resemblance to actual persons, living or dead, business establishments, events, or locales is entirely coincidental.

ISBN 978-1-338-16068-0

10 9 8 7 6 5 4   18 19 20 21

Printed in the U.S.A.   40
First printing 2017

Book design by Yaffa Jaskoll

CHAPTER 1

A lightning strike. A shark attack. Winning the lottery.

No. I lined through all the words. Too cliché.

I tapped my pen against my lips.

Rare. What was rare? *Meat,* I thought with a small laugh. That would go really well in a song.

My pen drew a couple more lines, blackening the words to unrecognizable before I wrote a single word. *Love.* Now *that* was rare in my world. The romantic version, at least.

Lauren Jeffries, the girl sitting next to me, cleared her throat. It was then I noticed how quiet the classroom was, how I'd slipped into my own space again, shutting out the world around me. I had learned how to keep my head down over the years, how to handle the occasional unwanted attention. I slid my Chemistry textbook over my notebook full of everything but Chemistry notes, and slowly raised my head.

Mr. Ortega's eyes were on me.

"Welcome back to class, Lily."

Everyone laughed.

"You were writing down the answer, I'm sure," he said.

"For sure." It was all about acting unfazed, like I had no feelings.

Mr. Ortega let it go, just as I hoped he would, and moved on to explaining the lab for the following week and what we'd need to read to prepare for it. Since he'd let me off the hook so easily, I thought I'd be able to slip out unnoticed when class ended, but after the bell rang he called out to me.

"Ms. Abbott? Give me one minute of your time."

I tried to think of a good excuse to leave with the rest of class.

"You owe me at least one minute seeing as how the last fifty-five were definitely not spent on me."

The last student filed out of class and I took a few steps closer. "I'm sorry, Mr. Ortega," I said. "Chemistry and I don't get each other."

He sighed. "It's a two-way street and you haven't been doing your part."

"I know. I'll try."

"Yes, you will. If I see your notebook out again in class, it's mine."

I held back a groan. How would I make it through fifty-five minutes of torture every day without a distraction? "But I need to take notes. Chemistry notes." I couldn't remember the last time I took a single Chemistry note, let alone multiple ones.

"You can have one sheet of paper, unattached to a book, that you will show me at the end of each period."

I clutched my green-and-purple notebook to my chest. Inside it lived hundreds of ideas for songs and lyrics, half-finished verses, doodles and sketches. It was my lifeline. "This is cruel and unusual punishment."

He gave a small laugh. "It's my job to help you pass my class. You've left me no other choice."

I could've offered him a list of other choices.

"I think we've come to an agreement."

Agreement wasn't the word I would've chosen. That implied we both had a say in the matter. A better word would've been *law, ruling . . . edict.*

"Did you have something else to say?" Mr. Ortega asked.

"What? Oh. No, I'm good. See you tomorrow."

"Minus the notebook," he called after me.

I waited for the door to close behind me before I opened that notebook again and wrote down the word *edict* on the corner of a page. It was a good word. Not used enough. In the process of writing, my shoulder slammed into someone, nearly sending me flying.

"Watch it, Magnet," some senior guy I didn't even recognize said.

Two years later and people still couldn't let the nickname go. I didn't react, but imagined throwing the pen in my hand like a dart at his back as he walked past.

"You look ready to kill someone," my best friend, Isabel Gonzales, said, falling in step beside me.

"Why do people still remember that stupid little chant Cade made up?" I grumbled. A stray piece of my dark-auburn hair escaped its hair-tie prison and fell into my eyes. I tucked it behind one ear. "It barely even rhymed."

"A chant doesn't have to rhyme."

"I know. I wasn't debating his chant-writing skills. I was saying that kids shouldn't remember it. Still. After over two years, when there's nothing catchy about it."

"I'm sorry," Isabel said, linking her arm through mine.

"You don't have to apologize for him. He's not your boyfriend anymore. Anyway, I don't want you to feel sorry for me."

"Well, I do. It's stupid and childish. I think people say it out of habit now versus really thinking about what they're saying."

I wasn't sure I agreed with that, but decided to drop it. "Mr. Ortega banned my notebook from class."

Isabel laughed. "Uh-oh. How are you going to live without one of your limbs?"

"I don't know, and in Chemistry of all classes. How can anyone be expected to listen in there?"

"I like Chemistry."

"Let me rephrase that. How can any *normal* person be expected to listen in there?"

"Are you calling yourself normal?"

I bowed my head, conceding her the win.

We both stopped as we reached the fork in the sidewalk

just past the B building. The pinkish rock landscape that lined the pathway looked especially dusty today. I lifted my red-sneaker-clad foot and toed a few rocks off the sidewalk.

The landscape was good for water conservation, but up close, Arizona scenery did little to inspire me. I had to observe it from a distance to find notebook-worthy lines. The thought reminded me to look up. The beige buildings and crowds of students weren't much better than the rocks.

"So, fake Mexican food for lunch today?" I asked Isabel as Lauren, Sasha, and their group of friends walked around us.

Isabel bit her lip, her expression suddenly worried. "Gabriel wants to meet me off campus today for our two-month anniversary. Is that okay? I can tell him no."

"Right, your two-month anniversary. That's today? I left your gift at home."

Isabel rolled her eyes. "What did you get me? A homemade book about why guys should never be trusted?"

I put my hand on my chest and gasped. "That doesn't sound like something I'd do at all. And the title was *How You Know He's A Selfish Pig*. But whatever."

She laughed.

"But I'd never give you a book like that for Gabriel," I added, nudging Isabel. "I really like Gabriel. You know that, right?" Gabriel was sweet and treated Isabel well. It was her last boyfriend—Cade Jennings, king of stupid chants—who inspired imaginary books.

I realized Isabel was staring at me, still worried. "Of course you can go to lunch with Gabriel," I said. "Don't worry about me. Have fun."

"You could come with us if . . ."

I was tempted to make her finish that sentence. To accept her invitation just to be funny, but I put her out of her misery. "No. I don't want to go on your anniversary lunch. Please. I have a book to write . . . *Two-Month Anniversaries Are The Start Of Forever.* Chapter One: At sixty days, you'll know it's real if he whisks you away from the drudgery of high school and takes you to Taco Bell."

"We're not going to Taco Bell."

"Uh-oh. Only one chapter in and it's not looking good for you."

Isabel's dark eyes glinted. "Joke all you want, but I think it's romantic."

I grabbed her hand and squeezed. "I know. It's adorable."

"You'll be okay here?" She pointed across the commons. "Maybe you could hang out with Lauren and Sasha?"

I shrugged. The idea didn't thrill me. I sat next to Lauren in Chemistry and sometimes we'd talk. Like when she'd ask what the homework assignment was or for me to scoot my backpack off of her binder. And Sasha hadn't said even that much to me.

I looked down at my outfit. Today I was wearing an over-sized button-down that I had found at a thrift store. I'd cut the sleeves to make it more like a kimono and tied a brown vintage belt at the waist. On my feet were beat-up red high-top sneakers. My look was quirky, not trendy, and I would stand out in a group like Lauren's where they were all perfectly put together in their slim-fitting jeans and tank tops.

I held up my notebook and nodded at Isabel. "It's okay. This will be my chance to work on a new song. You know I don't get any alone time at home."

Isabel nodded. Then, out of the corner of my eye, I saw him. And I froze.

Lucas Dunham. He was in the middle of a group of other senior guys on a bench, his hoodie zipped up, his earbuds in, staring into space. Like he was present and not present. A feeling I could relate to.

Isabel followed my gaze and sighed. "You should talk to him, you know."

I laughed, feeling my cheeks warm up. "You remember what happened last time I tried that."

"You got nervous, that's what happened."

"I couldn't say anything. Nothing at all. He and his cool hair and his hipster clothes scared me," I finished in a whisper.

Isabel tilted her head while she looked at him as if disagreeing with my assessment of his appearance. "You just need practice. Let's start with someone you haven't been pining over for the last two years."

"I have *not* been pining over Lucas . . ."

I trailed off when she leveled me with her knowing stare. She was right. I had been pining. Lucas was probably the coolest guy I knew . . . Well, I didn't really know him, but that probably made him more cool. He was a year older than us. He wore his dark hair long and his clothes consisted of band tees or old-school polo shirts, a contrast that made me unable to put him in a category.

"Double with me and Gabriel next Friday!" Isabel announced suddenly. "I'll find you a date."

"Pass."

"Come on. It's been a while since you've been on a date."

"That's because I'm awkward and weird and it's not fun at all for me or the poor soul who agrees to go out with me."

"That's not true."

I crossed my arms.

"You just need to go out more than once . . . or twice . . . with someone so they see how fun you are," Isabel argued, adjusting her backpack straps. "You're not awkward with *me*."

"I'm totally awkward with you but you're not under pressure to eventually kiss me, so you put up with it."

Isabel laughed and shook her head. "That's not why I put up with it. I put up with it because I like you. We just have to find a guy who you can be yourself around."

I put my hand over my heart. "And on that hot fall day, Isabel started on the impossible quest of finding a suitor for her best friend. It would be a lifelong quest. One that would test both her determination and her faith. It would lead her to the brink of insanity, and—"

"Stop," Isabel interrupted, bumping my shoulder with hers. "It's that kind of attitude that will make this impossible."

"That's exactly what I've been trying to say."

"No, I'm not going to accept that. You'll see. The right guy for you is out there."

I sighed, my gaze drifting over to Lucas again. "Iz, seriously, I'm fine. No more setups."

"Fine, no more setups. But be open or you might miss something right in front of you."

I flung my arms out to the sides. "Is there anyone more open than me?"

Isabel gave me a skeptical look. She started to answer when a loud voice called out from across the grass. "There she is! Happy anniversary!"

Isabel's cheeks brightened and she turned toward Gabriel. He jogged the rest of the distance separating them, and lifted her into a hug. They looked gorgeous together—both dark-haired, dark-eyed, and olive-skinned. It was weird seeing Gabriel at our school. He went to the high school across town and I associated him with after-school and weekend events.

"Hey, Lily," he said to me as he put Isabel down. "Are you coming with us?" His invitation seemed sincere. He really was a nice guy.

"Yeah, is that cool? I heard you were paying and I said, *I'm in.*"

Isabel laughed.

"Great," Gabriel said.

"It was a joke, Gabe," Isabel said.

"Oh."

"Yes, I'm not a charity case." I was beginning to think they thought I was.

"No, of course not. I just feel bad for not letting you know earlier," Isabel said.

Gabriel nodded. "It was a surprise."

"You guys are going to run out of time to actually eat if you keep coddling me. Go. Have fun. And . . . uh . . . congratulations. I recently read a book about how two-month anniversaries are the start of forever."

"Really? Cool," Gabe said.

Isabel just rolled her eyes and smacked my arm. "Be good."

I stood on the path alone now, watching the groups of students around me talking and laughing. Isabel's worry was unfounded. I was fine alone. Sometimes I preferred it that way.

CHAPTER 2

I sat on the school steps with my notebook in my lap, drawing. I added a few flowers to the sketch of the skirt, then shaded in the tights with a green colored pencil. My earbuds were in, and I was listening to a song by Blackout. The lead singer, Lyssa Primm, was basically both my style and music idol—a genius songwriter who rocked cherry-red lips, vintage dresses, and her ever-present guitar.

"Stretch out your wilting petals and let the light in," the song played in my ears. I tapped one foot to the beat. I wanted to learn how to play this particular song on my guitar. Hopefully, I could practice later.

The sound of the minivan was loud enough to drown out the music, and I didn't need to look up to know my mom had just arrived. I closed my notebook, stuffed it into my backpack, took out my earbuds, and got to my feet. I could see the two heads of my brothers in the backseat. Mom must've picked them up from school first.

I opened the passenger door, an old One Direction song filling the air, only to find the seat taken by my mom's bead organizer.

"Can you hop in the back?" Mom asked. "I have to deliver a necklace to a client on our way home." She pushed a button and the side door slid open, revealing my two little brothers fighting over an action figure. A plastic cup rolled onto the ground. I looked around to see how embarrassed I should be. The parking lot wasn't too full anymore. A few kids were getting into their own cars or shouting to their friends. No one seemed to be paying attention to me.

"Sorry I'm late," Mom added.

"It's fine." I shut the front door, swiped the cup off the asphalt, and patted my brother on the back. "Scoot over, Thing Two."

I wiped some Cheez-It crumbs off the seat and sat down. "I thought Ashley was picking me up," I said to Mom.

My older sister, Ashley, was nineteen. She had her own car, a job, and went to college. But because she still lived at home (stealing my opportunity of having my own room) she had to contribute to family obligations. Like picking me up from school.

"She's working at the campus store late tonight," Mom reminded me. "Hey, are you complaining about your super hip mom picking you up?" She smiled at me in the rearview mirror.

I laughed. "Do super hip moms use the word *hip*?"

"*Fly? Bomb? Awesome?*" In the middle of her list she turned to my brother and said, "Wyatt, you're ten, let Jonah have it."

"But Jonah is seven! That's only three years younger. He shouldn't get everything."

Jonah elbowed me in the stomach in his attempt to steal the Iron Man figure.

"It's mine now," I said, causing an outraged cry from both my brothers as I took the action figure and flung it into the trunk.

My mom sighed. "I don't know how helpful that was."

"My intestines appreciate it very much."

My brothers both stopped mid-whine and giggled, the desired result of my declaration. I tousled their hair. "How was school, Things?"

My mom slammed on her brakes as a black BMW cut into her lane. I reached over to keep Jonah from hitting his head on the seat in front of him. I didn't have to look at the driver to know who it was. But I could see him anyway, his wavy dark hair styled to perfection. Cade had the boy-next-door looks—tall, big smile, puppy-dog brown eyes—without the personality to go with them.

"Someone didn't learn safe driving skills," my mom muttered as Cade drove away. I wished she had laid on her horn.

"He didn't learn a lot of skills." *Including the ability to make chants rhyme.*

"You know him?"

"That's Cade Jennings. People call him Jennings the Jerk though." Now *that* was catchy. Alliteration. Magnet . . . *Lily?* How did anyone remember that?

"They do?" my mom asked. "That's not very nice."

"They don't," I mumbled. But they should've. It had a nice ring to it.

"Cade . . ." My mom's eyes narrowed in thought.

"Isabel used to date him. Our freshman year." Until Cade and I fought so much that my best friend basically had to pick a side. She'd claimed the breakup wasn't my fault, but I knew it probably was. Half the time I felt guilty, the other half I figured I had saved her a lot of heartache.

"I thought that name sounded familiar," Mom said, making a right turn. "Did we ever have him over to the house?"

"No, we didn't." Thank goodness. Cade would have no doubt mocked me about our constantly cluttered house. With four kids, it was in a never-ending state of disaster.

Isabel had dragged me to Cade's house once, for his fourteenth birthday. When we'd knocked on the door and he'd answered, his face had shown how he felt about me tagging along.

"Great birthday surprise," he called in a sarcastic voice as he headed back into the house, Isabel and I following behind.

"Believe me, I didn't want to come either," I'd answered back.

Isabel had hurried to catch up with Cade. Meanwhile, I'd come to a standstill in the entryway. The inside of the house was massive and shockingly white. Even the furniture and decorations were white. Nothing would have stayed white for a second in my house.

I'd turned a slow circle, taking everything in, when Isabel poked her head around the corner and asked, "Are you coming?"

My brothers' voices brought me out of the memory and back into the car with my family. They were now fighting over a fun pack of M&Ms. "I found it under the seat. That means it's mine," Wyatt said.

I pulled out my notebook and got to work on sketching the skirt again. "Hey, Mom, can we get some black thread? I'm out."

Mom turned onto the main street. "Can it wait until the end of the week? Your dad is finishing up a job."

My dad was a freelance furniture designer. The amount of work he got could be unpredictable, and so was our family budget. Basically everything about my family was unpredictable.

"Yeah, of course," I said.

☆ ☆ ☆

Back home, I stepped over the pile of backpacks just inside the door and made my way to my room. "I'm borrowing the laptop," I called out to anyone who wanted to listen, and grabbed the computer off the hallway desk.

Nobody responded.

I walked into my room . . . Well, half of it was my room. The clean half. The half with fabric samples and color palates pinned to the walls. Not the half with magazine clippings of makeup ideas and cute celebrities. Although I had found myself appreciating that half every once in a while.

But with Ashley not here now, I was free to flop down on my bed and pull up YouTube. I searched for an instructional video for the Blackout song. It wasn't a well-known song so I wasn't sure I'd be able to find someone teaching the guitar part for it. I had to scroll through several pages, but finally I found one. I positioned the laptop on my dresser.

I kept my guitar stowed under my bed in a hard case. It wasn't a precaution. With two younger brothers, it was a necessity. I slid it out and opened the case. This guitar, my baby, took me six months to earn. I had given up every Friday night to watch the neighbors' two-year-old twin boys. They were more difficult than any kids I'd ever watched. And considering the nickname I had for my own brothers, that was saying a lot. But it was worth it. This guitar was everything I'd dreamed it would be. Its tone was perfect. And playing it made me feel like I wasn't as awkward as usual. It made me feel like there was something I was meant to do. This. It made everything else disappear.

Well, it made everything disappear for a little while. I was positioning my fingers for the first chord when the door to my . . . our . . . room slammed open.

"Lily!" Jonah said, running in and sliding to a halt in front of me. "Look! I have a loose tooth." He opened his mouth wide and pushed on his top right tooth with his tongue. It didn't move at all.

"Cool, buddy."

"Okay, bye!" He was out just as fast as he came in.

"Shut my door!" I yelled after him, but either he didn't hear or didn't want to. I sighed, got up, and shut it. Then I focused back on the video and my guitar.

Two minutes later, there was a knock and then my mom appeared. "Your turn to unload the dishwasher."

"Can I just finish this?" I ask, nodding down toward my guitar.

"I can't start dinner until the sink is empty and the sink can't be empty until the dishwasher is."

I considered fighting for five more minutes but then I glanced up at my mom. She looked even more tired than usual.

"Okay, I'll be right there." I closed my eyes and played one more strum, letting the notes vibrate through my arms. My whole body relaxed.

"Hurry up, Lily!" my mom called.

Ugh.

☆   ☆   ☆

The next morning before school, I stopped in the kitchen to grab some cereal. Mom had already dropped off Jonah and Wyatt, and was folding laundry in the den. Ashley was still getting ready (it took her hours) and my dad was at the kitchen table, reading a newspaper.

I took a box of cereal from the pantry and was pouring some into a bowl when I saw something on the counter that made me shake my head. Two necklaces lay on the beige granite, a piece of paper beneath each one. The necklace on the right had two checkmarks on the paper. The one on the left had two checkmarks.

"No," I said.

My dad peeked over the top of his newspaper. "Just vote. It's not a big deal."

"You say it's no big deal but then you make it a big deal. Whose friend did you rope into voting this time?" I asked, noting there were already four votes without mine.

"Voting is a privilege. There is no rope involved. It's all in good fun."

"Then they're both equally pretty. I vote for both of them."

"Nope. You have to choose."

"You and Mom are weirdos. There is no hope for any of us when you two do weird things like this." I poured myself some milk and sat down at the table. Dad's newspaper was still in front of him as though he were reading. He was just trying to lull me into a false sense of security. Pretend like the competition didn't matter.

"You know Mom is not going to leave you alone until you vote," he said.

"Sure. It's Mom that cares. Just tell me which one is yours and I'll vote for it."

"That would be cheating, Lil."

"Why did you start this tradition? Mom doesn't take over your job and try to outdo your fancy carved furniture."

Dad chuckled. "She'd win for sure."

I took a bite of cereal. To get his mind on a different track, I asked, "Why do we still get the newspaper? You know you can find these same stories on the Internet . . . yesterday?"

"I like to hold my words."

I laughed, then stopped when I saw something on the page he held in front of him that changed my mind about newspapers.

Suddenly, I loved newspapers.

Songwriting Competition. Earn five thousand dollars and a three-week intensive with a top professor at Herberger Institute for Music. Visit our website for more details! www.herbergerinstitute.edu

"You ready to go?" Ashley asked, coming into the kitchen. She was yawning, but, as usual, she was perfectly put together, in skinny jeans, a pink scoop-neck T-shirt, and platform shoes, with her hair in a ponytail and her makeup flawless. Although we looked alike—same long, auburn hair, hazel eyes, and freckles—our style was totally opposite. Ashley would have fit in well with Lauren and Sasha at school.

"What?" I blinked at my sister, confused. "I mean, yes. I mean, Dad, can I have that?"

Dad looked at his plate, which had a half-eaten bagel on it, shrugged, and pushed it my way.

"Gross. No, the newspaper."

"The paper? You want to read the paper?"

"Yes."

Ashley came over and snatched the bagel off his plate.

"Hey, that was for Lily."

"No, it wasn't," I said. "I want the paper, not the bagel."

He grunted. "Nope, it still didn't sound believable the second time I heard it either."

"Funny, Dad."

"You can have the paper if you go vote."

I rolled my eyes, pushed my chair away from the table, and went back to examine the necklaces. The one on the right had feathers. My mom was going through a feather phase. I was normally a fan of my mom's jewelry but the feather thing was a little too hippie for my tastes. Other people seemed to like it though. I lifted the one on the left. "This is your winner."

My dad pumped his fist. "She voted for mine, Emily!"

I held out my hand.

Dad gave me the newspaper, kissed my cheek, and went off to find my mom, I was sure.

"It's funny how they think we don't know whose is whose," Ashley said. "Like the score would be so close every time."

"I know. We should really make Mom win by a landslide every time and then maybe they'd stop the competition."

"It's good for Dad's self-esteem. Now let's get you to school, little one."

I clutched the newspaper to my chest, hugging the words, and followed after my sister. Now I just had to write the perfect song and win this competition.

CHAPTER 3

There was something about Chemistry that stimulated every thought in my mind to fire at once. Maybe it was the mixture of boring subject, monotone teacher, and cold seat. I wondered if there was a chemical equation for that. Those three factors, combined, created slush brain. No, that was the wrong term. My brain didn't become lazy. It became full. Hyperactive brain. A brain that made it impossible to concentrate on the sluggish words exiting Mr. Ortega's mouth. Were his words coming out slower than normal?

Today, amidst all the usual thoughts and words that I now couldn't write down in a notebook, I had the song I had learned to play on my guitar the day before looping through my mind. It was a torturous song—one I loved and hated. I loved it because it was brilliant, the kind that made me want to write a song equally as good. I hated it because it was brilliant, the kind that let me know I'd never write a song anywhere close to as good.

And I kept thinking about that contest.

How was I going to win? How would I even *enter* it?

My pencil hovered over my paper—the single Mr. Ortega–approved page. If I could write the song down, it would get out of my head and let me focus on the lecture. This paper would go in front of Mr. Ortega in exactly forty-five minutes. *Forty-five minutes?* This class was never-ending. What was he even talking about? Iron. Something about the properties of iron. I wrote the word *iron* down on the page.

Then, as if my pencil had a mind of its own, it moved over to the fake wood desktop and jotted down the words playing in my head:

Stretch out your wilting petals and let the light in.

I added a drawing of a little sun, its rays touching some of the words. Now, just forty-three minutes left of class.

☆ ☆ ☆

I was in the midst of writing in my notebook and walking down the hallway—something I hadn't quite mastered, despite how many times I had done it—when I heard the laughter.

I thought it was directed at me, so I looked up. It wasn't.

A blond kid—a freshman, maybe—stood in the middle of the hall, books gripped to his chest. Balanced precariously on top of his head was a baseball bat. Cade Jennings stood behind him, holding his hands out to his sides like he had just let go of that bat.

"Toss me the ball," Cade said to his friend Mike, who was standing across from him and the poor freshman.

Mike did just that and now Cade was trying to figure out how he was going to reach the top of that bat to place the ball. The kid looked too terrified to move.

"I need a chair. Someone find me a chair," Cade said, and people immediately scrambled to do his bidding. The bat began to wobble, then fell, bouncing across the tile floor and coming to a stop against the lockers.

"You moved, dude," Cade said to the freshman boy.

"Try it again," someone in the watching crowd called.

Cade smiled his big, perfectly white–toothed smile. The one he used a lot, knowing its power. I frowned. I seemed to be the only one immune.

As much as I didn't want to draw attention to myself, I knew I should probably help the cowering kid.

But I wasn't sure what I could do. Being the center of unwanted attention thanks to Cade Jennings was something I was very familiar with . . .

I thought back to freshman year P.E. I wasn't one of those girls who thought she was horrible at everything. But I did know my weaknesses, and P.E. was one of them. And co-ed basketball was the ultimate form of P.E., so I did my best to stay as far away from the ball as possible.

For reasons that I later realized were probably malicious, the ball was constantly thrown to me. By my team, by the opposing team. And I could never catch it. It was like being the only target in a game of dodgeball. I was hit in the shoulder, the back, the leg.

That's when Cade, who had been sitting on the bleachers, shouted for everyone to hear, "It's like she possesses a force of energy that sucks the ball straight into her. A black hole. A Magnet. Lily Abbott, the Magnet."

He'd said that last part in a movie announcer voice. Like he had transformed me into some sort of clumsy superhero. Then all through the gym, everyone copied him. Using that same voice, and laughing.

They'd laughed and laughed, and the laughter had stuck in my ears just as the nickname "Magnet" had apparently stuck in everyone's heads.

And now that kind of laughter was happening again, in the hall, and it was directed at Cade's latest victim.

I cleared my throat and said, "Oh look, a game to see who is more thick-headed—Cade or his bat." I nodded to the side, trying to tell the kid to leave now that I'd distracted Cade.

Cade's smile doubled in width as he took me in, from the top of my hair—its waves feeling crazier under his scrutiny than normal—to my Docs with mismatched shoelaces. "Oh look, it's the monitor of fun. Is there too much of it happening here, Lily?"

"I only see one person having fun."

He glanced around at the hall crammed full of students. "Then you're not looking hard enough." He lowered his voice. "I get it. It's hard to see anyone beyond me, right?"

If I showed how annoyed I was, he'd just be winning. "I'm just here to rescue another soul from your arrogance," I said through gritted teeth.

24

Although maybe I wasn't rescuing anyone at all. The kid hadn't moved. I'd given him a wide opening to leave and he still stood there. In fact, he opened his mouth and said, "What if you put the ball on the bat first and then put the bat on my head."

Cade patted him on the back. "Good call. Where'd the bat go?"

I sighed. There had been no need for an intervention. The kid liked abuse, apparently. I resumed my walk.

"Next time, come by earlier. We wouldn't want things to get out of hand," Cade called, to more laughter.

Anger surged up my chest and I whirled around. "Have you ever heard of alliteration? You should try it." It was a lame comeback. An inside argument that he wouldn't get, but it was the only thing that came out. The kids around him laughed harder. I turned and it took everything in me to walk away at a normal speed.

CHAPTER 4

"I'm going to enter a songwriting competition," I said.

Isabel's hand paused while reaching for her pajamas.

It was Friday night and we were at her house about to watch a scary movie. I had held in this announcement since I'd read about the contest the day before, turning it over in my mind. Now I'd said it out loud. That meant I'd have to follow through. I *would* follow through.

"You are?" Her voice held more than a little skepticism.

I threw myself back onto her queen-size bed and stared at the poster of Einstein pinned to her ceiling. I wondered, like I always did, how she could sleep with him staring down at her like that. I always had a hard time.

But I still loved sleeping over at Isabel's. She was an only child, so her house was like an oasis of calm for me. We would eat dinner with her parents—tonight it was delicious home-made tamales with rice and beans—and then we'd come upstairs to hang out in her giant room, with its own pullout sofa, TV, and tiny refrigerator for stashing Diet Cokes and ice cream.

"You don't think I can?" I asked her now, frowning.

"It's not that, Lil. I'm sure your songs are great," Isabel replied, pulling her pajamas out of her dresser drawer. "I'd be able to tell you for sure if you would actually *share* one with me—you know, your best friend in the whole world."

I groaned. "I know. I'm sorry. I don't have one finished yet."

"That's what you always say. How are you going to enter a contest when you won't even share a song with *me*?"

I covered my face with my hands. "I don't know."

She sat next to me on the bed. "I'm sorry. I know you can do it, Lil. You just need to believe in yourself."

"Thanks, Mom."

"Don't be a brat. I'm trying to help."

I took my hands off my face and looked at her. "I know."

"Tell me about the competition."

I propped myself up on my elbows. "It's through the Herberger Institute," I began.

Isabel gasped, her dark eyes widening. "Oh wow. That's really prestigious, Lil!"

I nodded and tugged on a split end of my hair, feeling nervous. "I know. Anyway, there's a five-thousand-dollar prize, which would be so amazing, of course. But even better, the winner gets a three-week course with one of the professors."

Isabel smiled. "That's huge. Knowing a professor could help with admissions, right?"

I nodded. I was trying not to think too much about this fact. Not only would winning the contest get me some money to help pay for college, something my parents couldn't afford to do, but it might help me *get* into the college music program that I'd been dreaming about for years.

"So share something with me. One song idea, at least?" Isabel pointed to my green-and-purple notebook that sat on top of my overnight bag on the floor.

I felt a wave of shyness and shrugged. "I have a couple ideas. I need to make them better. I *do* want to share, just not right now."

She rolled her eyes then stood up to change into her pajamas. "Chicken."

I threw one of my socks at her then collapsed back on her bed again, the ceiling poster taking over my view. She was right. I was a total chicken. "I think Einstein is judging me."

"He probably is. Maybe he read your notebook."

I laughed and went to get my own pajamas from my bag.

Isabel changed the subject so I didn't have to. "One movie tonight or two?" That was code for "how long should we stay up?"

I smiled. "Two. We have all night."

☆　☆　☆

My phone buzzed against my thigh and I sat up on Isabel's pull-out couch, disoriented for a moment. The television hummed blue in front of me. Pale morning light shone through the cracks of the blinds. My phone stopped buzzing, then ten seconds later began again.

"Hello?" I answered groggily.

"Lily." It was my dad. "Your brother's last soccer game is today. I know you said you wanted to go to one. Just wanted to give you the opportunity."

"What time is the game?"

"At eight. As in, thirty minutes from now."

I yawned. Isabel and I hadn't fallen asleep until after three a.m. But I tried to pull myself together. "Yes, I want to go."

"Okay, I'll pick you up on the way in twenty minutes."

"Thanks."

"Who was it?" Isabel moaned from her bed. She sat up, her normally perfectly spiraled black curls smashed flat against her head.

I tried to tame my own hair, which always became more crazy curls than soft waves in the mornings.

"My dad. Go back to sleep. I have to run."

"What? Why? What about pancakes?"

"Next time. Thing Two has a soccer game I forgot about."

"He always has a soccer game."

"I haven't been to one yet this year. I promised him I would."

Isabel plopped back down on her pillow, her eyes already closed. "Okay. See you Monday."

CHAPTER 5

It took me four minutes to see it on Monday. I had unloaded my book, pencil, and single sheet of paper. Mr. Ortega had begun his lecture. My eyes went to the lyric I had written on the desk Friday. That's when I saw a line beneath mine written in blocky handwriting.

For the night will soon bring back its shadows.

It was the next line of the song. *What?* I was confused. Someone else that went to this school had actually heard one of my favorite indie songs? Apparently I wasn't the only one bored in this class.

I smiled and then quickly wrote beneath the line:

Blackout rocks. I want to be Lyssa Primm when I grow up. I'm impressed you know them.

I wondered how often the janitors wiped down these desks. That message probably wouldn't even make it to its intended target. It didn't matter, though; just knowing someone else in this school had excellent taste in music made me happy. I wondered if I knew them. Morris High wasn't a small school. But only the juniors used the Chemistry room—which ruled out the person I would've thought of right away—Lucas. He seemed like he might've been just as into obscure bands as I was. But he was a senior. That was just wishful thinking anyway. The odds it was someone I knew were low.

Mr. Ortega. What if he had written this message? Mr. Ortega, a Blackout fan? The thought made me laugh. Out loud. My eyes shot to the front of the room, but my teacher was in the middle of a sentence so thankfully he didn't seem to notice my outburst.

Lauren, sitting next to me, had, as evidenced by the look on her face. I knew that look. It was basically the silent version of *why are you so weird?* I thought about telling her I had pictured Mr. Ortega dancing, but I didn't think that would help. Besides, I'd already learned my lesson about saying things out of context, so I just shrugged.

Then I glanced back at the writing on my desk.

The rest of class seemed to pass by a little faster than normal.

🏮 🏮 🏮

I caught up to Isabel in the hall.

"Why are you so smiley?" she asked.

"I always smile."

She laughed then stopped. "Okay, actually, you do smile a lot, just not usually at school."

"That's because high school is a crusher of souls."

"Not to be dramatic or anything," she said.

"Exactly." But she was right. I was feeling light now, and I could only think of one reason why. "You know that band I've told you about? Blackout?"

We stopped at her locker and she took out some books from her backpack and shoved them inside. "No. What do they sing?"

I quietly sang a few lines of one song and when recognition didn't light her face, I switched to another. "No?" I had played them for her several times. It surprised me she hadn't remembered.

"Sorry, but you do like weird music," Isabel said, closing her locker with a grin.

"I think you mean *awesome* music, but whatever."

"What about them?"

"Someone else knows who they are."

"Well, I would hope for the band's sake that you're not their only fan."

I smiled. "No, I mean someone here at school. We exchanged a couple lines of lyrics on the desk. It was cool."

"You wrote on the desk? Are you trying to get in trouble?"

I sighed. She did not understand the significance of this revelation.

A loud laugh sounded from the opposite end of the hall. I turned to look and saw Cade and his crew. Sasha, the only girl in the group, was holding on to his arm. They must've been dating now. Not that it would last long. Cade seemed to have a new girl hanging around every week these days. He was looking at his phone while Sasha was talking animatedly to him. It brought back memories of his birthday party again.

After Isabel had snapped me out of my awestruck daze over Cade's entryway that day, I had followed her into the kitchen, which was at least three times as big as mine. The island was lined with silver food warming-trays that people in white jackets and bowties were removing the lids from. Who had a fourteenth birthday party catered? Cade had leaned against a far counter and was scrolling through his phone like he couldn't be bothered with his own party. It was Isabel on his arm that he was easily ignoring that day. She'd whispered something to him after a moment and he shoved his phone in his pocket as though angry at having been interrupted. The expression didn't last long; a second later he'd put on his fake smile and said, "Eat while it's hot, everyone." I'd nodded to the trays and said, "Most people serve pizza and cake." He'd looked at me with that smug arrogance of his and said, "I'm not like most people."

I'd said something rude back. Something like, "Thank goodness."

"Can't you just ignore him? Be nice?" Isabel had pleaded.

That day I couldn't ignore him, not after how he'd been treating Isabel. Today, I was going to prove to Isabel that I could. As we headed his way, toward the only way out of the building, I would not respond to whatever abuse he threw my way. But he just gave Isabel a dazzling and confident Cade smile, not acknowledging me at all. She returned it. I realized

I was glaring, so I smoothed out my features and kept my mouth shut. It was harder than I had imagined.

"Impressive," Isabel said when we had made it outside.

"What? I just did what I always do."

She laughed. "But you did notice that he was civil too, right? See what happens when you are nice?"

"Yes . . ." *Wait, what?* Was she implying that I always started arguments with Cade? He started it most of the time. I sighed. I sounded like my seven-year-old brother. Maybe she was right. If I were the bigger person, he'd at least leave me alone. I liked this thought—Cade leaving me alone. Us leaving each other alone. It would make school much more pleasant.

CHAPTER 6

My sister, Ashley, was waiting in a No Parking zone when I climbed in her car.

"Hey."

"Hi," she said. "How was school?"

"Same." For a second, I thought about mentioning the desk-writing, but decided against it. If Isabel didn't get the significance, there was no way Ashley would.

She waited for a group of girls to cross in front of us and then eased forward. "When I went to high school—"

"Last year," I interrupted.

"Yes. I had to take the bus home or have mom pick me up in the minivan."

"Mom picked me up in the minivan last week."

"Well, that was every day for me. Every day, Lily. And I still managed to have lots of friends. You're lucky I bought a car. A nice car that isn't embarrassing." This was a speech she gave often on the ride home. I'd worn out all my sincere responses already.

"Yes, I'm so lucky. Thank you, Ashley. However can I pay you back?" I leaned my head against the side window, wondering if she'd notice if I took a nap.

"Maybe I should work at the campus store more so that you have to experience the true torture of Mom every day." Ashley sighed and checked the rearview mirror. "She once honked for ten seconds straight when I didn't see her. And one time she made me take Jonah to the bathroom and he was screaming the whole time that he was going to pee his pants."

I laughed.

"You think it's funny because it wasn't you."

"I think it's funny because I have my own stories, Ashley. You're not the only one in this car who has three siblings and a weird mom."

"In this nice, almost-new car."

"Yes, it's the height of class and sophistication. So beautiful. What do they call this color? Cobalt blue or Arabian nights?"

"No gratitude whatsoever."

I smiled and Ashley turned on the radio. We did not have the same taste in music at all. When she saw me cringe, she rolled down the window and turned up the volume, wearing a smile of her own.

✿ ✿ ✿

"What is that?" Ashley asked as we walked into the kitchen and she set her car keys in a dish on the counter. I was behind her so I couldn't see what she was referring to. As I stepped to the side to look, a white furry thing streaked past my foot with my brother, Wyatt, chasing after it. Ashley screamed.

I dropped my backpack and jumped onto the counter, now sitting with my back to the cupboards, warily watching the floor.

Mom chuckled. "It's a meat rabbit." She looked up from where she sat at the table stringing a bead onto a piece of wire for what looked like an earring.

"A meat rabbit?" Ashley asked. "As in, we're going to *eat* it?"

"No, of course not. I saved it from that fate. The boys need to learn responsibility so I got them a pet."

I slid off the counter. "And a nice, normal dog wasn't in the running?"

The rabbit bounced its way into the kitchen again and Wyatt scooped it up, beaming. Jonah appeared at Wyatt's side and began petting the rabbit.

"It lives outside though, right?" I asked.

"Yes," my mom said, using her pliers to bend a section of wire. "It's just getting some exercise."

"Right." I picked up my backpack and grabbed an apple from the bowl on the counter.

Ashley, still standing where we came in, said, "That thing is gross. It has pink eyes."

"It's cute," Wyatt argued.

My bedroom door was halfway open when I got there. Not a good sign. I toed it open the rest of the way and looked around. Ashley's side, as usual, had a few jeans strewn across the floor, but other than that it looked the same. I kicked off my red sneakers and placed them in the closet. Just as I took a bite of apple and headed for my guitar, I stepped on something slightly wet. I picked up my foot and what at first looked like a pile of raisins, I soon realized was rabbit poop.

"Gross."

"What? Who's dying?" my mom asked when I got to the kitchen, a slightly mad look on my face.

"A rabbit, if I have any say in it. That thing pooped in my room. What was it doing in my room? Can you please keep the boys out of there?"

"Yes, sorry." She stood and went to what I hoped was either clean up the poop or tell Wyatt to do it.

I heard a noise on the back patio and opened the door. The rabbit was there in a black metal cage. It was big, not some fluffy little ball of fur, but a big, ugly rabbit. It stood on its hind legs and sniffed the air.

"Yes, you smell that," I told the rabbit. "That's the smell of your enemy. Get a good whiff. We are not friends." It could probably smell the apple I still held, not me. I bit off a piece and threw it into the cage, sending it a very mixed message considering the speech I'd given. "Just keeping you on your toes."

"Who are you talking to?" Ashley asked.

I shut the door and turned to face her. "Nobody."

"You might want to work on that." She headed past me and toward our bedroom. So much for my practice time today.

CHAPTER 7

Another message awaited me in Chemistry the next day. Beneath my—*Blackout rocks. I want to be Lyssa Primm when I grow up. I'm impressed you know them*—were the words:

Sorry, I already called dibs on being her. There was a crooked smiley face, and then: *Have you listened to The Crooked Brookes? The. Best.*

I'd never heard of The Crooked Brookes before. I assumed it was a band name or a song title. Our similar taste in music was over.

But my pen pal had left the first clue—she was a girl. It didn't help me narrow down her identity any more. If anything, it left me feeling even more clueless.

While Mr. Ortega's back was turned, I wrote, *No, I'll have to check them out.* My response took up the last bit of open space on the right side of the desk. The only side I could write on without it being obvious. It looked as though my distraction for Chemistry was done until the next cleaning day.

A hole in the cuff of my shirt drew my attention. The stitching had come undone. The perils of a thrift store find. I hadn't seen that before. I'd have to fix it later. I rolled the sleeve twice to hide the hole and then did the same to the other side.

From next to me, Lauren whispered, "You really shouldn't write on the desk like that." She was reading through the exchange. I wanted to cover it up so she couldn't, but that seemed silly. Anyone who wanted to could come in and read it.

"It's just pencil. It comes off." To prove my point, I erased the first letter of my very first message. "See."

That seemed to satisfy her and she went back to taking her own notes. I tried to take my own notes too but that missing *S* I'd just erased was distracting me. I filled it back in then listened very hard to what Mr. Ortega was saying.

✼ ✼ ✼

I hated newspapers. Newspapers that told me about contests. No, I hated contests. I had nothing. Less than nothing. I had no songs in this notebook I carried around all day writing song lyrics in. Sure, I had a few really good lines here or there, lots of words, and lots of ideas for songs. Well, *ideas* was a generous word. What had I even meant when I wrote *A song about monsters in trees would be awesome*? Monsters in trees? Had I really thought something in this book was worthy of a song competition?

"Why are you groaning?" Ashley asked from the driver's seat as she drove me to school. I had spent all night looking through my notebook. Sleeping hadn't made any more lyrics magically appear.

I looked up. She had just pulled to a stop at the front of the school parking lot. "I wasn't trying to groan."

"You seem to do a lot of things you aren't trying to do. Maybe you should try not to do things like that. You'd have more friends."

"Thanks, Ashley. Good tip."

I reached for the door handle just as a group of people walked in front of Ashley's car, Cade among them. He slid across the hood, landed on his feet on the other side, and then winked at her.

Ashley opened her mouth in disgust. "Who is *that* arrogant jerk?"

"Nobody."

She honked her horn three times.

"Ashley, stop."

She rolled down her window.

"Hey!" she shouted at Cade. "That was totally rude, what you just did."

I jumped out. "See you later."

I walked away to the steady stream of my sister's rant. I tried not to smile, but it was fun to hear someone tell Cade off for once. Nobody seemed to have the guts to do it at this school. He had turned as if actually listening to her, wearing his own smug smile. I picked up my pace so he wouldn't see me.

A minute later I heard a voice from behind me. "It runs in the family, I see." Had he jogged to catch up to me just so he could say that?

"Our feelings toward you?" I said, forgetting that I was supposed to be ignoring him. "Yes, must be genetic."

"I hear there are meds you can take for that."

I tilted my head. "Really? Do you sell these anti-Cade-annoyance pills? Is that how your friends manage it?"

"No, I was referring to your issues, but . . ."

I raised my eyebrows. "Yes, I won that round."

"So what's the score, you three, me two hundred?"

"You're keeping score?"

"Always." At that, he left my side, joining up with a group of friends.

Not worth it, I repeated over and over again in my head until he was safely out of sight. My jaw hurt and I realized I was clenching my teeth. I let a deep breath out and tried to relax. It helped when I saw Lucas walking alone twenty feet in front of me. I could practically feel all the tension leave my body as I watched his relaxed gait.

Ahead of Lucas, Isabel waved at me from across the rocks. She bounded over, her dark curls bouncing. By the time she was walking beside me, I'd forgotten all about Cade. And since I was still pretending he didn't exist, I was not going to tell her what had just happened. I was proud of myself for holding my tongue.

"Hey," she said, linking her arm through mine. Her plastic bracelets clinked together.

"Hey," I responded.

"I'm surprised he didn't feel you burning a hole in the back of his head."

"What? Who?"

"Funny. Like you don't know who you were just staring at."

My cheeks went hot and my gaze went back to Lucas, who was now almost to the lockers across the commons.

I was about to avoid the subject by asking Isabel if she finished the History assignment. But then four sophomore girls met up in front of us with a loud squeal. They all exchanged the lidded Starbucks cups they were holding. I was confused until Isabel whispered, "They each buy a drink in the morning and then they switch."

"Why?"

"Why not? It's fun." We walked around them. "We need a morning routine."

I gestured back toward the girls. "That morning routine?"

"Not that one. But something we do or say every morning when we see each other to start the day right."

"Um . . ."

"A handshake?"

I raised my eyebrows at her. " 'Hey' has been working pretty well for us for the last three years."

"But they're so cute," Isabel said, nodding toward the giggling girls.

"We're not cute enough for you?"

"No. We're not." She smiled.

"Just last night, before falling asleep, I thought to myself, *I wish Isabel and I had a morning tradition*. It would make our friendship so much cuter."

"And last night before I fell asleep, I was wondering how you got so lucky to have a best friend like me when you're such a brat."

"*So* lucky."

Isabel's eyes widened. "That's it! That's our tradition."

"To talk about how awesome you are and how lucky I am every morning?"

She shook her head. "No . . . Well, we can do that too. But how about the first thing we say to each other every morning is the last thing we thought of before we went to sleep the previous night?"

"That won't work. You'll just say 'Gabriel' every morning. You'll say it so much that soon I'll start to wonder if my name is Gabriel."

"That's not true." She stuck out her lower lip. "Fine, I guess we don't need a tradition. But, speaking of Gabriel, he wants to go out with us this weekend. You'll come, right?"

I tugged on the straps of my backpack. "I thought we already decided no setups."

"No, it wouldn't be a setup. It will be a group of us. Some of his friends and us."

I frowned, suspicious. "What will we be doing?"

"Go-karts."

The indoor track wasn't cheap. I calculated how much money I had saved in the jar in my closet. After I bought the guitar, the twins' mom hired a full-time nanny, so I was out of my regular source of income. Occasionally, I worked for my mom at craft fairs, but it had been a while. I couldn't remember if I'd spent all my money the last time we went to the movies with Gabriel and his friends.

"Okay, sure. I'll talk to my mom about it. Sounds fun."

"It sounds *awesome*." The bell rang. "See you at lunch. If you don't die in Chemistry, that is."

"Every day poses that risk."

"I believe in you."

She was ten steps away when I called out. "Iz!"

She turned. "Yeah?"

"We don't need any cutesy traditions. We're solid you and me."

CHAPTER 8

I wasn't going to die from boredom this time. It was going to be from shock.

In Chemistry, there was a hand drawn arrow underneath my final message from the day before. It pointed down, to the end of the desk. As if something was under there. My eyes went wide. *Was* there something under the desk? I looked on the floor but my high-topped red sneakers were the only things there.

What if . . .

While keeping an eye on Mr. Ortega, I ran my hand along the bottom of the desk, disgusted when it met a lump of what I assumed was chewed up-gum. Gross.

Still, I let my pencil roll off my desk and land on the ground. I used my sneaker to slide the pencil back toward me then ducked down to retrieve it. While leaning down, I craned my neck around. Sure enough, wedged under the strip of metal that ran between the desk legs was a piece of paper folded into fourths. I quickly grabbed my pencil and the paper then sat back up, the blood rushing back down my face.

As quietly as possible, I unfolded the paper and smoothed it flat. It was as if this was the most normal thing in the world, like this person and I exchanged notes all the time.

So, did you listen to The Crooked Brookes? What did you think? Maybe it was too dark for you. It is kind of a depressing band. But I thought if you liked Blackout you might like them. Sometimes listening to depressing songs makes me feel like my life isn't so bad. Reverse psychology or something. Ha. Well, hopefully this note distracted you for at least one minute. Writing back will take another couple. Then you'll only have . . . an eternity to sit through. Sorry.

I laughed quietly. So my pen pal liked Blackout and hated Chemistry. We were kindred spirits. I turned the paper over, trying to decide what to write back. This would be my third message to her, I realized.

I'd started a cute tradition with a total stranger completely unknowingly. It felt a little like cheating. No, this wasn't cheating. I'd already told Isabel about it. And this wasn't even a real friendship. It was a distraction. Besides, Isabel had other friends. I could have an anonymous pen pal. Anonymous friends were perfect for me.

I haven't had a chance to listen to The Crooked Brookes. Life at home is a bit . . . chaotic. I will the first chance

I get. I'm all for music that makes my life seem better.
And you're right, Blackout is depressing, but they're not
only depressing. Track 8 on their Blue *album, for*
example. I've never felt more alive than when listening
to that song. It makes me feel like I'm flying. Soaring
above my life and looking down on it. Being above it for
a while makes it easier to live when I'm back in the
middle of it, if that makes any sense at all. Anyway, I
better get back to the mind-numbing boredom.

For a moment I couldn't believe I had written that to a total
stranger. I even considered not folding the paper back up
and putting it under the desk. But two things made me do it.
One: When talking about music, I always found myself opening
up more than I might have otherwise. People who appreciated
music like I did seemed to understand that. I sensed my pen
pal would. Two, anonymity was freeing. I could say a lot when
I didn't have to sign my name at the end. And I didn't.

I stuffed the note back into place under the desk and got
to work on a few Chemistry notes that I was still required
to show Mr. Ortega at the end of each period.

I must've still felt a little guilty about the letter exchange
because at lunch, I blurted out to Isabel, "She wrote me a letter."

Isabel, known for her drastic subject changes, didn't follow
mine. "What?"

We were walking back from the food trucks with our
burritos and sodas. Isabel loved getting "fake Mexican food,"

as she called it, even though her dad made the best real Mexican food on earth. Maybe it was her form of teenage rebellion.

"Remember I told you about writing back and forth with that girl in Chemistry?" I began as we started toward the outdoor student commons. "The one who likes the same band as me?"

"Yes," Isabel said. "I thought it was a guy."

"No. She wrote something about wanting to be Lyssa Primm when she grows up."

"Who's Lyssa Primm?"

"The lead singer of Blackout."

"Aw, how cute, you found a new weird pen pal. The two of you are like the same person." She hip checked me.

"Two of me? Our school couldn't handle that."

"So true."

"But anyway, she left me a longer letter under the desk this time and I wrote back."

Isabel let out a hum. "Who do you think she is?"

"I don't know."

"Aren't you curious? Maybe it's someone you already know. It's obviously someone you'd get along with." She scanned the commons. Students were clustered in groups, divided by grade, eating and laughing and throwing balled-up napkins at each other. I spotted Lucas sitting with his friends, and tried not to stare. Especially since I got caught by Isabel last time. "We should find out."

"No." I knew it was silly to feel insecure about what others thought of me, but I couldn't help it. I was worried if this girl found out who I was, she wouldn't find me cool enough for her. Besides that, I'd already decided that anonymity made writing so much easier. And this letter exchange was my sanity in Chemistry. "It's just a fun distraction. I really don't want to know."

Isabel shrugged. "Okay. Fine. If it were me, my curiosity wouldn't be able to leave it alone."

And I wondered if her curiosity would be able to leave it alone even though it *wasn't* her. I gave her my best "we are not pursuing this" look and let it go.

"No anniversary lunches today, right?" I asked.

She smiled. "Yes, it's our two-month-and-five-day anniversary. You understand, right?"

We settled into our spot under a tree. I hadn't picked this spot because it had the best view of Lucas—that was just a happy coincidence. My eyes scanned the commons again. Maybe my letter writer *was* someone I already knew. But who?

CHAPTER 9

I scribbled in my notebook as The Crooked Brookes blasted through my headphones. I couldn't wait to write to my Chemistry friend the next day and tell her how awesome this music was. The song was raw and unapologetic and oh-so-depressing. But for whatever reason, it had inspired me. A song about secrets was twisting its way through my head and out of my pen.

If I tell you my secrets, will you just tell me lies?
If I say I believe you, does that make it all right?
It's hard to place my trust in someone new,
But that doesn't mean

A tapping on my back interrupted my thought. I looked over to see my brother, Jonah, standing by my bed.

I clicked off the music. "Hey, Thing Two, what's up?"

"Will you read me a story?" He was already holding the book.

"You can read."

"I like it when you read."

My notebook was begging me to continue, pleading with me as it sat there on my pillow.

"Sure, buddy," I said. "Come on up." I shut my notebook and Jonah climbed onto my bed with a smile.

He handed me the first Harry Potter. "And do the voices, too."

"So demanding."

I had been reading for twenty minutes when Jonah's attention wavered. His finger tapped the perfectly cut-out newspaper article about the songwriting competition I had pinned to my wall. "What's that?"

"That's just me dreaming . . . like always."

"Dreaming is fun," Jonah said. "I dreamed about dinosaurs last night. What did you dream about?"

My eyes darted to the notebook I had abandoned on my pillow, then back to my brother. "I dreamed about a little prince named Jonah who had three older siblings who always gave him whatever he wanted because he was the most spoiled prince in all the land."

Jonah stuck out his lower lip. "I am not."

"I wasn't talking about you. I was talking about Prince Jonah, from my dream. Do you think everyone is talking about you all the time?"

"Yes."

I tickled him. "Good night, Prince Jonah."

"I thought I was Thing Two."

"Only when you make messes." I gently pushed him off my bed with my feet. "Speaking of messes, how is that rabbit of yours?"

"Mom won't let him sleep in my bed."

"Mom makes good decisions sometimes. Have you given him a name?"

"Bugs Rabbit."

"You mean Bugs Bunny?"

He scrunched his lips together. "We call him Bugs Rabbit."

"Really? But then how are you going to remember it?"

"It's easy. His name is Bugs and he's a rabbit."

"Does nobody in the world use alliteration anymore?"

"What?"

"Nothing."

"Will you take us trick-or-treating Friday?"

"That's right, Friday is Halloween."

Jonah put his little fists on his hips. "Did you forget?"

"No, but I'm too old for trick-or-treating . . . so Halloween isn't such a big deal anymore."

"I'm never going to get too old for trick-or-treating."

I ruffled his hair. "Yes, of course I can take you . . . in exchange for a piece of candy."

Jonah gave a yelp of joy as he ran out of my room.

"One of the good ones!" I called after him.

I opened my notebook back up to the lyrics I'd been writing, but it was too late. The inspiration was gone. If I tried to write a song right now, it'd be about rabbits, dinosaurs, and Halloween candy. Almost as good as monsters in trees. I'd have to try again later.

✿ ✿ ✿

"Monsters in trees," I said to Isabel the next morning when I saw her by our lockers.

"What?"

"That's what I thought about before going to bed last night. Are we doing this or not?"

She clapped her hands, then bit her lip in thought.

I laughed. "Gabriel, right?"

"Shhh. There was something after that. I'm trying to remember. Oh! Nutella crepes."

"Now I'm hungry."

"And I'm confused," Isabel said, shutting her locker. "Monsters in trees?"

"Fake song idea. But I actually started a real song, one I'll read to you when I'm done."

"I'd like that."

"This is going to be a fun tradition."

She laughed. "It is. I feel our friendship getting cuter already."

✿ ✿ ✿

I may have started the morning tradition with Isabel because I felt guilty about how excited I was to read this letter.

The letter that I had retrieved from beneath my desk in Chemistry and was now unfolded on top of my desk.

> *Track 8 on Blackout's* Blue *album? I haven't listened to that one yet. I only have their first album. And even though it goes against my reverse psychology theory of how I handle life, if you think it's good, I'll try it out. Any other bands I should add to my "shutting out the world" playlist? I could use some of that to deal with my life right now. Does that make me sound pathetic? I'm not, most of the time. I'm actually a pretty fun guy when not at home.*

Guy? I blinked. My pen pal was a *he?* My eyes went back to the notes written on the desk—to the line that had made me think he was a girl. It was still there. His claim that he had dibs on wanting to be Lyssa when he grew up. So it had been a joke? He liked to joke.

He was a guy. A guy who liked the same music as me and was bored in Chemistry and had a sense of humor. We were soul mates. I smiled a little, then shook my head. The guy was bored and was writing me letters to pass time. He wasn't asking me out or anything.

I realized my brain had stopped mid-letter. I read the rest.

> *So what should we chat about that's not so depressing? I'm open to suggestions. Perhaps one of the following*

topics: Death, cancer, global warming (or is it climate
change now?), animal cruelty . . .

I turned over the page, but that was the end. We'd filled up an entire page with our back and forth communication. Which meant I got to keep this page. I folded it nicely and stuck it in my bag.

I stared at the new, clean sheet in front of me, and then wrote:

How about we discuss the fact that you're a guy. Let's
get married and have cute Indie Rock babies.

I bit the inside of my cheek to keep from laughing and dropped that sheet of paper in my backpack by my feet. I wasn't even going to mention the fact that he was a he. I was going to pretend I knew all along. Because it changed nothing.

I finally got a chance in the chaos that is my house to
listen to The Crooked Brookes. Brilliant. Track 4.
I must've listened to that one five times in a row. I wasn't
sure I could trust your taste in music before, but you
have now proven yourself. I will listen to anything you
suggest. I'll include a list of my favorites at the bottom
of this page. Do you play any instruments? I'm a
self-taught not-very-good-but-thinks-she-is guitarist.
Okay, you've convinced me, we can start a band

together. Unless you play the guitar, too. Sorry, but I
won't fight you for solo time.

I re-read what I wrote three times. It was me, but I wasn't
sure I *should* be me. I didn't have the best track record with
guys. But at least on paper he could read it in a smooth, confident voice, not in the way I would've delivered it in person:
awkwardly.

It didn't matter. Why was I suddenly worried about how
he would perceive me? I wished I hadn't found out he was a
guy. This had been fun until I learned that piece of information. I had actually been looking forward to Chemistry for the
last week. Something that had never happened before. And I
would continue to look forward to it. We still had anonymity
on our side.

CHAPTER 10

I opened another drawer of my dresser and flung several shirts onto my bed.

Where is it? I wondered in frustration.

I was the organized one in this room. I didn't misplace my favorite shirt. Especially when I saved it specifically for nights like tonight—nights where I'd be hanging out with Isabel, her boyfriend, and a bunch of his friends I didn't know.

I pulled the dirty laundry basket out of my closet and dumped it on the floor, then sifted through the pile of clothes. When I came up empty, I let out a growl. That's when I spotted my sister's laundry basket on the other side of the closet. I stormed over to it and after shifting a few clothes, found my favorite green shirt. I held it up. It was wrinkled and had a big dark stain on the right side.

"Ashley!" Anger made my eyes hot. I tore out of the room, taking my shirt and my anger with me.

Ashley was sitting on the couch eating a bowl of ice cream. Her eyes went wide when she saw me. "What?"

"This!" I held the shirt for her to see.

"I was going to wash it."

"Why were you wearing it? You didn't even ask. It probably doesn't even fit you right, anyway." Ashley was much taller than me.

She made a face. "You weren't home to ask."

"Ashley. Seriously."

"Fine. Chill. I'll ask next time."

At this point, Mom walked in. "What's going on, girls?"

"Nothing." I started to walk away. There was nothing I could do about the shirt now. I was meeting Isabel in an hour. I'd have to find something else to wear.

"Where are you going?" Mom asked.

She must've noted my hair, which I had managed to tame into relative smoothness tonight. "To finish getting ready," I said.

"Ready for what?"

Just then, Jonah came bouncing over, wearing a blue-and-red dinosaur costume. "Let's go, let's go, let's go!" he yelled louder than necessary.

My mom put her hand on his shoulder and he stopped bouncing. She continued to look at me, waiting for an answer.

"I'm going out with Isabel," I said.

"You didn't tell me that," Mom said.

I panicked, my mind rewinding through the week to try to pick out the conversation I could've sworn I had with my mom so I could reference it now. It didn't exist.

"You said you'd take us trick-or-treating," Jonah whined.

"Ashley can take you," I said.

My sister shook her head. "Nope. I'm going to a Halloween party tonight."

"Can't Mom take you?" I asked Jonah, desperate now because I knew how he got when he had his mind set on something.

Mom gave me her disappointed look but to Jonah said, "Yes, I'll take you."

The dinosaur head tipped forward as he looked at the ground in a pout. It was a really pathetic sight. As I clung to my stained shirt, I knew neither it nor I would be going out tonight. I sighed. Oh well. It was going to be a group date that I would have to spend my last twenty bucks on, anyway. Might as well save the money for something I really wanted to do.

"I'll take you, Jonah."

Jonah cheered.

"Thank you, Lily," Mom said, giving me a quick hug. "Tomorrow night is all yours."

"Sounds good."

I shuffled back to my room and called Isabel.

She answered on the second ring. "You better not be canceling on me."

"I'm sorry. I promised Jonah I'd take him trick-or-treating."

"What do you mean? We've been planning this all week. Why can't Ashley take him?"

"She's going to a party." I took my shirt to the bathroom where I treated the stain with an old toothbrush and soap.

"Lily," Isabel whined, sounding an awful lot like Jonah. "You promised."

I turned off the sink. "I know, but unfortunately my family has reigning power over my life."

"Didn't you ask your mom about tonight earlier?"

"I thought I had, but I guess I didn't."

She sighed. "Fine. I'll talk to you later." She hung up before waiting for me to say good-bye. I felt bad, but she had Gabriel. She'd be fine without me.

I glanced at my hair in the mirror. My waves were softer, straighter, tonight. When I put in the effort with a blow-dryer and a little bit of product, I could accomplish this look. I rarely did.

"How come you can't look this good when I actually end up going out?"

"Stop talking to yourself," Ashley sang out as she walked by the bathroom.

"I was on the phone," I called after her. Then I gathered my hair into a ponytail and left to grab my hoodie.

CHAPTER 11

When Isabel said she'd talk to me later, I hadn't thought she meant *that* night, on my porch, with two guys flanking her.

After taking my brothers trick-or-treating, I had changed into a pair of flannel pajama pants and a tee. I sat on the sofa with a large bowl of candy in my lap, in case any trick-or-treaters stopped by.

But when I answered the doorbell, I didn't find costumed kids out there.

I clutched the candy bowl as I stared at Isabel, my mouth doing the fish thing it sometimes did when words wouldn't come out.

"Hey," Isabel said, ignoring my expression. She adjusted the pair of cat ears on her head. "Trick-or-Treat. Can we come in?"

"I . . ."

She plucked a roll of Smarties out of the bowl I held and pushed past me, dragging Gabriel by one arm and the other guy, whose floppy hair and lanky frame looked vaguely familiar, by the other.

"Sure, come in," I said lamely, setting the candy bowl on the entry table.

They all slipped off their shoes at the edge of the tiled entryway.

"Oh, you don't have to take your shoes off. Our carpet is a mess anyway." I shut the door. They left their shoes off. "Okay. Let me just . . . um . . . put some jeans on."

My brothers, who had heard the doorbell, came running out of the TV room, holding the bowl of popcorn I had made them. It was leaving a white trail behind them as it spilled over the sides.

"Go watch your movie, Things. I'll be right back." I rushed into the bathroom where I ran my fingers through my now crazy waves, in hopes of flattening them, and applied some gloss. Then I headed into my room where I threw on a pair of jeans and the first decent top I could get my hands on—it was pale mustard with little birds on it.

By the time I got back in the living room, Isabel and the guys were sitting on the couch next to several piles of folded clothes, and my brothers had somehow managed to get the rabbit out of its cage and let it loose on the floor. It was hopping around, sniffing at the trail of popcorn.

"When did you get a rabbit?" Isabel asked me.

I had questions for her, too. Like, what was she doing here? Why didn't she give me any warning? "Um . . . last week. I think." I stacked the clothes and plopped them into the laundry basket on the floor.

"Hi, I'm Lily," I said to the stranger in the room before it became too late for introductions.

"I'm David," he said. "We were in Math together last year."

I looked at him again, closer, in this new context. Of course I knew him. We had Math together sophomore year. My brain hadn't registered that when I'd thought he was Gabriel's friend.

"You go to Morris High." I said it like an accusation. And it was. But it was meant for Isabel, not David. I shot her a look. She just smirked and shrugged. So this had been a setup after all. She'd set me up with a guy from school. No wonder she was so mad when I canceled.

"Yes?" David said, frowning at me.

"Sorry. I just thought you were a friend of Gabriel's."

The rabbit bounced around a spilled bin of Legos and over Isabel's foot. She yelped and pulled both feet on the couch before saying, "He *is* a friend of Gabriel's. But he also just happens to go to our school."

I shoveled the Legos back into the bin and righted it. The rabbit scampered to David and sniffed at the hem of his jeans.

"Things, go finish watching your movie. But first, put the rabbit back in its home before it has time to cast an evil spell."

"He's not evil," Wyatt said.

"Ah, see, he already has you hypnotized. The rest of us would like to keep our senses." I realized I was being stupid. I needed to shut up. But when I was nervous I tended to let all

64

my odd thoughts come out my mouth. Well, actually, most of the time I let that happen, but especially when I was nervous.

Jonah picked the rabbit up around its middle, its feet kicking wildly for a moment before they stilled, and the boys left the room.

"Your mom got them a rabbit?" Isabel said, staring after my brothers.

"Yeah, you know my mom. I guess she saw someone selling it on the side of the road and was worried it was on its way to a Crock-Pot . . . or a roaster or maybe a spit . . . how are rabbits prepared, anyway?"

Everyone was silent.

"Where *is* your mom?" Isabel finally said.

"When I said I'd stay home, she and my dad decided to go to some friends' Halloween party or something." I ran my hand through my messy hair and plopped down on the couch beside Isabel.

"Did they dress up?"

"Surprisingly, no. Unless their costume was just 'Weird Parents.'"

The doorbell rang and I went to answer it, this time dropping a handful of candy into the bags of excited little ninjas. When I sat back down next to Isabel, I said, "So . . . was there a plan? Or you just decided to come say hi."

Isabel turned to me, her dark eyes bright. "We decided to come say hi and introduce you to David. He is in the band at school."

This was supposed to be our common bond, I could tell by Isabel's proud smile. "Oh, cool. What instrument do you play?"

David pushed his floppy brown hair off his forehead. Considering how thin he was, he had a baby face—round cheeks and a wide nose. "The clarinet."

"Like the King of Swing?"

"What?"

"You know, Benny Goodman. Isn't he proof that clarinetists can actually make it somewhere?" The words were out before I realized how offensive they sounded. "I'm sorry. That was rude. There are lots of great outlets for the clarinet. Marching bands, orchestras." Now I just sounded patronizing.

"Lily plays the guitar," Isabel said.

"I try." Was it too late not to let them in my house? "Do you guys want something to drink?"

"Sure," Gabriel said.

"Isabel, help me in the kitchen."

She followed me in and when I was sure the guys couldn't hear, I whispered, "Why would you do this to me?"

Isabel sighed. "I thought that if you didn't know you were going on a date tonight, you wouldn't have time to stress. That you wouldn't practice lines in your mind and imagine outcomes."

"You thought my awkwardness was from preconceived plans to be awkward?"

"Yes, actually."

I laughed. "Well, now you know the truth."

66

She laughed too. "I guess I do. But come on. Isn't David adorable? And it's not like he's super smooth. You guys fit well."

I rolled my eyes.

"Give him a chance?"

I grabbed some cups down from the cupboard and scooped ice from the freezer into them. "Why not?"

"I'm sorry I didn't warn you. I really, really thought it would be better this way."

I knew her intentions were in the right place. "It's fine. Here, take these two drinks. Let me check on my brothers. I'll be there in a minute."

I opened the door to the TV room. Wyatt and Jonah were sitting on the couch, the rabbit between them. "Hey, I told you to put the rabbit away," I said. "He's going to pee and Mom won't be happy."

"He's watching this show. It's his favorite. When it's over," Wyatt said.

I smiled. "You two are strange." And I loved it. "As soon as it's over. Not one second later."

"Okay," they both sang out.

I went back to the kitchen and filled the remaining two cups with water. *Okay, self, you can hold a normal conversation with a group of people without looking stupid.* There. That was a good pep talk.

Back in the living room, Isabel had retrieved my guitar from my room and was strumming made-up chords.

"Oh, Lily, come here. Sit down," she said. "I was just telling the guys you would play for them."

I froze in the doorway, cups in hands. Not only because I wanted to rush in and take my baby from her and tuck it back in its protective case . . . I did let Isabel touch my guitar; I trusted her . . . but I did not want to play. At all. It was hard enough talking to new people, but playing, that was a different level. I taught myself the guitar so I could write songs, songs other people would play. I was not a performer.

Isabel met my eyes and I could tell she instantly knew my thoughts. "Never mind. I'll keep playing," she quickly said.

"Oh come on. Isabel's been bragging about you for months now, Lily," Gabriel said. "Let's hear it."

"I . . ." The cups in my hands were slipping. I put them on an end table and wiped my hands on my jeans.

"You don't have to," David said, and I gave him a thankful smile.

Isabel stood. "I'll go put it away."

"I got it." I reached out and took my guitar from her. After securing it in its case and stashing it under my bed, I joined the others again.

Isabel was sitting on the floor now, looking repentant. I gave her a smile so she knew I wasn't mad, and sat down next to her.

"Sorry," she said under her breath.

"It's okay."

Isabel dug her hands into the bin of Legos next to her. "We should have a ship-building competition."

"Yes," Gabriel said. "I am the King of Legos."

"Is that a self-proclaimed title or one that was appointed?" I asked.

Isabel laughed.

Gabriel acted offended. "Appointed, of course." He joined us on the floor and scooped out a handful of Legos. "By my father."

As I was about to respond that fathers are not fair judges, Wyatt ran into the room, holding something up. Jonah came in after him, crying, blood dripping down his chin.

Oh no.

"I got it out!" Wyatt announced. It took me a second to see he was holding a tooth and another second to realize it was Jonah's.

Jonah shoved him in the back. "*I* wanted to get it out."

I jumped up and slung my arm around Jonah's shoulder. "Whoa, vampire, you need to rinse out your mouth after feeding."

He laughed through his cry, but no one else was laughing. They looked horrified.

"He had a loose tooth," I quickly clarified. "Wyatt, next time leave his teeth alone."

"He was being a chicken. Mom said if he didn't get it out, he was going to swallow it in his sleep."

Just then the rabbit came hopping into the room. It went directly to David and proceeded to pee all over his socked foot. I wasn't sure if it was out of reflex or disgust, but David's foot flung forward, kicking the rabbit a good three or four feet across the room.

Jonah gasped. "You hurt him, meanie!" he cried. More blood oozed out of his mouth and dribbled down his chin with the exclamation.

I might have felt the need to apologize for my brother, but I kind of agreed with him. Who kicked a rabbit?

"Wyatt, take care of the rabbit," I said, then directed Jonah into the bathroom down the hall to help him clean up his face.

"Is Bugs Rabbit going to be okay?" Jonah asked.

"He's fine. He has a lot of fur. It protects him."

"You said you'd watch the movie with us, Lily, and now you're playing with your friends."

"I know, kid. I'll send them on their way."

But I didn't have to. After I'd finished helping Jonah and went out to the living room, they were all standing by the open door. Isabel was handing out candy to some trick-or-treaters, but Gabriel and David were putting shoes on.

When Isabel shut the door, she twisted her bracelet back and forth on her wrist. "We need to get going."

David wouldn't meet my eyes and seemed like he couldn't get out quick enough. He was holding his right shoe and walking on his tiptoes out the door.

"Well, when you get your special rabbit powers, give me a call," I said.

He tried to laugh but it came out more like a nervous cough.

Sorry, Isabel mouthed. I shrugged. I didn't blame her. My family was very overwhelming and only half of us were here. And besides, I didn't care. I was pretty sure David didn't even know who Benny Goodman was and for a clarinetist that was a sin as far as I was concerned.

David was somebody Isabel had picked out for her quest. And he only further proved my point that said quest was impossible.

CHAPTER 12

"Has anyone seen my blue-handled pliers?" my mom called out to the house in general. When six people lived under one roof, it was often the quickest form of communication. It didn't necessarily produce results, but it was the fastest. "Anybody?"

"No!" came the reply from Wyatt.

My mom poked her head in my room. I was sitting on my bed, in my pajamas, still contemplating whether I wanted to get up or not.

"I haven't seen them," I told her with a yawn.

"You want to come with me today?"

About once a month, my mom went to different outdoor craft fairs or flea markets where she sold her creations. "How far away?" I asked.

"This one's in town. The Fall Fest. You'd make twenty percent."

That was her draw for us to go help—twenty percent of the profits. It seemed like a good deal, unless she only earned fifty bucks, which wasn't unheard of. Then our take for an entire day's work was ten dollars. But sometimes she'd earn three hundred dollars and I could walk away with sixty dollars in my pocket. It was a gamble. One I was willing to take because I didn't only go for the money incentive.

I went for the people-watching. People-watching inspired me, and I could use some inspiration. Ever since scribbling down a couple of great lines while listening to The Crooked Brookes the other night, I couldn't conjure up any more good ideas. The newspaper clipping taunted me from the wall next to my bed. It reminded me that I had less than two months to write an entire song—music, lyrics, everything. And I'd barely completed a few lines.

"Yeah, I'll go," I said, finally getting up.

Mom nodded. "We leave in thirty minutes."

✿ ✿ ✿

The kettle corn cart was closer to our booth than normal and the sweet smell in the air almost made up for what I'd discovered upon arriving at the Fall Fest. In the booth right next to ours was Cade Jennings. His father owned a very successful insurance company and they were giving out quotes today right in the middle of all the craft booths.

I scowled. Wasn't there a different section for that kind of thing?

My mom was unloading her trays onto the table and I was trying to think of any excuse to leave this booth. "Should I go get us drinks?" I asked.

"I brought some water bottles." She pointed to a bag under the table.

"Snacks?"

"Are you hungry already?"

It was nine in the morning and we'd eaten breakfast before we left. It was a valid question. "No, I guess not."

"There's another case of rings below. Why don't you put them out?"

"Okay." I pulled up the tablecloth and slid out the boxes. "How come we aren't selling any of dad's pieces today?" I meant his furniture pieces; Dad's furniture was really nice, even nicer than the necklaces he made that he tried to pretend were better than Mom's.

"He's working on a contracted job—some kitchen cabinets for a house up in Scottsdale."

"Oh, that's good." Contracted jobs were steadier pay and better money.

I glanced to our right. Cade hadn't seen me yet. Or at least I assumed he hadn't, by the lack of rude comments. He was unloading some sort of flyers into a plastic stand. I'd never seen him dressed up before. He was wearing slacks, a button-down, and even had a tie on. I felt more shabby than normal in my homemade short floral skirt and denim vest. I would not try to hide half my outfit by sitting down, even though I was very tempted to do just that. I did not care what Cade thought of me.

A man who looked nothing like Cade walked up to the front of his booth holding two lidded cups. He handed one to Cade.

Maybe Cade took after his mother. Or this man was his father's business partner. He mumbled something to Cade, who then dumped the flyers he had just arranged out onto the table and refilled the plastic stand with different ones.

My mom began discussing the potential crowd today with the lady to our left. Cade met my eyes then, like he knew I'd been staring all along and a slow smile spread over his lips.

"Are you taking notes?" he asked me. "This is what success looks like." His eyes swept over the jewelry on my table, pausing on the tray with all the feathered necklaces. He raised his eyebrows. "You'll probably need more than notes."

I pretended to write on a pad of paper. "First step, dress like a forty-year-old man. Second step, treat people badly. Third, act like the world revolves around me. Did I miss any?"

Cade smirked. "Actually, you missed quite a few. Don't pretend like you know everything, don't write and walk at the same time, and think about other people every once in a while."

"What? Me think about other people? What's that supposed to mean?"

"No hidden meaning there."

I narrowed my eyes, about to say something I probably shouldn't have, when my mom placed a hand on my shoulder. "Do you go to school with that boy?" she asked me. "How fun." Then, much to my horror, she called out, "Hi. Nice to meet you."

Cade brought out a smile that might've looked sincere to my mom, but actually was completely mocking her.

"Hi, booth neighbor," he said, and my mom laughed like that was some super witty line.

"What a cutie," my mom said under her breath. "Do you know my daughter?" This she said at a volume he could hear. I cringed.

Cade met my eyes, and a playful sparkle lit his up. "I do. We go to school together."

"That's great. If it's slow today, you two won't be so bored now."

"Lily definitely keeps things interesting," Cade said.

"We feel the same way," my mom said as if he hadn't just insulted me.

Today was going to be awful.

🎋 🎋 🎋

The day wasn't going as badly as I originally anticipated. Cade minded his own business and I did mine. And now, he wasn't even in his booth. He'd left about an hour ago and hadn't returned. Maybe Isabel was right. Maybe I did start things more often than I realized.

A woman with a coin purse and several stripes of colored hair stood at our booth, checking the circle price tags on each item and then counting her change. Every time she'd come up short then move onto the next item. There had to be a song in this situation somewhere. *If a penny can bring luck and a dime can grant a wish, how come my eleven cents hasn't bought me what I need.* I chuckled at the lame lyrics.

"What's so funny?" my mom asked.

"Oh, nothing."

"You ready for a lunch break?"

"Sure."

She handed me a ten. "I want one of those big veggie burritos."

"Okay, I'll be back."

I weaved my way through the crowd as I headed toward the food trucks at the end of the street. I had been standing in line for a few minutes when I saw Cade sitting off to the right at a long plastic table with one of his friends, Mike, from school. They were a stone's throw away and even though I wasn't trying to listen, I could hear their voices perfectly.

"Do you think Coach expects us to be at every club practice plus the games?" Mike was saying.

"Yeah," Cade answered. "At least you don't have mornings here and afternoons there."

"True. How many more of these do you have to work?" Mike asked.

"As many as the company decides to do," Cade answered.

"It's not too bad. This is a good place to meet new girls. Unlike club baseball."

"Really? Have you noticed the average age of the buyers here? Not really my age bracket."

"I noticed that one chick from school in the booth next to yours . . . you know . . . what's her name . . . Lily. That could be interesting. She's weird, but cute."

I tensed up.

"Lily Abbott?" Cade said. "You think Lily Abbott is cute?"

"You don't?"

"No."

"Then maybe I'll go talk to her."

"Believe me. Avoid her at all costs. She's not worth your time at all. She's a——"

Before I could hear how Cade ended that delightful sentence, the person standing in line behind me snapped: "Are you going to order or are you just looking?"

"Oh, I'm ordering." Flustered, I stepped up to the window, glancing once at Cade to see if he'd seen me. He raised one eyebrow at me, then took a drink of his soda. I hurriedly placed my order and waited on the opposite side, far away from Cade.

My thoughts were swirling. That Mike guy thought I was *weird, but cute*? I wouldn't have expected that. I didn't think boys thought of me at all. But I wasn't really surprised by Cade's response.

I could see why Cade hated me. I really could. In his mind, I had broken up him and Isabel. And I might've been able to deal with his hatred if that was the only reason for it. But his attitude toward me wasn't new. It wasn't *post*-Isabel. It had started when he and Isabel started. His jerkiness all along was what made me want him out of Isabel's life. His attitude was the precursor to mine. He'd created my loathing with his. And I couldn't for the life of me understand why.

78

CHAPTER 13

Chemistry used to be the class I had to get through. Now it was the class I couldn't wait to get to. Monday morning seemed to drag on forever. Math was nothing short of torture. Composition, my favorite class ever, was slow, and in English, Ms. Logan decided we should read *Romeo and Juliet* out loud, the entire period, with English accents. A few drama students were the only ones who made it halfway entertaining. Everyone else butchered it. Two more classes until I would get to read today's new note.

Fourth period I was an office aide——the much-coveted position that usually only seniors got. It was basically busy-work and no homework, not the noblest elective, but a free period was a free period. And helping out Mrs. Clark wasn't so bad.

I was making my way through the crowded halls to the office when I saw Lucas ahead of me. He was several inches taller than everyone around him. He turned at the end of the hall. I turned, too. It was time to say something . . . *anything* to him.

The second I made that decision my heart kicked up a notch.

It's okay, I said to myself, *Just say hi, make sure he knows you exist.*

That wouldn't be hard. *Hi* was a harmless word.

Lucas pushed open a door on his right and I nearly followed him right through it until it swung shut and I saw the blue symbol of a man on the outside of it. I had almost walked right into the boy's bathroom. Apparently I was a stalker now.

I doubled back around and bumped into Isabel. Which was a relief. I needed an intervention or, at the very least, a lecture about why silently following boys was creepy.

Only Isabel wasn't alone. A boy was beside her. David. Isabel smiled eagerly at me.

I sighed. Were we really going to do a take two? Isabel didn't know how to give up.

"Lily!" Isabel said in a fake innocent tone. "Look who I ran into."

"Hi," I said.

"Hey," David replied, hands in his pockets. "How are you?"

"Pretty good. Did you get all the pee out of your sock?"

"I threw it away."

"Oh. That was another solution." A bit of an overreaction in my opinion, but maybe it smelled worse than I imagined it might.

I looked at Isabel. She had a smile on her face like she was witnessing the cutest thing she'd ever seen. Isabel made a horrible matchmaker. I hoped she didn't have her heart set on this as a career.

"I didn't mean to kick it, by the way," David added, looking at the ground. "The rabbit. I just . . . it just surprised me."

I smiled. "My brother will be relieved to know this. Although you should probably avoid him for a while. My brother, that is. Oh, and the rabbit, I guess." Not that David would ever want to go to my mad house again.

"She's just kidding," Isabel clarified.

"Yes. I am." I had probably sounded rude. I was glad Isabel got my sense of humor so she could translate for me.

"So . . . anyway, about that Chemistry assignment," David said, turning to Isabel, and I realized this was how their conversation had probably started, how she had gotten him to follow her over here.

"I can help you with it. Lily and I meet in the library on Wednesdays after school to work on Chemistry," Isabel said.

We most certainly did not.

"Why don't you join us this week?" Isabel went on.

"Okay, sure." David smiled a little at me and I softened. Maybe he was just shy and uncomfortable. I could understand that and have some sympathy for the poor guy. We could be friends. Maybe a few more conversations would bring out his real personality. "Mr. Ortega is going to be the death of me."

"Me too," I said. "Do you guys have Chemistry together?" I glanced from David to Isabel.

"No," Isabel said. "I have it fourth period, and David has it second."

"And I have it sixth," I said, almost to myself. We were each in one of the three junior Chemistry classes. The only three that existed. So my mystery pen pal was in one of their periods. One of them knew exactly who sat in my seat. All I had to do was open my mouth and ask . . . and forever ruin Chemistry. This was the one thing I'd been looking forward to for the past week and a half. I was not going to ruin that with my curiosity. I'd already told Isabel I didn't want to know who my pen pal was. And I really didn't.

The late bell rang then. David, Isabel, and I all went our separate ways. I smiled as I hurried toward the main office. I was one step closer to Chemistry class.

🌟 🌟 🌟

I didn't have to look under the desk to find the note anymore. My hand went straight to it. I'd even become an expert at unfolding it quietly and placing it just so under my single sheet of notepaper. I didn't even think Lauren realized what I was doing. I held my breath and read:

> *Track 4 is my favorite too. And also, Track 8 on* Blue *is amazing. You were right, not depressing at all. (I'm not just saying that because the cool guitarist in my new band said she likes it the best.)*
>
> *By the way, I don't play guitar so there will be no stealing your solo time here. That means it's official, right? We need a band name now. Something overly*

sweet like Rainbows & Roses. Then all our songs should
be angry. It will make for a good contrast. I have a lot of
angry material right now——awful stepdad, distant
mother, and absent father. That's some solid fodder, right?
Here, I'll come up with a good first line right now . . .
Parents (a pause in lyrics for a dramatic guitar solo for
you) are (pause for drum solo) lame. Hmm . . . maybe
I shouldn't be the lyricist either. My musical skills don't
translate to a band. Where does that leave me? I can
stand in the background and dance. Oh, also, if
Mr. Ortega catches me writing you this letter, I am
committed to shoving it in my mouth and swallowing. I
hope I can count on the same commitment from you.

I smiled. After the buildup of the whole weekend and all
morning anticipating this letter, I was worried it would dis-
appoint. It did not. It was cute and funny and a little sad. I
wished there was something I could do about the sad part to
make him feel better.

I took out a fresh sheet of paper because now that we were
saying more personal things, I didn't want someone to find a
long exchange under the desk. If discovered, it was better to
have less.

We're already to the swallowing-paper-for-each-other
commitment level? You may be moving a little fast for
me. And yes, your lyrics could use some work. What are

these other musical skills you mentioned? Maybe we can integrate them somehow.

That is some serious material for lyrics. It will make a great song. Capitalizing on your sad life is cool, right? But seriously, I'm sorry. I don't know if I can help much, but feel free to vent. I'm a good listener. Especially in letters, because I have no other choice.

You want to hear about a sad life? My best friend brought a guy to my house, kind of like a setup, and he basically ran away screaming. That's how crazy my family is. Has your family ever accomplished such a feat? I doubt it.

I wasn't sure that making light of his situation was the way to go, but he seemed like the type who appreciated humor. And it felt good to get my frustration about the weekend off my chest. I couldn't vent about it to Isabel because I knew she'd just tell me that it was fine and that nobody thought my family was crazy—even though I was sure they all did.

I folded the letter and carefully placed it back in its spot. Now I had to wait twenty-four hours for a response. This was so much less gratifying than texting.

No, that wasn't true. There was something about the secrecy and the anticipation and the possibility of getting caught that made it much more exciting than texting.

The next day I was just as excited when I pulled his response from beneath the desk.

No, I can't say that my family has ever sent anyone away screaming. That would require them actually being involved in my life in some way. My parents divorced seven years ago and my dad moved. He moved to get away from her and me. If my mom hadn't mentioned where he moved a couple times, I wouldn't even know. Also, he might be dating someone four years older than me. I only know this because my mom screamed it into the phone about a year ago. I think she got remarried to make my dad mad, because there is no way she likes the jerk of a guy she married. He is impossible to impress. Everything has to be better and more and perfect for him.

How's that for venting? Remember, you asked for it. I don't know if I buy your "good listening because it's a letter" thing though. Technically you could just skip to the end of a letter and pretend you read it. Is that what you did? Here, I'll give you some key words so that you can fake a response: five-state buffer zone, man cougar, loveless marriage. (Those sound like song lyrics. Look at that, I'm getting so much better. I'm back on for lyricist.) I was going to call him just a plain cougar, but they only use that term for women, right? That's sexist. What do you call men in their fifties who date women who are practically teenagers?

I hid my smile so Lauren wouldn't notice. My pen pal had this way of making even the saddest things funny somehow. I looked up at Mr. Ortega. I had to pay attention for five minutes before I could write back. It was my method of secrecy—listen, write, listen, write . . .

I think they're called perverts. And I'm sorry. I wish I were more than a good listener who reads entire letters and not just the highlights. I wish I had awesome advice to give you about how trials make you stronger or build character or something like that, but I know that doesn't help. So if you want advice, you'll have to find some other desk defacer. Me, I'll just wallow with you.

I'm impressed you've kept a sense of humor through all this. You haven't let it make you a bitter, angry person. Or have you? Do you walk around punching lockers and kicking small animals? Or writing angry songs (for real)? That's how this whole topic started, right? We're going to use the injustices against you to make some awesome songs! Okay, so the first one can be called "Left Behind." I'll try to figure out how we can use the words man cougar in it.

I hoped he was okay with me trying to make his sad topics funny too. Because before I'd added the last sentence, I'd stared at that song title for a few minutes. "Left Behind." The title that represented his father leaving him without looking back, and a pit formed in my stomach that I'd had to combat.

I folded the letter and secured it beneath the desk.

CHAPTER 14

I hadn't been serious about writing a song inspired by my pen pal's life. It was supposed to be like the jokes I'd always made with Isabel about writing a book based on her dating situations. But that wasn't what happened. What happened was that the title "Left Behind," along with his words, brought so many images into my mind that I found myself that night, notebook on knees, writing.

First I'd filled in the margins with notes about what he'd said about his life. Then I'd let those words inspire lyrics.

> *I've turned waiting into a form of art.*
> *Tied twisted lines around my broken heart.*
> *Because I always thought you'd be back one day.*

The door swung open and Ashley walked in and dropped onto her bed with a loud sigh.

"What's wrong?" I asked.

"I just completely and totally humiliated myself in front of the guy I have a crush on at work."

"How?"

She showed me her teeth. "See that?"

"No."

"Exactly. Earlier there was a big, huge food chunk right here." She pointed at her front tooth. "And nobody told me. Nobody. Oh wait, Mark told me after I'd been talking to him for five minutes."

I laughed.

"You would've told me, right? Tricia should have told me. It's girl code. I think Tricia likes Mark, too. That's the problem here."

"Maybe she didn't see the food."

"Lil, people on the space station saw this chunk of food. It was massive. And right on my front tooth."

"That was rude of the people on the space station not to tell you about it."

"Ha-ha."

"He probably thought it was funny," I said.

Ashley groaned. "That's exactly what he thought. That's why this is a nightmare. If you want a romantic relationship with a guy, first he has to find you mysterious, then intriguing, then funny. In that order. If it's in any different order, you are forever labeled *friend*."

I frowned. "That's an interesting theory."

"Tried and proven. And the funny has to be intentional. None of this making a fool of yourself business."

Huh. Maybe that's why I'd never had a romantic relationship. I was always making a fool of myself.

Ashley rolled off her bed, crawled forward, and sat on the floor with her back facing me. "Braid my hair. I want it to be wavy tomorrow. Plus, it will make me feel better."

"You're so needy." Sometimes, it felt like Ashley was the younger sister.

"Please? I'll straighten yours for you."

"Get me a brush."

She hopped up and walked out of the room.

I looked at my notebook. "We'll never have enough alone time together, will we?" I asked it with a sigh. "It's as if people are trying to keep us apart."

My sister came back in swinging a hairbrush like a pendulum between her thumb and forefinger, a straightener tucked under her other arm. "Who are you talking to?"

"Myself."

"You do that a lot."

"I know. I'm the only one who understands me."

Ashley threw the brush at me, narrowly missing my leg, then plugged in the straightener and positioned herself on the floor by my bed. I begrudgingly closed my notebook.

My sister had long, beautiful hair. It was the same color as mine, but unlike my crazy waves, hers was perfectly straight.

"People spend a lot of time to make their hair look exactly like yours," I said as I ran a brush through it.

"And people spend just as much time to make their hair look like yours."

"I guess everyone wants what they don't have."

As if I had been making a statement about her love life, Ashley said, "Boys suck."

"Amen," I said.

Ashley tipped her head back. "What? You're agreeing with me? Spill."

"You want to feel better about your supposedly embarrassing situation that in reality happens to everyone?" I asked.

"Not everyone."

"Everyone at some point or another has had food in their teeth. But I bet your pet rabbit has never peed on your date's foot."

Ashley laughed.

"Yeah . . . exactly," I said.

Ashley didn't stop laughing. She put her forehead to her knees, causing me to let go of the braid.

"Keep on laughing," I said.

"Okay, I'm sorry, I'm sorry." She sat back and I separated her hair again and began to braid when she broke out into laughter again.

"I'm not braiding your hair anymore," I announced, sitting back.

"No, no, no," she said. "I'm sorry."

I gathered her hair. Two minutes passed, then she said, "Do you call him Pee Foot now?" and burst into laughter.

I let go of her hair and shoved her. "You're a brat."

She stood and let out a happy sigh. "Your stories are the best, Lil. Your social life is so funny. Thanks for making me feel better." With that she left the room.

"Yes, that's me, the girl whose social life makes everyone feel better about theirs," I said to nobody.

I yanked the straightener's cord out of the wall, turning it off, and then picked up my notebook. I flipped to the back and titled the last page: *Suspects*. I didn't have that sad of a social life. I had a fun and perfectly normal relationship with an anonymous pen pal. Okay, so an anonymous pen pal didn't exactly sound normal, but I would ignore that fact. Maybe it was time to figure out who he was.

CHAPTER 15

"Mrs. Clark, did you have rules when you were dating?"

I was beginning to wonder if I was the only girl in the world who didn't have dating rules, and if this was part of my problem. I was sitting at a desk in the main office fulfilling my aide duties, which today consisted of transferring the handwritten sign-out sheet from the day before into the computer.

Mrs. Clark looked up from her computer. She was about my mom's age, and pretty, with long blonde hair and glasses. I could almost picture her as a teenager. Almost.

"Rules?" Mrs. Clark asked, furrowing her brow.

"You know, like 'be mysterious but not too mysterious,' 'don't laugh at your date,' things like that."

She smiled. "Do you make it a habit of laughing at your dates?"

"Only when they do something funny."

Mrs. Clark thought for a second. "When I was dating, my girlfriends and I used to say, 'Don't cry in front of him before date three.'"

"Cry?" I echoed, frowning.

"Yeah. Guys gets skittish when you cry."

"I don't think I have to worry about that one."

"You don't cry?"

"I don't make it to date three."

She smiled again, like I hadn't been making a joke. I had been. Sort of. "Rules are silly," she said. "Just be real."

"Easier said than done." I entered the last sign out into the computer, then filed away the hardcopy. "Done."

"Oh, good." She pointed across the room. "Can you grab the keys and drop this packet off in Mrs. Lungren's room?"

"Sure." I got to my feet. "Why do I need keys for that?"

"Mrs. L locks up during fourth. Prep period."

"Where are the keys?"

"Have I never had you drop things off in locked rooms before?"

"No."

She gave a grunt like she was surprised. "Well, you're responsible, so I can trust you." She winked and went over to a cabinet at the very back of the office, retrieved some keys, and then placed them in my hand.

"Super responsible," I promised with a smile.

So responsible that after dropping off the packet in Mrs. L's classroom, I found myself in the Science building, heading toward room 201. The room where I had Chemistry. I'd just look in the window, I told myself. See who sat at my desk. True, Isabel had Chemistry fourth period, and I could have just asked her. Why was I doing this? My best friend would've mentioned if she'd seen someone writing notes the whole class.

She noticed things like that. Especially because she knew I was exchanging notes with someone. My pen pal had to have it second period.

Still, I wanted to look.

My heart was racing when I reached the room. But it was dark, and locked. Why? The keys I held dug into my hand and I was so tempted to use them. But for what purpose? To retrieve the note early? To see if my note was already gone? Both seemed too pointless to risk it.

I turned and rushed off before Mrs. Clark realized I had been gone way too long and took my future key privileges away.

☆ ☆ ☆

When it was time for my Chemistry class, I arrived at the door to find it locked again, and the classroom still empty. This time I noticed a sign taped to the door. Had it been there earlier? It must've.

LAB TODAY. MEET IN ROOM 301.

Lab. I'd forgotten about lab. That meant there would be no note today. It also meant he hadn't read *my* note from the day before. I didn't remember exactly what I had written. I vaguely remembered trying to make a few jokes. Would he think I was laughing at him? Was I trying too hard to be funny?

It didn't matter. I wasn't trying to date the guy. I didn't even know who he was. I wasn't going to overanalyze it. Besides, rules were stupid.

"It says: *Lab today. Meet in room 301.*" Cade said each word of the sign slowly.

I turned, wanting to throw an elbow as I did, but kept my arms safely at my sides. "Yeah. I got that."

"You were standing there for so long I wondered."

"Are you stalking me now?"

He held up his hands and stepped to the side. "I was just trying to be helpful. It's who I am."

"You should reevaluate your definition of help."

He smiled and started ticking words off on his right hand. "To assist, to save, to be handsome. I think I have them all."

"Pretty sure you only possess the one that doesn't even fit the definition."

"I'm glad you think I'm handsome, Lily. I always knew you did."

My cheeks went pink as I realized I had walked right into that.

He leaned close. "That makes it two hundred and one . . ." He pointed at himself. "To three." He pointed at me. "Since you're keeping score."

I gave him a little push and walked away. "I have at least five points," I mumbled.

I got to the lab and settled into my seat next to my lab partner, Isaiah. I knew there would not be a note under the long lab table. I looked anyway. There were only tubes leading up to the Bunsen burners. My pen pal and I probably sat in completely different seats for lab. But that didn't mean I wasn't disappointed.

Isaiah handed me a pair of goggles and said, "I should probably control the fire this time. Your paper dragon last time almost set off the smoke alarm."

"Thanks," I sighed, and got to work.

CHAPTER 16

I was the first to arrive at the library after school. I found a table near the back and placed my backpack in the center. This was already off to a better start than the last time I hung out with David because it was taking place outside of my house. No spilled Legos and stacks of laundry, no bloody-chinned brothers and definitely no rabbits with bladder control issues.

Okay, I told myself as I settled back in the chair. *Isabel is trying really hard in her self-appointed quest to make you dateable. You can try, too.* I wasn't sure what trying consisted of. Not talking?

As I sat there thinking about how to be normal, I realized I was staring in the general direction of a guy sitting two tables over. Not just any guy, but Lucas. I caught my breath.

His attention was fully focused on the book in front of him, his finger scanning the page. This was my opportunity to say hi or to ask him if he knew where the nonfiction section was or something. I could do that.

Just as I convinced myself that I really could do that, David arrived.

"Hey," he said, placing his backpack next to mine.

"Hi."

He sat down and pulled books out of his bag. I gave one last useless look at Lucas and then sat down as well. I unzipped my bag and pulled my book and notebook out. This not-talking thing was working well so far; it made things less awkward.

"Silence is kind of awkward, don't you think?" he said.

Oh. Or not. "No. I'm okay with silence. We're in a library after all. This is the birthplace of silence."

"The library is the birthplace of silence?" David asked.

"All the words are being used by the books. When I was little, that's what I used to think. That people were told to be quiet so that all their words didn't get stolen by the books. I thought books needed words to exist. Well, obviously they do, but I thought they needed spoken words. Yeah . . . I was always weird."

"And here I thought libraries were quiet because people were trying to study," David whispered.

"That might be another explanation."

He laughed a little and my eyes met his. It seemed like he was genuinely amused. That was a good thing. Or was it too early for that?

He opened his book. "So is Isabel normally this late?"

"Normally . . . That's such a subjective word." Especially since she and I never met in the library to study.

"Is it?" He looked at his watch.

Before I had to answer, Isabel came rushing in. "Hi, guys. Sorry. I got held up in Math class because Sasha needed notes from yesterday."

"Sasha?" I said. "Cade's girlfriend?"

"I don't think she and Cade are together. Are they?"

"I thought they were." I looked at David to back me up but he was turning pages in his Chemistry book as if he hadn't been following the conversation.

"I guess they could be. She's never said anything." Was that jealousy in Isabel's voice? Why would Isabel be jealous of Sasha?

"I didn't know you and Sasha were friends," I said, feeling sort of jealous myself.

"We're not, really," Isabel said, opening her books, "but everyone always asks me for notes. I'm a good note taker." She looked from me to David. "Did you guys get started?"

I smirked. "Yes, the people who need help in Chemistry went ahead and taught each other. We're super good at Chemistry now."

Isabel rolled her eyes.

Over Isabel's shoulder I could still see Lucas. He looked up, a small smile on his face. Had he been following our conversation or was he amused by something in his book?

Isabel hit my arm. "I hope you've learned by now that Lily likes to joke," she said to David.

"I have," David said.

"You have?" I said.

"Yes."

Isabel moved her eyebrows up and down at me. I ignored her.

"Why are we extending the torture of Chemistry beyond school hours again?" I asked, picking up my pen.

"So we don't have to retake the class next year?" David offered.

"Good point." I opened my book.

"What are you guys up to this weekend?" Isabel asked, instead of focusing on Chemistry. "We should all do something."

I glanced at David. I wondered if he knew that Isabel was trying to set us up.

"What day?" he asked.

"I don't know," Isabel said. "Whatever day we all have open."

I said nothing.

David flipped through the pages of his textbook. "The band is playing for the home game on Friday."

"You're playing at the football game?" Isabel asked, widening her eyes. "Fun. We'll totally go watch you. Right, Lily?"

"Um . . . I'll have to make sure I'm not stuck babysitting again, but sure," I said hesitantly. "Sounds fun."

"And maybe we could all hang out after the game?" Isabel added. She was so persistent.

David nodded and tentatively looked at me. I couldn't read him very well. I wasn't sure if he wanted me to give an encouraging look or if he was trying to get out of this plan.

I smiled, just in case that would help when really I just wanted to say, *Yeah, I'm trying to get out of this too, but you don't know my best friend very well if you think there is hope for either of us.*

"We'll be doing our marching band performance at half-time," David finally said, glancing back at Isabel.

"I love watching the marching band," Isabel exclaimed. "It's so cool to see all those formations. How long do you have to work on those?"

"Months," he said.

"Lily likes anything with music."

Apparently I was still going with the "not-talking" strategy. I finally found my voice. "It's true."

David smiled. "Music and chemistry. Bringing people together."

For some reason, I blushed. *Music and chemistry.* Why had he said that?

I thought about the *Suspects* page in the back of my notebook. I had written down two possibilities so far: A guy named George from my composition class who yesterday morning was going on and on about his parents' divorce and how he was going to write a song about it. When I'd heard him say that, my heart had jumped. George wasn't that cute, but he seemed smart. I was willing to consider him. The other suspect was Travis from P.E.; I'd overheard him telling his friend that reverse psychology works well on teachers. My letter writer had said something about reverse psychology. I guess I was grasping at straws.

But now, sitting in the library, I wondered if I could add a third name to the *Suspects* list: *David.*

CHAPTER 17

*F*inally, I thought, as I settled into my seat in Chemistry on Thursday. I couldn't listen to Mr. Ortega for the normal five minutes I usually did before reading. I unfolded the note right away.

> *I hadn't realized it was lab yesterday. It surprised me.*
> *Maybe I should start paying more attention in class.*
> *I blame you for the distraction. The problem is that*
> *you're making me look forward to Chemistry or*
> *something. In what crazy world does anyone look*
> *forward to Chemistry? Can you stop being so amusing? I*
> *think that will help. Did you start on our first song?*
> *"Left Behind." It's hard to tell if someone is kidding or*
> *not in a letter. Are you actually a songwriter?*

That last sentence made me pause. I wanted to be a songwriter. But I really wasn't. I hadn't even written a full song. I had partial lyrics, and incomplete melodies, but nothing finished. I shook off the thought and continued reading.

*If so, I'm impressed. If not, maybe you should be. You
seem passionate about music and you have a way with
words. Sometimes I wish I were passionate about something real. Something I knew I could succeed in. Right
now all my dreams are a little far-fetched. Oh no,
Mr. Ortega wants us to complete a worksheet with our
seat partner. Gotta go.*

I smiled, and checked up to see Mr. Ortega writing some
endless formula on the board. I immediately produced a
fresh piece of paper and wrote:

*You think songwriting is a realistic dream? That was a
joke, right? Like you said, it's hard to tell from a letter.
But yes, I am passionate about it. Now, if only I could
actually write a complete song, I might feel like I could
call myself a songwriter. For now, I'm just a far-fetched
dreamer like you. It might stay that way until I get out
of my house. It's impossible to write there.*

*What is this far-fetched dream of yours anyway?
Something your home life prevents, like mine? How are
things at home? Any improvement with your mom or
dad? You said your dad left and you haven't seen him in
a while, but you have talked to him, right?*

*Ugh, now Mr. Ortega is asking US to complete the
worksheets. Gotta go too.*

☆ ☆ ☆

Twenty-four hours was a long time to think about what answers my pen pal would give to my questions. I found myself worried about him the rest of the day and that night, wondering what his far-fetched dreams were that he didn't feel he could believe in.

The next day, his reply read:

My dad calls me once a year around my birthday. I think he may have forgotten the exact date. It was hard the first couple years, now it's kind of amusing. I make a bet with myself about how close to the real date he'll actually get. His closest so far has been within two days. Not bad. This last year I was a jerk to him. I felt guilty and then I felt guilty for feeling guilty. If that makes any sense. I've written him off. Now he's just someone that used to be in my life. He actually pays child support, which is big of him, right? Maybe that makes him feel better about himself. It felt nice for me when my mom let me buy a car with some of it. The unfortunate side effect of this choice is that now every time I drive, I'm reminded of him.

And that's enough whining for one letter. You'll stop writing me if all I ever do is complain. And then where will I be? Stuck listening to Mr. Ortega again? So

what about you? I think I need some more complaining
on your end.

I frowned down at the letter, my heart hurting. His dad had forgotten exactly when his birthday was? What kind of father did that? The kind that would move five states away and never visit.

Something about the way my pen pal wrote made him easy to open up to. I found myself doing just that as I wrote back.

Complaining? My complaints seem minor now compared
to what you have to deal with. And again, I have no
sage words of wisdom to offer. Hang in there? Chin up.
What are some other cheesy, not-helpful slogans?

My main complaint about my own life is that I have
no time to myself, at all. My whole family seems to
dictate every second of my day. When I go out, eat,
think. I'm living a collective life. Everyone around me
decides my fate and sometimes I feel like I'm just along
for the ride.

I see what you mean about a maximum quota of
whining per letter. I feel like I just reached mine. I need
to end with something lighter. Today is Friday. That's
good, right? Although, by the time you read this it will
be Monday and Mondays suck. So that's not a happy
letter-ender at all. How about the fact that there are

only three more weeks of school before Thanksgiving
break, when we get a week off? Happy thought for you,
or no? I can't decide if I were you if I'd rather be at
school or at home? I'm sorry, that was insensitive. I'm
really not doing well here. Music. That's the universal
language, one I usually can't mess up. Go listen to a band
called Dead's the New Alive. Track 9 off their new
album. That will help. At least, for three minutes and
forty-four seconds.

I folded the note, finding myself a little depressed as I stuck it in its place. Fridays were the worst. I had to wait all weekend before I'd get a reply. Was I really already looking forward to Monday? That was backward thinking. I should've been excited about the football game that night. The one my mom had said I could go to. David. Yes, I could get excited about seeing David. That would make Isabel happy. And maybe I'd get some more clues as to whether his name belonged on my *Suspects* list or not.

CHAPTER 18

The night was my favorite kind of night—cool enough for a jacket, but warm enough for it to be a thin one. Now, if only we weren't headed for a stadium full of screaming fans. Watching a football game wasn't exactly my favorite activity.

Gabriel and Isabel were a couple steps ahead, arm in arm, talking too quietly for me to hear. I wondered if they were plotting the after-game activity where they expected David and me to fall madly in love.

Isabel noticed I had fallen behind and slowed down, hooking her free arm in mine. "This is going to be awesome," she said as we reached the ticket booth.

"I guess," I said. We paid and headed inside, climbing the steps to the stadium. Some of the kids were all decked out in paint and holding signs. I was glad Isabel hadn't insisted we do that. When we reached the top, the noise that had somehow seemed muffled on the way up hit me like it was a living, breathing force.

"There's the band," Isabel said.

Gabriel looked at me, like I should have a response to that.

"Cool hats," was the only thing I could think of.

★ ★ ★

It was five minutes to halftime when Gabriel said, "We should get food before David's thing."

"You guys go ahead. I'm good." I loved Isabel and Gabriel, but I needed a break from the overdose of affection the two of them were displaying.

"Are you sure?" Isabel asked.

"Positive."

They left for the food vendors. I sat back and looked for lyrics in the sights around me. *Lights in the blackness. Waiting for the score. Putting on a face. Flirt a little more.*

That last line, unfortunately, had been inspired by Cade. I'd happened to see him chatting with some girl. When he noticed me looking over, he caught my eye and winked. Ugh. I stood, deciding I wanted a drink after all, and pivoted toward the aisle to catch up with Isabel. I nearly ran face first into a chest. Even over the noise of the crowd, this close to him, I could just make out the beat coming from Lucas's earbuds.

He tugged on the cord, freeing them. "Sorry . . . Lily, right?"

His presence here shocked me silent. Although to be fair, his presence always seemed to do that. But what was he doing at a football game? I didn't know a lot about him but I did know this wasn't his scene.

I tried to answer, to think of something clever . . . or just something . . . to say, but my mind was blank. I managed to shut my mouth, which had been open for at least one second too long.

"You okay?" Lucas asked. "Did I hit you?"

I shook my head no. His earbuds were dangling near his shoulders and I was so tempted to pick one up and put it to my ear and finally learn what music he was always listening to, but thankfully I stopped myself. I was already acting crazy enough. *Quick, brain, think of something clever to say.* My thoughts were flying around, uncatchable.

Lucas smiled, a perfect, gorgeous, disarming smile. All the tension that was holding my thoughts captive eased out of my body. I was going to talk. I was going to say something funny and clever. Finally. I took a deep breath and opened my mouth.

"Lucas." Cade appeared at his side. "Can I interest you in a friendly wager?"

"What?" The irritation on Lucas's face as he glanced at Cade made me like him even more.

"Trust me, this is better than anything going on over here." He nodded his head toward the game, and for some reason that worked. Lucas followed him away, leaving me with only a small wave.

Cade had just led away my first real chance at talking to Lucas. Even more reason to hate him.

"Nachos?" Gabriel asked, holding up a tray of chips and gooey cheese. Where had he come from?

Isabel tugged on my arm, carrying a drink in her free hand. "You're missing the show."

Oh. Right. I sat back down, trying to make out David on the field. But the whole time I was fuming about Cade and Lucas.

☆　☆　☆

After the game was over, Isabel, David, Gabriel, and I went to a park near Isabel's house. Gabriel was pushing Isabel on a swing and David and I were sitting on a picnic table.

I picked up David's marching band hat that he had set next to him. It had a long black feather on top. "What's with the feather?"

"It makes us taller." He was still wearing his full band uniform and it looked uncomfortable and sweaty. But cute.

"Really? I should probably wear one of these all the time then." I placed it on my head.

"I think it really has to do with the history of marching bands," David explained. "Marching bands used to be used in wars. The musicians wore certain uniforms so the opposing army could identify who not to shoot or something like that."

"Nice. I'm glad you won't get shot in a war."

David smiled and shook his head. "Now it's just tradition."

I tipped my head back so I could see under the brim of the hat. "Do you like being in the marching band?"

"Sometimes. It's a lot of work."

"It looked good tonight even though I couldn't really see you out there." I wasn't sure that came out right. "I mean, you did a good job . . . I think. I guess what I mean is that no one stood out, which is what you want, right? It's supposed to look all . . . uniform." How come when faced with Lucas, no words came out, and for David, I had no filter?

"Yes. Thanks."

David wasn't much of a talker and I still couldn't decide if it was because he was shy or because he really didn't want to be here. I took the hat off, twisted it once between my palms, and set it back down.

"So, I know nothing about you," I blurted. "Except that you play the clarinet and you hate Chemistry. What else is there to know about David . . ." I paused. "I don't even know your last name."

"Feldman."

"Okay, David Feldman, give me the bullet points."

"The bullet points?"

"You know, your life in ten points or less."

"Okay, um . . . my parents are divorced. I have a much older brother and a sister. They're both married and moved out. My favorite books are Harry Potter."

"That counts as seven."

"Really?"

"No, but that's awesome. I love Potter, too."

He smiled and with it I decided that he was just shy.

"Keep going," I said.

"I haven't been sick since the seventh grade and—"

"Wait, that one needs some expounding. Do you have a super immune system or do you just mean you haven't thrown up in that long?"

"I haven't had a cold or the flu since the seventh grade."

"Why?"

He shrugged. "I take lots of vitamin C."

"Text me your diet and habits please." I was kidding but he pulled out his phone like I'd been serious and handed it to me. I assumed he wanted me to enter my number so I did.

"Is that ten yet?" he asked when I handed it back.

"If you're done it is, but I think I interrupted you in the middle of one."

"I was just going to say that I hadn't missed a day of school since seventh. One of the bad side effects of never being sick."

"True. Plus, how can you ever appreciate your health when you're always healthy? Maybe you should try to purposely get sick. Go around kissing sick people or something."

Why had I said the word *kiss*? His cheeks darkened. Had he never been kissed? Not that I was all that experienced in the kissing department, but I had done it before. And I could at least say the word without blushing.

"And you?" he asked.

"I'm not sick right now so I can't help you."

"N-no, I meant the bullet points thing," he stammered.

I blinked. Okay, maybe I was blushing a little. "Oh. Right. You've been to my house so you know like eight of mine. But let's see, besides the guitar and the siblings and the crazy house, I like to sew. I shop at thrift stores and have no problem buying used shoes. I talk to myself too much and at school they call me——"

"Magnet," he finished for me. "Why?"

"Long story. Basically the school jerk, who for some reason is popular, bestowed the name upon me because I'm horrible at P.E.—oh, there's another bullet, I'm horrible at P.E.—and it stuck."

"Who's the school jerk?"

"You don't know? Do people really not know? You go to our school." Remembering how Cade had pulled Lucas aside, I gritted my teeth. "He's actually probably warned you to stay away from me." Cade seemed to be on a one-man mission to do just that.

David shook his head no.

"Who do you think the school jerk might be?" I held up his hat again when it seemed like he wasn't going to answer the question. "You're telling me that you walk around wearing this and you've never been picked on?"

He laughed. "Are you making fun of me?"

"No. Hey, I would totally wear this hat to school if it went with my outfit."

"You would, wouldn't you? But you're confident like that."

I gasped and then coughed. "That's funny."

"You don't seem to care what anyone thinks of you," David said seriously.

"Just because I wear weird clothes doesn't mean I'm not worried people aren't judging me for them. Now, stop trying to avoid the question. Who is the biggest jerk?"

"Pete Wise."

"That big water polo guy?"

"Yes."

I growled. "Okay, second-biggest jerk then."

"Lyle Penner."

"Really? Lyle's your number two? How about third?"

David's eyes widened. "How many people do you think pick on me?"

I laughed. "I don't know. I figure we're at least tied. But you still haven't named the biggest offender. He picks on everyone. If you're walking around in this hat, there's no way he hasn't given you a name."

"I only wear this to games, Lily," David said.

I sensed I had told one too many hat jokes. "Fine. Never mind. I'm supposed to be pretending he doesn't exist anyway."

"You're going to leave me in suspense?"

I still couldn't believe he hadn't guessed. "Cade Jennings."

"Cade? *He* named you Magnet?"

"Yes. He's a jerk."

David seemed to consider that label then said, "I guess I can see how he'd come off like that. He's a little full of himself."

"A little?"

"And he's loud and over the top. But he's never been mean to me like Pete or Lyle."

"Well, he's been mean to me," I said. "And always when there's an audience. He's the worst kind of jerk, the kind that

115

pretends he's doing something for your benefit, including you in some funny joke, when really he's making you the butt of a joke."

David nodded and I could practically see the memories of all the times Cade had done just that to many people, working their way through his mind.

From across the playground where I could've sworn Isabel and Gabriel had been too concerned with each other to worry about us, Isabel yelled, "Stop talking about Cade, Lily!"

"Mind your own Bs, Isabel!" I yelled with a laugh.

"I take it this isn't a new discussion," David said.

No, it wasn't. And I really shouldn't have been dwelling on it. "You want to race down the bumpy slides?"

He looked down at his uniform. "It might not be a fair race. This material makes a super slick surface."

I laughed. "I'm willing to take my chances."

He smiled and led the way to the slides, where after a few races, I really had forgotten about Cade and how he'd embarrassed me in front of Lucas at the football game. Maybe a guy I couldn't talk to wasn't the right guy for me, anyway.

When we all left the park together, Isabel dropped me off first and I wondered if David would walk me to the door. I'd had a really fun night. But David didn't even move toward his handle when the car stopped. I climbed out and walked the path alone.

CHAPTER 19

The next week of notes in Chemistry were amazing and I counted my days by them.

Monday from him:

> Dead's the New Alive is something I listen to once a week. I can't believe you know that band. We speak the same music language. Is that rare? How many people have you met that speak your same music language? I have met maybe one other. (That sounds like a song, right? You speak my music language, baby. You have to admit that would make an awesome lyric.) Okay, so since you gave me a music coping strategy for my parental problems, here is my cure for your overbearing family. Track 11 of Serendipity. This one will make you feel like you are in the middle of a forest completely alone.
>
> To answer your other question: I am pro Thanksgiving break. As pathetic as I've obviously made my home life seem, a break from school is a break from school. I don't usually hang out at home anyway. I go out with friends,

drive, walk, read. Now, as for Thanksgiving day, when I'm forced to stay home and celebrate, that's a joke. My mom and stepdad order a bunch of "homemade" food, my grandparents come over, their friends come over. Someone ends up yelling, usually the stepdad, my mom ends up drinking too much wine, and we all wish we would've pretended it was just any other day. What about yours? Hopefully your Thanksgiving traditions are better than mine.

My response:

Is being crazy considered a tradition? Because that's what our tradition is. Okay, we actually have a real one: The double-blind taste test. First, both my mom and dad make pumpkin pies. Different ones, mind you, but both pumpkin. Then they cut the pies in the other room and put pieces on different plates. One each for everyone there. Then they force us—force us—to eat it blindfolded. Then we have to tell them whose is better. We can't say they both taste the same or they are equally good. Nope. We HAVE to choose a side. It's quite obnoxious. So my siblings and I have a little competition of our own. We always try to even up the score so someone has to be the tiebreaker. But anyway, the winning parent brags about it the entire year. My parents are strange.

Other than that, it's loud and disorganized and exhausting. But the food is actually homemade and we do laugh a lot. So I think I win. But . . . hang in there.

I'm convinced we do speak the same music language because Track 11 on Serendipity *is on my favorites list. (As for your "song" about us speaking the same music language. Just . . . no.) I wonder if we compared our playlists what percentage would be the same. I wouldn't want it to be one hundred percent because that's too similar. You have to bring something new to the table to help balance out my music tastes or I'll learn nothing. You did introduce me to The Crooked Brookes so I think we're safe for now.*

Tuesday from him:

Good thing we're safe. I didn't realize the music list conversation could put us in jeopardy. I feel the need to present a new band to you so we're safe for another couple weeks. Maybe I have that backward. I already did my part. Where is my new band from you? I could really use one. I've had a bad couple of days.

Have you ever tried so hard to live up to expectations only to fall short every time? That was vague and cryptic, wasn't it? Okay, so my stepdad. He's a super demanding jerk and I feel like if I could do or be what he expects me to be, then he'd be nicer to my mom or happier, or something. He's been in my life for six years and I still

119

can't figure out exactly what it is that he expects of me. He'll ask me to do things, I'll think I do exactly what he asks, but he is never satisfied. I know you said you're not good at sage advice, but what would you do in this situation?

Tuesday from me:

I don't know. I'm a bit of a people pleaser so I'd be horrible in that situation. It sounds like maybe you are too. I guess if I were trying my hardest, that's the best I could do. But it sounds like it's his problem, not yours. If you haven't figured out what his expectations are then they are undefined, which makes them impossible to live up to. Have you tried talking it out with him? Asking him?

You need a new band to help you deal with this? How about Better Than Yesterday? Are they new to you or are we in sync again?

Wednesday from him:

They aren't new to me but I love them, of course. However NSYNC better not be on your list or we might be done.

Ask my stepdad. Now there's an obvious solution that I haven't tried yet. I just thought if I kept running as fast as he said for as long as he said that eventually

I'd catch him. I don't know why I care what he thinks so much anyway. Like I said, he's a jerk to both me and my mom. I shouldn't worry about it, especially because it doesn't help. But for whatever reason his approval still means something to me. I do like your advice though. I should try that. Does it work for you when you talk to your parents? Are you a parent whisperer? (More lyrics: She's a parent whisperer and that's why she rules the world.) Tips would be helpful.

Wednesday from me:

Hey, I just give advice, I don't take it. Tips for talking to parents . . . hmm . . . maybe write a letter so they have to listen and can't interrupt. I don't know. I talk to my parents a lot. For example: Can you pass the butter? Can I stay home from school today? Can I borrow the car?

No, but in all seriousness, sometimes I do talk to my mom about things that matter. And half the time it helps. The other times, life is too crazy for her to hear me. I'm not the only one who has no space in my house.

Okay, enough of the minor problems in our lives. Back to the real issue: finding an awesome band you've never heard of. Oh! How about End Game or Flight and Fight? Also, please, please stop making up song lyrics. It's killing me.

Thursday (him):

Flight and Fight? I haven't listened to them before.
You finally found one. This means our playlists aren't
perfectly matched! We're safe. I know you secretly like
my song lyrics. How can you not? They're brilliant. And
besides, I don't see you offering up any lyrics. Do you
have any to share? You said you'd written parts of songs.
You should include some lyrics in a letter so I can read
them.

  As far as writing my stepdad a letter, that's a
really good idea. One I might be able to do. I mean, I
know a girl who just skims letters, but unlike her, he
might actually read the whole thing.

Thursday (me):

I hope you're not referring to me when you say you know
a girl who skims letters. I read at least half. That's
much different than skimming. I measured this week in
letters so I think you've underestimated their importance
in my life. Well, at least their importance in my
Chemistry class. That's almost the same as life. And now
that it's almost Friday, I'm already dreading the
no-letter weekend. No, but really (do I say that a lot?)
I think a letter to your stepdad is a great idea. You
should try it and if it works, let me know. Then maybe

this will become my go-to form of communication with
my parents from here on out. Talking is so overrated,
I am learning.

And there is no way I'm including lyrics in a letter.
I don't share my unfinished songs with anyone. When
I write the perfect one, then I will share.

Friday, him:

You don't share your songs with anyone? As in, no one
has read any of your song lyrics? How are we supposed
to write songs if you don't want anyone to hear them?
We must work on this.

I loved Flight and Fight. They only have three songs
though. Unless I'm missing something. Tell me that they
have more hidden songs somewhere. And I'm with you on
measuring this week in letters and the two-day drought
we are about to experience. If only there was a way to
transport letters faster, through some sort of electronic
device that codes messages and sends them through the
air. But that's just crazy talk.

Friday from me:

Sending letters through the sky? Like when airplanes
attach notes to their tails? I thought they only adver-
tised for going-out-of-business sales. But perhaps our

letters would be okay up there as well. I wonder how much they charge per word.

Nope, no hidden songs from Flight and Fight, unfortunately. Maybe you should offer them some of your lyrics for their next song. Considering how awesome your lyrics are, I'm sure they'll accept. I should stop teasing you about that, considering I won't share lyrics with you . . . or anyone. You're right, it is something I need to work on. Confidence. I'm bad at it. I get too self-conscious. Especially about things that mean a lot to me. I feel like if I hold things close, never share, then I never give anyone the opportunity to judge me.

CHAPTER 20

I sat on my bed, strangling the neck of my guitar and staring down at the lyrics I had finally been able to write. I was now trying to find the perfect melody for them:

I've turned waiting into a form of art.
Tied twisted lines around my broken heart.
To keep me hanging on for one more day.
I've painted on a crooked smile.
Hung the tears to dry awhile.
Because I knew that you'd come back to stay.
But my . . . arms are empty.
And my . . . heart's in pieces.
And my . . . soul is twisting.
And my . . . throat is aching.
Because I've finally woken up to find:
That I've been Left Behind.

The song wasn't finished, but I was satisfied with the first verse and chorus. I patted the newspaper clipping on my wall.

"I'm getting closer," I told it.

Now I only had to work up the nerve to actually let someone else hear the song. One step at a time.

An image had worked its way into my mind as I wrote. It had inspired the *crooked smile* line. Lucas. The way he'd looked at me at the football game. I knew he wasn't my letter writer—as a senior, he didn't take Chemistry—and therefore not who this song was about. But his face was inspiring me. That, and the letters. Apparently my pen pal was good luck. His letters put me in the mood to write songs. And even with the interruptions constantly happening at my house, if I would reread one of his letters, I was back in the moment. It was amazing. It made time fly by. I didn't even mind that Isabel was out of town and that I stayed home all weekend. I got to stay in my little bubble of writing and daydreaming.

If I hummed in the school halls on a Monday, would I get kicked for it? Mondays weren't for humming. It was probably better to keep the song in my head. My heart was singing too, bouncing around in my chest as I headed to Chemistry. When I walked into the classroom, a wall of noise hit me. People were chatting, texting, laughing. My eyes went to the front of the classroom to see a substitute. Then my eyes were on my seat. Sasha, who normally sat in the second row, was sitting next to Lauren.

My heart dropped.

I reminded myself that we had a seating chart that the sub would have to use to take roll. So I went to claim my place. Sasha and Lauren were in the middle of a conversation I couldn't help but overhear.

"I tried that," Sasha said. "It didn't work. What else does he like? I swear I've never had to work this hard for a guy to ask me out in my life."

"Why don't you ask *him* out?" Lauren suggested.

"I tried that, too. He laughed it off. Like I was joking or something."

Were they talking about Cade? Maybe Isabel was right. Maybe he and Sasha weren't dating yet.

I reached the girls and cleared my throat. I offered Sasha a smile when she looked up at me.

"Oh, hi, Lily," Sasha said. "Let's switch. Mine is row two, fourth seat over."

"I'm sure Mr. Ortega left the sub the chart."

She shrugged. "We're both here so it won't matter. It's not like he'll know which one of us is which."

"Right." *I just wanted to read my letter.* I could see the penciled words on the desk, as obvious as if they'd been written in neon lights. That arrow pointing to the bottom of the desk, basically showing her there was something waiting there, was as obvious as ever. Why hadn't I erased the desktop?

She widened her eyes at me. "What?"

If I said something now, she'd discover the note for sure. "Nothing."

I turned and forced myself down to the second row, thinking about how Sasha and Cade would be perfect for each other.

I glanced over my shoulder again. Maybe I didn't have to worry about her finding the letter at all. It was possible my pen pal had gotten displaced today, too. Maybe there wasn't a letter.

Or maybe Sasha was about to find it because her eyes were now on the desktop, her head tilted as she read the words there. My heart was pounding. Lauren whispered something to her and Sasha laughed, her focus changing direction. I took a breath of relief.

I looked over my shoulder so much throughout the rest of class that finally Sasha let me know exactly how she felt about it with a rude hand gesture. I hadn't meant for her to notice.

Toward the end of class the door squeaked open and in walked Cade Jennings. Great.

"Can I help you?" the sub asked.

Cade's eyes scanned the room, landing on Sasha. She smiled and he winked. Looks like she hadn't needed to worry after all. Cade walked a few steps forward and addressed the sub. "Yes, I was told to inform you that your class should get out ten minutes early today to give the students time to get to the assembly."

"Really?"

While Cade was playing whatever prank he and his friends decided was funny, I figured I should probably write my pen pal a letter even though I hadn't read his yet. I didn't always need to be the responder. I'd write him a letter, then leave it on my way out.

I pulled out a sheet of paper while the sub looked through his notes on the desk, trying to confirm Cade's claim.

> *Almost out of time. Haven't read your note yet. Long story.*
> *Remember a while back, I was trying to leave you*
> *on a happy note and I ended up talking about Mondays*
> *and how they suck . . . sort of defeating my purpose?*
> *Well, I take back my labeling of poor, innocent Monday.*
> *I found myself humming this morning on my way to*
> *class. Is it illegal to hum on a Monday? I blame you.*

"I see nothing about this," the sub said.

"That's why I'm here telling you," Cade answered with his big smile.

"Your name?"

"Jack Ryan."

He said it in a casual tone, not in the deep voice that would indicate he was mocking the teacher. Sasha snorted from behind me and that's when the teacher's brow went down.

"Young man, wait here for a moment."

"I would," Cade said, "but I'm on a secret mission." He headed for the door and waved to Sasha on his way out. She laughed and then he was gone.

The sub looked around at the classroom in annoyance. "Who in here is willing to give me his name?"

Nobody said a word. I was so tempted to. I wanted Cade to have some consequences once in a while. But I stayed quiet with the rest of the class.

The bell rang and I grimaced. I quickly jotted down a closing line on the piece of paper.

> *Sorry it's so short, started too late. I'll make up for it tomorrow.*

I folded the letter and slowly packed my things. I just needed to wait until everyone was gone. I stood up and nearly ran into Sasha's chin.

"Do you have a problem with me?" she snapped.

I took a step back. I should've known looking at her for the first half of class wasn't going to be tabled with one rude gesture. "No. I don't."

"You were mad about me stealing your seat? You don't think Lauren is your friend, do you?"

I hadn't been expecting this. "No," I snapped back.

"I'm glad you know your place."

"Is there a problem, girls?" the sub asked.

Sasha's smile made its first appearance as she unleashed it on the teacher. "No, we're just talking about meeting up later. See you." She turned and took her long legs and perfect hair out of the room.

"I wouldn't want either of you as friends anyway," I said way too late.

"What?" the sub asked.

"Nothing." I walked to my normal seat and squatted down, pretending to tie my shoe. Then I exchanged the notes.

I lingered for a moment, staring at the desktop—my initial exchange with my pen pal. The sub was busy writing on the whiteboard so I took out a pencil and erased as much as I could as quickly as I could. Satisfied I didn't have to worry about someone like Sasha reading it ever again, I got up and left.

I ducked around the first corner and hugged the letter I'd retrieved to my chest. It was nice to have a distraction. My heart was still beating fast from my confrontation with Sasha and from the hurried erasing session. I unfolded the letter.

Yes, you should stop mocking me about my song lyrics. I think Flight and Fight would welcome my suggestions. I was just getting ready to write a song about all the things I hated about Chemistry. It would've been a really good song. Okay, fine, I'll stop. Maybe. But only if you start writing down some of your lyrics for me. I want to read them. Don't be self-conscious. I'm sure I'll love them. I get it, though—the holding important things close. I have a hard time sharing private things too . . . except with you for some reason.

I was thinking about the Thanksgiving tradition you told me about a few letters back and how fun that sounded. Maybe I'm just craving pumpkin pie. Maybe I'm just craving a crazy home life. It seems like we have

the opposite problems. My family ignores me, yours is
too present. Maybe we can get them all together and
somehow they will balance each other out.

Maybe we would balance each other out . . .

The wall against my back was doing a good job of keeping me steady. I felt wobbly. Maybe my pen pal and I *would* balance each other out. Maybe we were perfect for each other. I smiled, read the letter again, then carefully folded it in with his other letters that I kept in my backpack.

My head was in the clouds for all of two seconds until I realized we'd have to *meet* if anything else was going to happen. Me on paper was not the same as me in real life. I mean, I was exactly the same, but less awkward. My mind went to both the times I'd hung out with David and how horribly awkward I'd been. Whoever my pen pal was, he'd want nothing to do with me once he found out who I was. Or maybe getting to know someone through letters first was a good idea.

This could go well . . . or horribly.

Okay, calm down, Lily. It's not like he was asking to meet. He just said it was possible that we could balance each other out. That was just an observation. We'd continue on how we were. It was fine. We were fine. Letters were perfect.

Or . . . I could suck it up, face my fears, and meet him.

My phone vibrated in my pocket. It was a text from Isabel.

Where are you? Were we meeting somewhere else today?

On my way, I wrote back.

The halls were empty as I hurried to meet Isabel for lunch. So when I rounded the last corner before the door, I stopped in surprise when I saw one person standing at the end alone. Lucas. He wore dark jeans and a tee today. His headphones were in and he was flipping through a textbook. My heart pummeled my ribs as I forced myself to walk forward. It would be too obvious now if I avoided him.

Maybe I should say something. I'd start with something clever like, *You're listening to music. Cool.* I laughed a little at myself. *So clever, Lily.* No, I could think of something that was actually clever. His T-shirt. It would probably be an awesome band tee, hopefully one I listened to, then I could quote a lyric to him or something.

I reached him and looked at his shirt. Across the front in faded blue was the name Metallica. Not helpful. My eyes went down in disappointment. Then I noticed he was holding a Chemistry textbook. He took Chemistry? But he was a senior.

My brain gave me the warning that I had been standing there silent too long. My eyes shot up to his. He was looking at me now, his earbuds out. When had he done that?

"Hi," I said.

"Hey."

"We're in the hall alone." *What, brain? That's what you chose to spit out? Thanks for nothing.*

But when Lucas gave me his crooked smile, I decided it wasn't the end of the world.

"We are," he said. "Cool shoes."

I lifted up my foot as if he wanted to see my Docs closer. "Thrift store."

He pulled on his T-shirt. "This too."

"Nice."

"You're in Chemistry," I said.

"Second time's a charm."

"You're taking Chemistry . . ."

My phone buzzed in my pocket again. I was sure it was Isabel. Lucas must've heard it as well because his attention was drawn there.

"Isabel is waiting for me."

He smiled again and nodded as if I was trying to get out of this conversation. That wasn't my intent. But now I felt like I should follow through with that.

"I'll—I'll see you around," I stammered.

"Sure." He stuck his earphones back in as I walked away.

My whole body felt like it was soaring. Lucas could really be . . . no. I wasn't going to let my brain give me some unrealistic scenario just because I wanted it to be true. But . . . it could've been true. I could now add Lucas to the list of possibilities at least. I flipped to the back of my notebook and added his name, big and bold. As I went over all the clues it made much more sense than anyone who I'd written there before. My heart jumped in my chest. This could work. We could work.

CHAPTER 21

I woke up the next morning smiling and didn't stop even when I got to school. I was determined to write a letter in Chemistry suggesting that my pen pal and I meet in person. He seemed to be hinting at that and I was ready now, too. It would be perfect. I'd even tell him where we should meet that day after school, by the composition room. It would symbolize what had brought us together in the first place—music.

I let out a happy sigh, imagining Lucas waiting for me by the composition room. Then I went back to sorting mail into the teacher's boxes in the main office. This was one of my regular duties as office aide fourth period. A pretty mindless duty, lending itself to daydreaming. Although, really, what didn't lend itself to daydreaming?

Mrs. Clark came in holding a cardboard box. "Lily, I need you to deliver these to Mr. Ortega. They're his review packets he wanted printed off."

"Right now?"

She smiled. "No, next period when you're not here. Of course right now."

"But Mr. Ortega has class right now. Next period is his free one. Maybe the next office aide should take them."

Mrs. Clark shook her head. "He needs them right now. He's using them. Right now."

"Oh."

She pushed them into my arms. "Quickly please."

I stood, the box throwing me off-balance for a moment. I was almost certain that my pen pal was in second-period Chemistry. Still, I felt a surge of nervousness.

I made my way out of the office, through the halls and to the C building. Then I entered the Chemistry room where I now stood at the back, not wanting to take another step forward. I could see Isabel in the front row. The front row was not a very good vantage point for observations. And in the back row, in my seat, was a boy, his head bent low, writing. Maybe just taking notes. He was taking notes.

Mr. Ortega waved me forward and pointed to his desk. I rushed there and set the box down.

"Thanks," the teacher said, and continued his lecture.

Isabel smiled and waved at me. I tried to return the gesture and began walking toward the door. I could see the front of the boy in the back row now, his hair flopped over his forehead as he furiously wrote on his paper. He was so obvious about it. Why wasn't Mr. Ortega calling him out? Because he was just taking notes, I told myself. Really intense . . . apparently funny . . . Chemistry notes.

I was good at pretending.

I could also pretend it wasn't Cade Jennings even though that was just as obvious as the fact that he wasn't taking notes.

All my pretending had to stop when I watched him fold up the paper into fourths and tuck it beneath the desk. I rushed out of the room before he saw me and didn't look back.

CHAPTER 22

Cade couldn't be my pen pal.

He couldn't.

Cade was an insensitive, selfish, arrogant jerk. He was not a funny, thoughtful guy with exceptionally good taste in music. *Lucas* was supposed to be my pen pal. I had all but convinced myself of that the night before.

Cade was definitely not someone who would balance me out. He made me my most unbalanced self.

Why did I go into that classroom? I asked myself, furious, as I tore down the hall. Why hadn't I found someone to make the delivery for me? I could never unknow this. I could never go back to getting anonymous, perfect letters again. I wanted to cry. I wanted to scream. I wanted to go back in there and tell Cade that he wasn't allowed to be two different people.

I found the nearest bathroom to get my emotions under control. I refused to cry. Cade Jennings didn't get to have this much power over me.

I leaned back against the tile wall, letting its coolness seep through my shirt and chill me out. Across the room, on the opposite wall, was a full-length mirror. My hair was a wavy mess today, a little more unruly than normal. I wore a plain brown tee with a pair of skinny jeans and white high-tops with hand-drawn pictures on them. It was one of my more plain outfits. I took off the necklace I wore, one Ashley had made me ages ago, and looked at the charms—a butterfly, a cat, a flower, a music note. There was no rhyme or reason to the things she'd picked to put on the necklace. Just everything she'd thought was cute when she was ten. She made fun of me for wearing it now, but I loved it.

I squeezed the necklace in my fist, hoping to gain some sort of positive energy or something from it. But my sister was right, it was pointless.

I slid down the wall and hugged my knees to my chest. I hated Cade Jennings. Now more than ever.

Why does he always have to ruin everything?

I knew that thought made no sense. The fact that Cade Jennings wrote the letters should've made me realize he wasn't the person I'd always thought he was. But I'd never understand how the person in the letters could be the same person who mocked those he considered beneath him, who'd mistreated me and my friend. He wasn't. He wasn't the same person.

Two girls came into the bathroom, laughing. They both stopped when they saw me. I stood, brushed off my jeans, and left.

In Chemistry I very slowly pulled his letter out from under the desk. I was shaking. For the first time ever, I dreaded reading it.

> *Humming on a Monday? Has that ever happened before in the history of Mondays? I'll take the blame for that if you'll take the blame for making me laugh in the middle of a Chemistry lecture.*
>
> *Too bad there's not a way for us to exchange letters during break. A week is a long time. I mean, your idea of airplanes carrying our messages was a good one, but I was referring to that new thing some kids do these days called texting. What do you think? Or am I just the guy who keeps you entertained during Chemistry? I'm totally fine with that title, by the way. Chemistry entertainer. No, that was bad. You'll think of a better name for me I'm sure, being the word girl. Word girl? I think maybe you were right about banning me from writing lyrics.*

The letter should've made me laugh but it only made me want to punch something. I refolded it exactly like he had and stuck it back under the desk. Cade didn't know he was writing to me. So as far as he knew, the recipient of his notes wasn't in school today. And I wouldn't be in school for the rest of the year. I was not going to write back to Cade Jennings. Ever.

When class was over, I got up to leave. "Lily," Mr. Ortega called. "I need to speak with you."

My heart stopped. Had he figured out the letter-writing thing? Was I about to get in trouble for writing on the desktop and wasting my time in class? Was Cade about to be the bane of my existence *again*? If I could've I would've grabbed the letter I'd left tucked under the desk and made a run for it. I didn't want Mr. Ortega reading it. As the class emptied out, I slowly walked to the front where Mr. Ortega sat behind a long table.

He cleared his throat. "I got a not-so-glowing report from the sub yesterday. I have to say, I'm very disappointed."

"What?" I asked.

"He said not only were you and Lauren talking the entire class but that you gave someone a rude gesture, and then picked on another student after class."

It took me too long to realize that the sub, because of our seating mix-up, thought I was Sasha. "Oh. We changed seats," I said. "He thinks I was someone else."

"He also said a young man came in at the end of class, pulling a prank. He was one of your friends, but you wouldn't tell him who it was."

"He is *not* one of my friends," I said, my face flushing. I pictured the note stuck under the desk.

"Then who was it?"

Why wouldn't I just tell him? I owed Cade nothing. Nothing at all.

"It's not my place to say."

Mr. Ortega frowned. "I'm very disappointed. After-school detention for two weeks. I'll shorten it to one if you change your mind about coming clean and taking responsibility for your actions."

"But—"

"That'll be all."

🐾 🐾 🐾

"What's wrong?" Isabel asked me at lunch.

All I wanted to do was tell her what had happened. It was all I could think about. But I didn't know how she'd react. What would I even say? I imagined how our conversation would go.

Remember that pen pal I told you about in Chemistry? It's your ex. I've been exchanging letters with your ex.

The one you hate?

Yes, the one you broke up with because he hated me and I hated him. The one I still hate. Apparently we're okay on paper. Perfect, actually. So maybe I'll date him through letters the rest of our lives. Cool?

Of course it's cool, I mean, I've made out with him and talked to him for hours on end for months on end, but hey, he's all yours now.

No. That wasn't how it would go at all. It would be better to have this delicate conversation off school grounds. Just in case I did cry, or if she punched me or something equally as dramatic.

"Can we talk later?" I asked Isabel. "After school. I need to tell you something."

Her brown eyes grew concerned. "That sounds so cryptic. Are you okay?"

"Later. I'll tell you later."

She squeezed my hand. "Okay. Later."

CHAPTER 23

The already-long day ended an hour later than usual because of detention.

Ashley looked over at me as she pulled into our driveway. "You're mopey today. Detention isn't a big deal. I was in there like every other month. It's a great time to get homework done."

I didn't want to tell her this had nothing to do with detention and everything to do with my letter-writing world being shattered.

"Good idea," I muttered.

"Guess who asked me out?" Ashley asked brightly.

Like I wanted to hear about her—or anyone's—love life at the moment. "Who?"

"Mark. The boy who saw the food in my teeth. Apparently I'd already made it through the first two stages. Thank goodness."

"He told you that?" I glanced at my sister. "He said, 'Ashley, first I found you mysterious, then I found you intriguing, and then when that food was on your tooth, I found you adorably funny. So now I can ask you out?'"

Ashley grinned. "Yes, that is basically what he said."

144

"How?"

"By asking me out."

I grabbed my backpack and climbed out of the car. "It probably went more like this: 'Huh, that girl is cute, I should go out with her. Because guys don't care about anything else. They don't care about personality or intrigue.'" I could hear the bitterness in my voice but I didn't try to stop it.

"Wow." Ashley raised her eyebrows at me. "Jaded?"

"Yes, I've unlocked that achievement. Leveled up."

"What?"

"Nothing." I headed for my room, needing some time to unwind on my guitar before I called Isabel.

I reached my bedroom. I should've known something was wrong when the door was wide open, or when my guitar case was only halfway under my bed. I should've, but I didn't. I pulled the case out, very calm. The latches were undone, but I figured I'd just left them undone the night before. I flipped open the lid.

The first thing I saw were all the strings loose, a couple broken completely. That didn't have me panicking, just a little angry. Strings were easy to replace. But then I saw the jagged line across the neck of the guitar, close to the body.

"No, no, no, no." I pulled it out and only the neck came— the end as spiked as a rake. The rest stayed in the case, completely severed. My face drained of all feeling. "No! Mom!"

My mother arrived at my door, breathless. "What? What's wrong? Are you okay?"

I held up the bodiless neck for her to see.

Her expression went from panicked to sympathetic. "Oh no. What happened?"

"What do you mean, what happened?" I exploded, feeling tears threaten. "Jonah happened! I've asked you a million times to keep him out of my room."

Mom frowned. "Jonah did that?"

"Who else? I certainly didn't do it."

"Don't jump to conclusions."

"I don't have to jump to anything. I'm holding the conclusion." I threw the broken piece into the case and sank onto my bed face first.

"Oh, honey. We'll figure something out."

"What?" I said, my voice muffled by the mattress. "You can't afford to buy me a new guitar. This one took me six months to earn. What's left to figure out?"

"Is it repairable?"

"It's splintered. It's not a clean break."

The mattress sank down as my mom sat next to me. She rubbed my back. I shrugged her hand off. She got the hint.

"I'm sorry, Lil. You can have first dibs on all the fairs," she said softly. "I'll help you earn it back."

I lifted my head, brushing the tears away from my eyes. "Why should I have to earn it back?" I said. "Shouldn't *Jonah* be working the fairs to buy me a new one?"

"He's seven."

"Old enough to know better."

"Honey . . ."

"Mom? Can you leave? I want to be alone."

"Okay."

I didn't say anything and she stood and left my room. I heard her call for Jonah as she shut my door. Then they had a conversation in the hall. I listened in, my face pressed back into the mattress.

"Jonah, did you break your sister's guitar?"

"What? No."

"Did you go in her room and break her guitar?"

"No! I didn't."

Right. Give him the chance to say no, Mom. Good call. She should've just led with, "I know you broke her guitar." But whatever. It didn't matter. It was broken. Jonah admitting it wouldn't change that fact.

There was a rattling on my handle followed by my mom saying, "Leave her be for now. You can talk to her later."

Mom must've told everyone to leave me be because no one bugged me for the rest of the evening. Not a single person. After years of trying to get some alone time, I finally had it.

I pulled my notebook out and stared at the song I had started. I couldn't write that song right now. It was about *him* . . . about *Cade*. I shuddered. I could only write one song about Cade. I turned to a fresh page and positioned my pencil.

You claim you want to be heard.

So you write your hollow words.

You fill your life with deception.

Because it's all about perception.

The world sees you one way.

And they listen to all you say.

You crave their attention.

To feed your addiction.

You have two sides.

Two faces.

You're trying to hide.

In two places.

And I hate you, Cade, because you're the biggest jerk in the world and you should go away forever and stop writing me stupid letters where you pretend to be nice and misunderstood.

"Ugh." Even my angry Cade-inspired songs were better than anything I'd written before him. I scratched two deep lines in an X across the words. Then I flipped to the back and crossed out all my suspects. *Why couldn't it have been you?* I thought as I x-ed out Lucas's name.

I reached up, ripped down the newspaper clipping from my wall, and crumpled it into a tight ball. Even if I still could finish any song, I wouldn't be able to write the guitar part for it. And there was no way I was using a song that had anything to do with Cade. I threw the paper across the room. I was being dramatic, but for once I felt like I was justified. Everything had gone wrong.

I dug my phone out of my pocket and called Isabel.

"Hey, Lil!" she answered.

"Hey." I thought I'd kept the tears out of my voice but when she added, "What's wrong?" I realized I hadn't.

"Jonah destroyed my guitar."

"Oh no! How?"

"I don't know. He's denying it, but it's broken. Completely broken."

"I'm so sorry," Isabel said softly. "I know how much you loved your guitar. How hard you worked to buy it."

"Yeah."

"Your mom will probably replace it, right?"

"She can't afford that, Iz. She couldn't even afford a spool of thread for me before payday." Tears came to my eyes again. "This is not a spool of thread."

"That totally sucks."

"I know."

"Aw, Lil. It'll be okay."

"It's just, this was my thing, you know?" The tears fell down my cheeks now and I couldn't stop them. "It was the one thing I was really good at. The one thing that brought me perfect peace and happiness. I don't need much, but I need this." I wondered if I was only talking about my guitar.

"Then you'll find a way to get another one," Isabel said with determination. "It might take some time, but you'll do it."

I knew she was right. "Yeah."

"If I could, I'd buy you one."

I smiled through my tears. "I wouldn't accept something like that from you, Iz."

"I know."

I sniffled and wiped my nose on my sleeve.

"So was that the thing you wanted to tell me at lunch?" Isabel asked after a moment.

I paused, and realized I wanted to have this conversation in person. "Are you busy?" I asked. "Can I come over?"

"Of course you can."

"Okay. I'll tell you when I get there."

I hung up, gathered the letters from Cade, and headed for the door.

CHAPTER 24

I was staring at Einstein on Isabel's ceiling because I couldn't look at her. I'd rather have Einstein judge me.

"I have to tell you something."

"Okay . . ." Isabel moved to her desk chair.

"Remember how I was exchanging letters with someone in Chemistry?" I said to Einstein.

"Yes. That girl?"

"Girl?" It had been so long since I'd thought my pen pal was a girl that it took me a while to remember that I had at first. "No. I mean yes, but I found out she wasn't a girl."

"How'd you find that out?"

"He said something about being a guy in one of the letters. Sorry. I thought I told you."

"It's okay."

I waited for a moment. Waited for her to give a little excited squeal or happy hum. Something that would indicate that she thought this was a good thing—my pen pal being a guy. But she didn't. She was silent. Probably because I seemed so distraught.

I sat up then to face her. Her expression was as serious as mine.

"Remember years ago when you gave up a boy because he was coming between us?" I asked in a rush.

She nodded. "You mean Cade?"

"Yes."

She laughed a little. "Yes, of course I remember." She paused and added, "I don't want you to think that you were the only reason Cade and I broke up. The two of you both complained about each other to me all the time, and I got tired of it. But Cade and I wouldn't have worked even if you weren't in the picture."

I nodded, then blurted. "Cade is my pen pal."

Isabel didn't answer. "Cade Jennings," I repeated for effect, barely believing the words myself. "He's the one who's been writing to me in Chemistry."

I pulled my shoulder bag, which I had flung onto her bed when I first walked in, onto my lap. Then I dug out all the letters and held them out to Isabel. But my best friend didn't move to retrieve them.

"And I'm going to stop writing him. Now," I said. "I didn't write him today even though he wrote me. I'll never write him again."

She still said nothing and I noticed something missing from her expression—surprise.

That's when it hit me.

Isabel knew.

I'd told her I had a pen pal. And Cade was in her Chemistry class writing letters without the tiniest bit of discretion. And she knew. Isabel was observant like that.

I stood, shoving the letters back into my bag. "Why didn't you tell me?" I demanded.

"Because you hate him and you seemed so excited about the writing."

"How long have you known?"

"Not very long. I swear."

"*Why didn't you tell me?* It felt like being slapped in the face today when I saw him at that desk. A little warning would've been nice."

Isabel held up her hands. "I know. I'd hoped after a while that his letters would show you that he wasn't someone you wanted to continue writing to. Because you hate him."

I frowned. "I do hate him. But his letters are different . . ."

Isabel's expression went a degree darker. "Wait. You like him? Because of his letters?"

My heart jumped. "No! I don't. What? Not at all."

Isabel nodded, looking relieved. "You like David, right?"

"David . . . He's fine . . . nice . . ."

Isabel sighed. "You two would be perfect for each other if you'd both give it a chance."

"Why are you insistent on getting me and David together?" I asked, putting my hands on my hips.

Isabel shrugged, but her expression said it all. "I thought he was a better match for you."

"Better than who?" I asked.

"The alternative."

"Cade?"

"Yes!"

The air seemed to fly out of me and I was rendered silent. She was jealous. She didn't want me to know I was writing to Cade because she was jealous. Even though she and Cade had dated two years ago and she didn't like him anymore, she was still jealous.

"I'm sorry," she said again, her voice softer. "But it shouldn't matter. You wouldn't ever like Cade, would you? It would be too awkward, considering the whole history. I mean, I gave him up for you two years ago."

"But you didn't give him up for me . . . you just said that."

She looked at the floor then back up quickly, but not before I knew the truth. She *had* broken up with him because of me. Because I couldn't get along with him. I always suspected that, but she'd always contradicted me. And now I knew for sure.

"Well, I won't stand in your way anymore," I snapped. "Go get him back."

She gasped. "I'm with Gabriel now. I don't want him back."

"You just don't want me to have him."

"You said you didn't want him."

"I don't." What was wrong with me? "I need to go." I headed for her door.

"Lily, wait."

"I can't do this right now."

"We'll get through this, right?"

"Yes," I answered right away. "Just not right now."

☆ ☆ ☆

It was only eight thirty at night but I was already in bed, staring at my own ceiling now. There were no judging eyes up there, only a blank wall, but I felt just as bad. I sighed.

Why was I so mad at Isabel? I knew one reason—because she'd been lying to me. On purpose. That hurt. Would I ever believe her again?

But . . . was it more than the lost trust that was bothering me?

Maybe, just maybe, I had wanted her to say it was okay for me to like Cade.

Not that I did. At all.

But in a sense I could understand Isabel's possessiveness. Two years ago, I'd driven her and Cade apart. I wasn't a good friend.

The sounds of the house around me were loud—my brothers getting ready for bed in the bathroom next door, my mom yelling to make sure they brushed for two minutes, Ashley laughing on the phone in the hall, my father asking her to keep it down. I forced my eyes closed, listened to the noise of my family instead of the noise in my head. Tomorrow would be better than this day had been. It had to be.

CHAPTER 25

Do you know how disappointing it is to pull out a note expecting a letter from someone, only to see your own handwriting staring back at you? It sucks. You must be sick. Which I'm sure is not very good for you, but think about where that left me. I'm sorry you're sick. I hope you get better soon.

Okay, so, um that looks like a deformed turtle or something but it was meant to be a bowl of soup. That thing that looks like the turtle's head is a spoon. Do you see it now? No? I won't attempt to draw again. I apologize for making you suffer through that and when you're just recovering from being sick.

Okay, quiz. What music do you listen to when you're sick? Is it different than or the same as your everyday music? I listen to really sappy music when I'm sick. I don't know why because I don't like that music when I'm healthy. Maybe it

helps me wallow a little bit more. We need to think of some
sappy song lyrics for our fans to listen to when they're sick.
Something like . . . You thought I was going to make up
some song lyrics, didn't you? I learned my lesson. I'm not.
  How's home life?

I closed my eyes. I would not write back. I would not. The
letters were from *Cade*. He hated me. I hated him.

I folded the letter up and put it back. If I stopped writing he
eventually would as well. I needed to stop reading, too. I knew I
did. It wasn't fair to give up on my end of the letter writing but
still participate in the reading. The part that, despite knowing
who had written it, still gave me a thrill. It still had me nodding
my head in agreement and smiling in amusement.

I did not want to relate to Cade. I did not want to find him
funny. I knew the other side of him. And I didn't care why he
acted like he did in public. He was old enough not to treat
people like garbage, regardless of how he'd been treated by his
dad and stepdad.

And I was old enough to be honest and tell him that I
couldn't write anymore.

I took out the two letters that were under the desk,
dropped them in my bag, and stared at the empty sheet of
paper in front of me. I didn't have to be mean. I didn't want to
humiliate him or anything, even though that's exactly what he
liked to do to me. I was bigger than that.

I wasn't sick but thank you for the turtle bowl anyway. It
was so awfully drawn that it almost crossed the line that
made it art again. Almost. I've had a bad couple of days.

Tears pricked my eyes as I wrote that last line. I wanted to tell him everything that happened. I wanted to say, "First I found out that you were you. Then my brother broke the one thing that might've helped me deal with that fact, then my best friend and I got into the worst fight of our friendship so she can't even help me through this." But I couldn't. I wondered what advice he'd give me about my brother, about Isabel. This was Cade Jennings. He had millions of friends. Backups for his backups. Isabel was my one.

I got in a fight with my best friend. Plus my little
brother broke something very important to me.
Something I can't replace and I was so angry that
when he tried to hug me this morning to say sorry, I
turned my back on him. And I hate myself for doing
that, but I'm still angry.

This time a tear fell and I swiped it away quickly. I still felt guilty for turning my back on Jonah that morning. He'd looked so sad and I couldn't get over my anger to comfort him. And I didn't think I should've been expected to comfort him, though it was obvious my mom thought so by the look she'd given me. That kid got away with everything.

Maybe he needed to learn that not everything could be hugged away. See, here I was again trying to justify how I'd acted that morning.

> *But then I think: it's just a thing. You know? And my brother is a person. A thing is not more important than a person . . .*

And you, Cade Jennings, are not more important than my friendship. And I hate you even more for coming between us. That's what I should've written. But I didn't, I finished with:

> *Anyway, I wasn't sick.*

This wasn't the note I had set out to write. The note I had set out to write was supposed to include the words: *I won't be writing you anymore.* This note did not come anywhere close to including those words. Then why was I folding it up and shoving it in place?

I just needed one more. This last letter. Then I'd end it officially.

☆ ☆ ☆

I needed to talk to Isabel. We could work through this. We just needed to talk it out more. I'd left too fast the day before, hadn't acknowledged my fault in anything. That's what I realized as I left Chemistry. I just needed to tell Isabel that I was sorry for breaking up her and Cade because I was too immature to deal with him back then (and maybe now) and that she had every right to not want me to write to him. I hoped that admission would fix everything.

Only Isabel wasn't waiting at our meeting spot for lunch. She didn't answer my texts either. I couldn't find her anywhere. She was probably giving me space.

I wandered toward the food cart. I'd get some food and find a quiet place in the library to eat and think.

David was leaning against a tree to my right so I cut left and went the long way around. I sensed David had only gone out with me as some sort of favor to Isabel. To keep me from the "alternative." I did not need pity dates.

There were three lines for the sandwich cart and I picked the wrong one. I didn't know it at first. But after a few minutes, Cade, Sasha, and crew were in line right behind me.

I wanted to leave but it would be too obvious . . . and weak.

I pulled out my phone and pretended to read texts.

From behind me came a voice. "Nice shorts." That was Sasha. I knew she was referring to mine. They were jeans I had cut off and sewn patches on. I didn't want to turn around and acknowledge that she'd been talking about me, but when Cade laughed, a rush of anger made me turn.

He had his arm around Sasha, which was different than past times I'd seen them together where she was the one hanging on to him. I wondered what changed. I looked him straight in the eyes, like he was the one who made the comment and said, "I'm sorry, what was that? I don't speak jerk."

He didn't flinch, just cocked his head and said, "And here I thought you were fluent."

It shouldn't have hurt. I was used to it. I'd heard much worse. But it did hurt, and I didn't want him to see that. I left the line, not sure where I was going, when I saw Lucas sitting beside his friends, listening to music. Present but not present.

I marched over. When I arrived in front of him I tugged on the cord to his earphones. They fell into his lap and his eyes met mine in surprise.

"You want to go do something?" I blurted out.

"What? Now?"

"No. Friday—this Friday. The day after tomorrow. There's a concert at the all-ages club in Phoenix. A new band is playing. You want to go with me?" My nerves were catching up with me, overriding the bravado that had propelled me here. All of Lucas's friends had gone silent and were staring at me. He was staring at me.

"Sure," he said.

"Sure?"

"Yes, I'll go. Should we meet there at eight?"

"Okay. Friday at eight."

I managed not to let out any form of happy yelp or excited jump as I walked away.

CHAPTER 26

The next morning Isabel jogged toward me as I walked to first period, determination in her eyes. When she reached me we both stopped.

"Time's up," she said.

I smiled and she handed me some sheets of paper. Had she written me a letter?

"What's this?"

"The last thing I thought about before I went to bed last night."

I unfolded the papers. They were ads, printed off of Craigslist. *Gently used acoustic guitar. In great shape. New strings. Plays perfectly. $150. Or best offer.* There were several more similar to the first for different prices.

I smiled. Those prices were a lot more doable than four hundred, but they still seemed impossible. I glanced up at Isabel tentatively, knowing this was her peace offering, feeling bad for not having one of my own.

"I'm sorry," we both said at the same time. Then we both smiled.

"Let me go first," she said. "I should have told you it was

Cade." She looked around and dropped her voice. "I'm so sorry I didn't. It was wrong of me and I can only imagine how you felt when you learned who you'd been exchanging your thoughts with. And it hadn't even occurred to me that you might have been telling him things that you wouldn't want him to know. I really just thought they were letters about music."

"I'm sorry, too. I should've shown you the letters and then you would've known. And I'm really sorry for getting in between you two when you were together."

She shook her head so hard that her hair went one way and then the other. "No. Please don't apologize for that. You can't get in between something that isn't already broken."

I gave her a hug, choosing to believe she was sincere. Even though I now knew that on some level, she really did think it was my fault. But I'd own that because I knew in some ways, it was. "You're the best friend on the planet." I held up the Craigslist ads. "And thank you for this."

"I know they aren't your guitar," Isabel said, nodding. "You'd saved up for a great one. But it's something, right?"

"Yes. It's perfect. I might be able to afford one like this in a couple weeks." *Maybe in time to still make the deadline for the competition*, I thought, feeling a rush of hope. If I won that, I'd be able to afford a guitar and more. "Thank you, Iz."

She smiled. "You're welcome."

I put the papers in my backpack just as the first bell rang. "So . . . I asked Lucas out."

Isabel's eyes widened. "You did? When?"

"Yesterday," I said, feeling a jolt of nerves. "I asked him to a concert this weekend." I turned to her. *"Please* tell me that you and Gabriel will go with me."

"Of course!" Isabel put her arm around me. "I can't believe you asked him out."

"I can't believe it, either! And he said yes." I was still in shock.

"Of course he did." Isabel nudged me. "That's what I've been trying to tell you. You don't need anonymous letter writing when you are Lily Abbott."

I laughed, blushing. "Let's not get carried away."

"So how did that go, anyway?" she asked.

"How did what go?"

She shot me a sidelong glance. "You stopped writing Cade, right? I know you. You probably felt the need to explain why in a letter. What did you say?"

I wrung my hands together. "I haven't been able to explain why yet. But I will. I will."

"I know you will. I mean, it's Cade Jennings. Mortal enemy number one." She laughed, gave me another hug, then turned around and headed to her first class. "See you later."

Yes, exactly. Mortal enemy number one.

✿　✿　✿

I'm sorry. It sounds like you were worse than sick—you were depressed. Is there anything I can do? I haven't had

a blowup with a best friend, but it can't be fun. I'm
sure it will work out.

What did your brother break? I don't have any
younger siblings so I never have to worry about that
stuff. I know how kids can be, though. Every year since
freshman year I have to help coach a kids' sports
league——"volunteer" service. The kids can be punks
but I actually really enjoy it. They're fun. Wait, this
started off as me commiserating with you. Kids suck. We
should be born adults. Better? No, but seriously, if I had
something irreplaceable and it was broken, I know I'd be
mad. It's understandable. Don't beat yourself up about
your reaction to your little brother. What was the
awesome advice you gave me a few letters back? Hang in
there. Chin up. Also, that song you made me listen to a
few letters back, brilliant. Listen to that.

This was it. His last letter that I'd read. So it was okay to smile
a little at the contents of it. But then remembering his "fluent
in jerk" comment the day before at lunch made me angry
again. Then rereading the letter made me soften. This was so
messed up.

I couldn't help but wonder how he was doing. We'd spent
the last few letters talking about me. I wondered if he hoped
every holiday season that his dad would call. What an awful
feeling to be abandoned like that by someone who is supposed
to love you. And here I was, preparing to abandon him.

I shook my head. I hated him for making me feel sorry for him. For showing me a different side to him. I had a feeling that this—the person in the letters—was his real side. But what good was knowing that? He'd never reveal that side in public. I wrote back.

> *You know, your awesome advice was just what I needed.*
> *I'm now hanging in there and the second I put my chin up*
> *I felt one hundred percent better. Who knew those bits of*
> *advice actually worked? Also, "made" is such a strong word.*
> *I think I merely suggested that you listen to that song. If my*
> *suggestion creates an undying desire to act, that's on you.*
>
> *No, really, I feel a little better today. My friend*
> *and I made up this morning. I think we're good. If not*
> *all the way, we will be soon, I'm sure. My brother and I*
> *are at a standoff. I know I'll soften soon because he's*
> *the prince of the house and as aggravating as he is, I*
> *love his face. He still won't admit to what he did,*
> *though. I have a hard time with people who do one*
> *thing in one situation and a completely different thing*
> *in another. Once he aligns himself, I'll feel much better.*

Okay so that was a totally passive-aggressive statement but I couldn't help it. I needed to get that off my chest. I stuck the letter in its home and was actually able to focus on Chemistry the rest of class.

CHAPTER 27

"**Y**our detention is really making my life hard."

"Hi, Ashley, nice to see you, too." I shut the car door and my sister peeled out of the parking lot. "What's the hurry?"

"I have to get to work."

"Then why didn't Mom pick me up?"

"She has some craft fair out of town."

"On a Thursday afternoon?"

"I don't know all the details. Ask her."

I stopped talking. I could tell my sister was done. I reached up and pulled out the elastic band holding my hair back then ran my fingers through my waves.

"Mom said somebody is picking up Wyatt in a little bit for his first club baseball practice," Ashley added, "so make sure he eats something right away."

"Okay."

"And I guess dinner is whatever you want."

That meant cold cereal. "Okay."

She barely stopped enough for me to climb out of the car before she was off again. "Thanks for the ride," I said to her taillights.

Inside, I yelled into the TV room, "Wyatt, eat. You have baseball practice." Then I went to my room and changed my jeans for a pair of loose shorts, my blouse for a tank top and my flats for a pair of wool socks that went up to my knees—the socks because I wanted to dress like it was summer when technically it was heading toward winter. Arizona winter, but still. I felt better until I tripped over the edge of my guitar case. I snarled at it and kicked it all the way under the bed. My door creaked open.

"Uh, knock, please," I said. When I turned around I could see Jonah standing in the small opening.

He pushed open the door but didn't breach the threshold. I should've opened my arms and let him run to me but I didn't. I offered him a stiff smile. "Yes?"

"Can you get me some cereal?"

"You know how to get your own cereal, buddy."

He frowned at the space under my bed. "I didn't do it."

I sighed. "Jonah. It's important to take responsibility when we do the wrong thing. If you can't tell me what you did, then how am I supposed to believe that you're sorry?"

His bottom lip stuck out. "I'm sorry that you hate me."

I sighed. "I'm mad that my guitar is broken and I'm mad that you touch my things without asking. But I don't hate you. I will never hate you."

"I didn't do it."

It was a lost cause. One day the truth would come out. And even then, it wouldn't matter. My guitar would still be broken. "Okay, go eat."

I sat down on my bed and docked my phone on my stereo, turning it up as loud as I could stand. Listening to Blackout didn't necessarily accomplish its intended purpose of relaxing me—because now they made me think of Cade and the letters. But I would not let him ruin my favorite band for me. I turned the music up another notch.

I opened my notebook and stared down a sketch I had started in detention. I wasn't sure what I wasn't liking about the design.

Jonah appeared at my door, his mouth moving but only music sounding. I switched off the song.

"Someone's at the door," he said.

"Oh, okay." I stood up. I figured it was the mom of one of Wyatt's teammates, coming to pick him up.

When I rounded the corner though, Cade Jennings was standing in the open doorway.

I'm sure my face fell in shock. Cade's expression was also one of utter surprise.

I was so shocked, in fact, that I slammed the door in his face.

What was Cade doing here? Did he figure out the truth about the letters? My heart was pounding. It was probably too late to go run and change my clothes. He'd already seen me and my knee high socks. I took one step back and then I heard Cade knock three times. I tried to pat down my crazy hair once before giving up and opening the door again.

Cade's initial look of shock had softened to his normal look of smugness. He took in my hair and outfit.

"Shut up," I said.

"I didn't say anything."

"Your face did."

"Really? And what did my face say?"

"You know what your face said."

He laughed a little and shrugged.

"Why are you here?" I demanded.

"I'm Wyatt's club coach. We have practice today."

"Oh." Ugh. Cade was my brother's coach? No wonder he'd been surprised to see me. He probably hadn't realized I was Wyatt's sister. "Okay. Just be nice to my brother . . . please," I added.

I wouldn't have felt the need to add that if the real-life Cade was like the one in the letters. But he wasn't, so I did.

Cade shrugged with a smirk. "I will. He can't help who his sister is."

I let out an exasperated sigh. "Right. I'll go get him."

I hoped Cade would stay by the door but instead he followed me into the kitchen. Wyatt wasn't there, though; only Jonah sat at the table, eating his cereal.

I glanced back at Cade, and saw that he was looking at the underside of his expensive sneaker. He'd clearly stepped on the crunched-up pile of Fruity Pebbles on the floor. Great. I watched as he brushed his foot against the kitchen tile, then leaned against the counter, almost knocking over a bunch of bowls that were still half-full of milk.

I groaned inwardly. Cade was in my house judging me all

over again with new criteria to add to his list. I stacked the bowls and set them in the sink.

Wyatt came running into the kitchen. "Hi, Coach!" he said to Cade. "I'm ready!"

"You must be Wyatt."

My brother nodded, then glanced at me. "What's wrong, Lily?" he asked. "You look mad."

"I do?"

"Are you still mad that Jonah—"

"Ate all the Lucky Charms?" I quickly interrupted. "Yes. I am."

"I didn't eat all the Lucky Charms!" Jonah protested from the table.

"Then where are they?"

Jonah hummed an "I don't know" and kept eating his cereal.

Wyatt scrunched up his nose and was probably about to contradict me when I said, "You better be on your way. You don't want to be late."

Cade headed for the door and I stopped Wyatt. "Hey," I whispered. "Don't mention my broken guitar to your coach, okay?"

"Why not?" Wyatt whispered back.

Because if he thought about it too hard, he might figure out that my brother breaking my guitar was too similar to a certain letter he'd read recently. "Because I don't want him to think badly of Jonah."

"He wouldn't like Jonah if he knew?" Wyatt asked.

"We just don't need to talk badly about Jonah to people."

"Okay," Wyatt said, and hurried out the door.

For two hours I waited anxiously for my brother to get home. I tried to distract myself with sewing and then writing and then sketching, but each attempt was useless. When I saw Cade's car pull up around seven thirty, I opened the front door and stood on the porch as Wyatt came running up. I waited for him to turn and wave to Cade. As soon as Cade drove away, I said, "So? How was it?"

Wyatt was beaming. "It was great! I love baseball. We all got nicknames. Want to know mine?"

Of course Cade would give them all nicknames. "Yes," I said, already worried.

"Pink Lightning!"

"Pink? Lightning?"

Wyatt held up one foot. Across the side of his baseball cleat was a hot pink Nike swoosh. My mom must've picked them up at the thrift store like she did a lot of things.

"Yeah. The kids thought it was funny when Coach Cade said it. They laughed. But then everyone was cool with it."

I swallowed the anger in my throat for my brother's sake. I did not want him to feel bad. That was a name everyone was going to laugh at every single week and have to keep remembering they were cool with.

"That's a fun nickname," I said at last.

"Yeah. It's good."

"Well, go shower."

He started to walk away then stopped. "Lily?"

"Wyatt?"

He looked down at his feet. "Um . . . never mind."

I frowned. Had Cade made him feel stupid? I didn't want to ask him that if it wasn't true. But I wanted my brother to be able to talk about it with me. For him to know he wasn't alone in that feeling.

"Are you sure you don't need to tell me something?" I asked gently.

Wyatt nodded slowly. "Yeah, I'm sure."

Wyatt may not have needed to talk about it, but *I* was going to talk about it. With the source.

*   *   *

I searched the halls before school on Friday, not sure what Cade's morning routine was. I'd seen his car in the parking lot, so I knew he was here. I usually tried to avoid him. Today would be the opposite. My blood was on fire. Even my eyes were hot.

He was standing alone at his locker, staring at it, like he'd forgotten the combination or something.

I marched straight up to him and poked his shoulder with my finger. "How dare you."

He turned to me, a tired look on his face. "What do you want?"

"You named my brother Pink Lightning? Let those kids mock him?"

Cade's eyebrows went up. "Is that what he said? That the kids were mocking him?"

"Yes. He said they laughed at him."

"For one second."

"Well they wouldn't have at all if you hadn't given him that nickname," I spat out.

"Really? That's what you think? Did you see the sneakers your brother was wearing? I knew they would make fun of him. I needed to cut them off at the pass."

"By beating them to it?"

"By making it seem purposeful. Cool, even."

The next words I'd planned, whatever those were, left my brain. I stood staring at Cade.

"You're welcome," he said. "Are we done? Have you rid the world of all your perceived injustice?" Before I could respond he started to walk away. Then he turned and added, "Who bought him those cleats, anyway? They're the person you should be yelling at." He didn't wait for my answer before walking off again.

I growled then looked at his locker, the one he hadn't opened. Had he forgotten since I interrupted him or had he gotten something out before I came? If so, why had he been standing there staring at it when I walked up? No, I was not going to worry about Cade. He didn't need my worrying. He took care of himself just fine.

CHAPTER 28

Picturing Cade's face now as I read his letters was both infuriating and oddly satisfying. Infuriating because he was cute and he knew it, which made me angry. Satisfying because it was nice to put a face with words. It made them more personal.

Even if that face infuriated me . . .

> Have you and your brother made up yet? It is almost
> Thanksgiving. I don't know what that has to do with
> making up with your brother but the holidays always
> seem like a good time to do . . . well, anything, I guess.
> It's the Fourth of July, let's eat and get the family
> together. It's Easter, we better make up with the
> neighbor who ruined our fence. It's Presidents' Day, let's
> buy a couch. My mom actually did buy a couch last
> Presidents' Day. I didn't even know we needed a couch.
> I really think she bought it just because it was a holiday.
> Anyway, I'm going off the path here. My point? It's
> Thanksgiving (almost). Time to do that thing you've
> been meaning to do. I'll do my thing, too.

And that's how he ended the letter. In that vague way that left me dying to know what his thing was. What had he been meaning to do?

I bit my lip. Hadn't I sworn I wasn't going to write him back? But what was one more exchange really? In the scheme of things.

What thing have you been meaning to do? Listen to the entire Pink Floyd library in one sitting? I've been meaning to do that. Maybe that needs to be my Thanksgiving thing because my brother and I have sort of made up. Or at least I've accepted that he'll never admit to what he did, but he is my brother. So yeah. All that's left in the make up is the official hug-it-out. That has to be part of every make up because hugs are full of magical healing powers.

Also, I didn't know we were supposed to buy couches on Presidents' Day. My family has some catching up to do. Speaking of catching up . . . How are you? Everything okay?

I tucked the letter into place, angry at myself. I felt like some addict who couldn't kick a habit. And this made me even angrier at Cade. But this was the last day before Thanksgiving break. A weeklong break would surely cure me of my need. It would be like a detox. An even better detox, I thought with a smile, would be going out with Lucas. In about eight hours, I'd be doing just that.

⚜ ⚜ ⚜

Day four of detention. Only six more days to go. It hadn't been too bad so far, I thought as I opened the door to start my time.

And then I walked in and saw Sasha sitting in the seat I normally sat in, toward the back of the room.

Of course she'd steal my seat. It's what she did.

I wondered what she'd done to land in detention today. She should've been the one here all along considering I was fulfilling *her* sentence.

I claimed a seat on the opposite side of the room. There was a pretty senior girl sitting next to Sasha. I didn't know her name but the two of them were chattering away. I tried to drown them out by sketching a shirt design into my book. Shirts were much harder to sew than skirts, but I was ready to try my hand at it. I'd come up with a cute wide-necked crop-top idea. I had pulled out my sewing machine the night before and found the best material in my scraps. I just needed to figure out how to piece it all together.

I was doing an excellent job in my goal of shutting out Sasha's loud voice when I heard her speak his name: Cade.

My ears pricked up.

"Are you and Cade together now?" the senior girl asked Sasha.

177

I was curious about that as well. My pencil paused on the bow I was drawing.

"Yes," Sasha said happily.

"How'd that happen?"

"The other day, out of the blue, he asked me out. It was adorable."

"Why?"

"Why what?"

"Why did he ask you out?"

"Why not? You should be asking what took him so long. He finally realized what he was missing."

I continued drawing. Fine. Great. Sasha and Cade were together. The world was now well ordered. Cade had found his perfect match.

CHAPTER 29

The band, Frequent Stops, was loud but awesome. I would definitely be downloading some of their songs when I got home. I wondered if Cade had ever heard of them before. I'd have to write to him and tell him to add Frequent Stops to his playlist—

No. I wouldn't do that. What was wrong with me?

I glanced at Lucas. His club wardrobe wasn't much different than his school one, minus the earbuds—jeans and a tee. We'd been here for an hour. Gabriel and Isabel had driven down to Phoenix with me, Isabel talking the entire time, seeming to know how nervous I was. The nerves were mostly unfounded. Lucas was waiting for me outside, with his adorable shaggy, long hair, and he'd given me a slow smile. I'd introduced him to Isabel and Gabriel and we'd all gone inside together, a red underage bracelet attached to each of our wrists.

Now we all stood fifteen feet back from the stage, a little too close to the speakers to hold a normal conversation. I told myself that I hadn't led us there on purpose.

I'd prove it by talking. "Do you like the band?" I yelled to Lucas.

"What?" He put a hand to his ear and leaned closer.

"Do you like the band?"

He nodded.

"Do you listen to a lot of this kind of music?"

"What?"

"Is this your taste in music?" I asked when he leaned in again, his shoulder brushing mine.

"I like variety," he replied.

"I wonder how similar our playlists are."

"What?"

"Never mind." Maybe I *had* placed us here on purpose.

Isabel tapped my arm then mimed drinking from a cup. "Getting water. Be right back."

"Okay."

Lucas said something I couldn't understand. Maybe we both needed to take a cue from Isabel and start miming.

"What?" I leaned close to him this time.

"Do you want something to drink, too?" he asked, gesturing toward where Isabel and Gabriel were walking toward the bar behind us. It was a small crowd tonight, like it usually was with lesser-known bands.

The lead singer on stage was wailing into the microphone, sweat dripping down his temple.

"I'm okay. Maybe when they break," I told Lucas.

Lucas either heard me that time or understood my hand motions because he turned his attention back to the front as well.

My ears were still ringing and my chest still buzzing even though we were all outside now, on the far end of a parking lot across the street. The night was calm around us. Concerts always left me buzzing in the best ways. I wasn't someone who needed to be up there in the spotlight, performing. If I could just hear my words being sung, my chords being strummed by someone breathing life and passion into my ideas, I would be so happy.

We had stopped by Lucas's car, a navy Ford Focus. Not the car I would've imagined him in. He seemed more like a beat-up Corolla guy to me. Not that most people I knew matched their cars. I drove my mom's minivan most of the time . . . Okay, well that kind of fit.

Isabel plugged and unplugged her ears several times with her pointer fingers. "They need to issue earplugs on our way in the door." Her voice was loud, her ears probably ringing.

"You sound like a grandma!" Gabriel teased, but he was speaking extra loud, too.

I giggled.

"That was great," Lucas said, his crooked smile on.

I smiled. "Amazing. Had you ever heard them before?"

"No, I think they're local. Pretty new."

"Now we can say we knew them way back when once they get big."

"Yes. We'll be smug about it, too," Lucas said, and I laughed.

Gabriel nodded. "Maybe by then Lily will be just as big and she can be equally smug."

Lucas spun his keys once around his finger then stopped it with his palm. "Are you in a band?" he asked me.

"No. Not even close."

"She plays the guitar and writes music," Isabel put in.

I shuffled my feet. "I used to—well, I tried to. But not anymore. My guitar is broken."

Lucas tipped his head to one side. "Is it fixable?"

"Not sure. It's splintered pretty bad."

"I know a girl at the music store who does guitar repairs. I'll get you her info."

"Really? That would be amazing. Thank you."

Lucas nodded. "A broken guitar is the worst."

I paused, about to agree, when I processed what he said. "Wait, do you play?"

"I do."

"Cool," I said.

"Really cool," Isabel said, giving me a big smile.

"I'll try to get her info for you this week," Lucas told me. "The store might not be open, with Thanksgiving and everything."

"That's fine. After this week will be good."

"I'll send you a message if I get it."

"Like in the sky?" I asked with a laugh.

"No, like a text?" he said, confused.

"It was a joke . . . airplanes . . . sales . . . never mind, yes, a text would be great." *Stop referring to your letters like everyone should understand what you're talking about, Lily.*

We exchanged numbers then he unlocked his car and held out one arm. I wasn't sure what the one arm was offering but I slid in for a side hug. "Thanks for coming. That was fun."

"It was. See you later."

When he left I squeezed Isabel's hand and she squeezed mine back. I'd gone on a date with Lucas! And we'd exchanged numbers. And hugged!

It had been perfect.

I could finally move on from my pen pal.

CHAPTER 30

"Why is he in the house?" my dad asked, stepping over the rabbit. Ashley and I were in the living room, watching a documentary on fire ants (her idea, not mine) that I was finding oddly fascinating.

My mom, who sat at the table, stringing beads onto a necklace, said, "He needs some exercise. If he had a bigger cage . . ." She gave Dad her pleading eyes.

"I'm not building a mansion for a rabbit."

"Did I say mansion? Girls, did I say mansion?"

I held up my hands. "Leave us out of this. That rabbit is evil. I'm on dad's side."

"There are no sides," Mom and Dad both said at the same time.

Ashley looked at me, raised her eyebrows, then said, "So we don't have to vote anymore? Ever?"

My dad laughed. "Those are just fun and games. Get ready to vote on the best pie in two days. I've perfected my recipe."

Ashley stood up. "Come on, Lily. Let's take a walk."

"But I don't want to. The fire ants." I pointed to the TV.

She pulled on my arm. "Come on."

"Fine. We're going for a walk."

We were halfway down the block before she said, "Why did you throw away the newspaper clipping?"

"What?" I asked, even though I had heard her perfectly.

"The one I saw on your wall for weeks."

"I didn't throw it away," I argued. "It's still in the corner of our room somewhere . . . in a tight crumpled-up ball."

Ashley bumped my hip. "I thought you were finally going to get over your fear and share your songs."

"I was. But my guitar is broken so I can't now." I didn't mention that Lucas might know someone who could fix it. I didn't want to get my hopes up just in case that didn't come to anything.

"Get a new guitar," Ashley said as we rounded the corner.

"You know I can't afford that."

"Rent a guitar."

"I . . ."

She tapped a mailbox as we passed it, like it had taken her side in the argument. "That's what I thought. You jumped on the first excuse available to get out of the competition."

I scowled in annoyance. "Ashley. My guitar is broken. The thing I have to use to write half of the song. I think that's a pretty good excuse."

"Fine. If that's the only reason, you can share the words to the song you've been working on with the family on Thanksgiving."

I paused then said, "Fine. I will."

"Good. Grandma and Grandpa are going to be there, too."

"I know."

"And Aunt Lisa and her kids. And Uncle James and his kids."

"I know." Was she trying to talk me out of this or just make me admit I was terrified?

"And Mark."

"I know . . . wait . . . who?"

"The guy from work. We're getting serious."

"Really?" My sister never got serious with anyone so that surprised me. "The guy that saw food on your teeth?"

She shoved my arm. "Shut up."

I laughed. "Just kidding. That's cool, Ash."

"So I invited him over for Thanksgiving dinner."

I nodded. A boyfriend at Thanksgiving would be new. "If you like this guy, keep him far away from our house," I said. "Especially on holidays."

She laughed like I was joking but then her laughter trailed off into a worried expression. "Oh no. You're right. I've made a mistake."

I nodded. "It's not too late to tell him to stay home."

"Our family can all be normal for one day, right?" Ashley asked hopefully. "That won't be hard. We've been normal for a stretch of time before." She sounded doubtful.

"It's your funeral."

"It'll be fine." She waved a hand in the air. "I'll be there to run interference."

"Pay no attention to the man behind the curtain."

"Do not say things like that when he's over."

"I can't quote *The Wizard of Oz*? Everyone knows *The Wizard of Oz*. And if he doesn't then you should be glad that we found out so early in the relationship."

She put her hand to her forehead. "You're right. He needs to stay home."

"Exactly."

"He'll stay home . . . but you're still sharing your song on Thanksgiving."

❋   ❋   ❋

"You did *what?*" I was pouring hot gravy into the dish and nearly spilled it on the counter. A little splattered on my wrist and I wiped it quickly before it burned me.

"Please, Lily," Mom said with a sigh. "Let's not get dramatic about this. I thought you knew him."

"I do know him and that's why I don't want him over here for Thanksgiving dinner."

"Well, your brother invited him and he accepted."

Ashley popped an olive in her mouth. "Wyatt invited him to Thanksgiving dinner? Weird."

"See. It's weird," I said. "Just call Cade and tell him there was a change of plans."

Because Cade Jennings, my enemy, my former secret pen pal, could not show up at my house for Thanksgiving.

"Who's Cade?" Aunt Lisa asked, a baby on her hip while she stirred yams. She and her three kids, along with my grandparents, had arrived an hour earlier. My uncle, his wife, and their four kids had arrived the night before. And we were still waiting on my mom's other sister.

And Cade, apparently.

"Lily's friend," my mom said.

My face went hot.

"No. *We are not friends*. He's Wyatt's baseball coach." I placed the gravy boat next to the potatoes. "Mom, our family is too crazy to have guests over," I tried to argue. And why couldn't Cade go to Sasha's house for Thanksgiving? Couldn't he torture another family?

Ashley, now raiding the vegetable tray, said, "He and Mark can talk."

"What? I thought you'd convinced Mark to stay home," I said.

"No, I didn't. But everyone be normal today, okay? Normal!" Ashley marched out of the kitchen, probably to give the "be normal" instructions to the rest of the family. My family didn't know what normal was. She'd have to be a bit more specific than that.

I wiped my hands on a dish towel and found myself heading to the bathroom and analyzing myself in the mirror. My analysis ended with me applying more mascara, a dusting of blush, and some lip gloss. Not for Cade, but because it was Thanksgiving.

The doorbell rang and I closed my eyes, giving myself a pep talk.

I am glad Cade can spend Thanksgiving away from his house. He needs this. And I can handle him for one afternoon.

Right?

The doorbell rang again.

Did nobody else know how to answer the door around here?

It was probably better if I answered it, anyway. I could let Cade know what he was in for or better yet, turn him away.

I opened the front door and stepped outside while Cade's fist was in the air, getting ready to knock again. He wore a nice pair of pants and a button-down short-sleeved shirt. His hair was combed and he held a wrapped box in his hand.

He looked at the closed door over my shoulder and then said, "Your brother invited me."

"I know. Did he warn you about how crazy our house is?"

"No."

"Well, here is your warning. You can leave now before anyone even knows you're here if you want to." I wanted to add that I wasn't sure our house was exactly a better alternative to his. But that would mean giving away that I knew he was my pen pal.

"I told your brother I'd come," Cade said.

"Fine. But I want to have a nice day so let's call a truce, okay? Let's not fight today . . . because it's Thanksgiving."

"Because it's Thanksgiving?" he asked, one eyebrow going up.

I hadn't meant to quote one of his letters again. It just came out. But he wouldn't possibly guess that I was quoting him. I was the last person he would think was exchanging letters with him.

"Unless that much self-control is too hard for you," I added, trying to cover.

"You've already broken the truce with that comment," Cade pointed out with a half-smile.

"The truce doesn't start until you enter the house."

"And it ends the second I leave?"

"Yes."

"Deal." He held out his hand like we should shake on it.

I almost walked away from his outstretched hand but figured I should get a head start on playing nice.

I shook. "Good."

When I tried to pull my hand back, he held on. "You look nice."

"What?" I spit out. "No need to overdo it. I said no fighting. I didn't say we had to think of compliments."

A slow smile spread across his face. "This is going to be fun. And I sense it might be harder for you than it will be for me."

"Because you're used to being fake?" I bit my tongue before I said more.

"No, because you seem incapable of being nice." He dropped my hand and opened the door, leaving me on the porch staring after him.

So had we called a truce or not? Sealing a truce with insults didn't seem like a very promising start.

He was right, I wasn't sure I could do this.

"Cade's here, everyone!" I called, walking in behind him.

"Coach!" Wyatt came running down the hall. It looked like he was tempted to hug Cade, but then he held up his hand for a fist bump instead. Cade complied. Jonah appeared as well, and wanted his own fist bump.

"I'm Jonah. I'm seven and you'll be my coach in two years," he told Cade.

"Hopefully," Cade said. "I might be away at college by then."

"You can come back to coach me," Jonah assured him.

"I hope I can. Wyatt, direct me to your mom. I have a gift for her."

"Why did you bring her a gift?"

"Because it's polite to bring people gifts when they have you over."

"I've never done that before," Wyatt said thoughtfully. "Except for birthday parties, but this isn't a birthday party."

Cade draped his arm over Wyatt's shoulder. "You're right."

They left and I took a deep breath. I could do this. I'd just imagine Cade as the guy I'd been exchanging letters with, the one my brother looked up to, not as the one who mocked me in the halls and warned guys away from me.

Just as I was about to see if my mom needed help in the kitchen, the doorbell rang again. I turned around and answered it. A guy holding a bottle of sparkling cider stood on the porch. His dark hair was a mess, but his clothes were wrinkle-free and dressy so I assumed the hair thing was purposeful. Considering my own hair on most days, I really should've been more forgiving of unruly hair.

"Hi," I said.

"I'm Mark."

Ashley's friend . . . boyfriend? "Oh, right, food teeth guy."

His brow furrowed. "Excuse me?"

"Nothing. Come in. I'm Lily."

"Ah," he said as if he now understood some mystery. What had my sister told him about me and how could I already have proven whatever that was in two sentences?

"Ash!" I yelled, stepping inside. "Your . . . boy is here!"

Ashley came sweeping into the room in a cloud of perfume and hairspray. I wasn't even sure what about her hairstyle required hairspray, but she'd used a lot of it. "Mark! Hi! Oh is that for us?" She gestured toward the bottle he held. "Thank you." She threaded her fingers between his and led him away.

When had our house become the destination for Thanksgiving visitors? The type that brought gifts? This was going to be the strangest Thanksgiving ever.

CHAPTER 31

Just because our visitors had some form of etiquette training didn't change my family's manners. The second my father uttered the word *amen*, my brothers and little cousins dive-bombed the counter where all the food was laid out. They were digging through turkey pieces before anyone had a chance to move.

The kitchen became a flurry of activity—my mom taking lids and foil off of everything, my dad calling out for the dark meat, my sister pouring drinks, my grandparents directing from their places at the table, my aunt wrestling her daughter into a high chair while the baby screamed bloody murder and her other two kids ran circles around the counter, my uncle barking orders at *his* kids. Cade stood as if frozen to the tile, unsure of what to do. Visits to my house needed to come with a training manual.

I looked at the clock on the stove. It was 2:05 in the afternoon. One hour—that's how long Cade would last before he made an excuse to leave. I'd bet my broken guitar on it.

I gave him a smirk. "I warned you. And if you want any food, you'll have to take the plunge."

He did just that. In two steps he had a plate and was filling it expertly. He wound in and out of bodies until he arrived at the end of the counter, where Ashley held up a drink for him. I was the only one frozen to the tile now. The empty roll basket mocked my amateur move of waiting too long. Wyatt's plate had three rolls precariously stacked and I snagged one as I walked by.

"Hey!"

I patted his head and took a bite, then grabbed a plate. The table was already full as were the bar stools at the counter. So after I filled my plate, I went outside to the picnic table where it was possible to eat comfortably in November, because it was Arizona—the state that tried to kill its inhabitants every summer but made them forget about its attempt by being exceptionally kind every winter.

I dropped a green bean into the rabbit cage as I walked by. Then I sat down. Soon I was joined by Ashley (and her boy). And then Cade came out. My stomach dropped. He was Wyatt's guest. Shouldn't he have stayed inside with him?

Mark looked a little deflated, his wild hair flatter than it had been upon arrival. "It's much quieter out here," he noted, looking around in relief.

"Not for long," I said.

"Well, I can't stay too long, anyway," he said.

Wow, ten minutes and Mark was already laying down the exit strategy.

"You can't?" Ashley asked.

"I told you, right? My grandparents are expecting me soon."

I waited for Cade to say something similar, jump on the easy excuse, but he was too busy eating.

"I don't think we've officially met," Ashley said to Cade. "You're Wyatt's coach, right?"

Cade looked up, and swallowed. "And Lily's friend," he said, winking at me.

"You two are friends?" Ashley asked, the surprise in her voice a little insulting.

"More like acquaintances," I said coolly. *Who hate each other*, I almost added but stopped myself in time. "We hang out in completely different groups."

The back door flew open and Jonah and two of my cousins came running out. The two little ones went straight for the grass but Jonah went to the rabbit cage.

"Hey, Coach!" Jonah called. "Do you want to see Bugs Rabbit?"

"You mean Bugs Bunny?" Cade said.

"No, it's a rabbit."

Cade looked at me and I smiled. "It's a rabbit," I echoed.

"Of course it is." Cade nodded to Jonah. "Yes, I see him. Very cool."

Jonah opened the cage and both Ashley and I said, "Leave him inside."

"I'm just holding him." Jonah brought the rabbit out and over to show Mark and Cade.

"Have you ever eaten rabbit?" Mark asked. "It's actually pretty good."

Jonah's mouth fell open and Ashley shoved Mark's shoulder with a laugh. "He's just kidding, Jonah," she said.

A second too late, Mark nodded his head. "Yes. Just a joke. We won't eat Bugs Bunny."

"Bugs Rabbit," Cade said before Jonah could. Cade scratched the rabbit behind the ears and Jonah must've taken that to mean he wanted to hold him because he dropped the rabbit in Cade's lap. Cade let out a grunt, obviously surprised, and couldn't wrap his arms around the rabbit in time. It hopped up onto the table and somehow managed to step in every plate in under five seconds, each one of us reaching for but missing it.

Finally, I stood and picked it up. This was my first time picking up the evil pet, though, and apparently I didn't know how because its back legs became like mini saw blades, its nails chewing into my arms. I let out a shriek and dropped the rabbit and it took off across the yard.

I studied my arms. Most of the cuts were surface scratches, but one longer one beaded with a few drops of blood. When I looked up, Cade was chasing Bugs with Jonah on his heels.

"Seriously, rabbit is tasty," Mark said then chuckled at his own joke. "Just sayin'."

Cade dove, arms outstretched, and managed to land perfectly, capturing the little pest. Jonah cheered and my two cousins who had joined in the chase jumped up and down, clapping. Cade, on the ground, rolled onto his back, bringing the rabbit onto his chest. The rabbit now looked like a docile kitten as Cade stroked its fur.

"He's going to pee on you," I called.

Cade laughed as if this was a joke, now with all three of the kids sitting in the grass at his sides and petting the rabbit. No, it wasn't the cutest thing ever. I refused to admit that.

Cade picked a few strands of grass and was trying to feed them to the rabbit.

"He doesn't like grass. He eats carrots and lettuce and pellets," Jonah informed him.

"What are pellets?" Cade asked.

"I don't know but they smell gross."

Cade laughed again, a deep genuine laugh, and all the kids joined in. I was glad he was enjoying himself. The letter about his normal family Thanksgivings was not a happy one. I guess I could be glad for him today. Tomorrow, all bets were off.

Jonah relieved Cade of the bunny and tucked it away in his cage. Ashley and Mark took the contaminated plates inside. My little cousins went back to picking weeds that looked like flowers. Cade stayed on his back on the grass, hands clasped behind his head, ankles crossed. My feet had a mind of their own because they walked to stand next to him.

He squinted up at me. "Your brother's cute."

"He knows it, too. Kind of like someone else I know," I muttered, before I could stop myself.

Cade laughed. "You're not talking about me, right? Because we have a truce."

It had been a joke . . . sort of . . . but he was right, we had a truce. "You have grass stains on the knees of your pants now."

He lifted one leg and looked, then put it down and patted the grass next to him. "Sit down."

I didn't take kindly to commands but, again, my brain didn't seem to be in control of my body. I sat. Cade rolled onto his side to face me, propping himself up with one elbow. Then he just stared at me. For so long that I began to squirm under the scrutiny.

I didn't want to be the first person to say something but I couldn't help it. "You should look into catching rabbits for a living. You're not half bad at it."

He smiled. "That would be almost as manly as becoming a cowboy."

I laughed. "What are your career plans, anyway?" I asked, realizing we hadn't ever talked about that in our letters before.

Cade sighed. "You sound like my dad."

I noticed that he didn't say stepdad, even though I assumed that's who he was referring to. "Was that supposed to be an answer?"

"Baseball. Those are my plans for now. Let me know if you hear of any rabbit catcher openings though."

I knew a non-answer when I heard one. But I was used to Cade sharing with me (in his letters, at least). And, even though it made no sense, it hurt a little that he wasn't willing to do that now, in person.

But of course he wouldn't open up to me, Lily. I wasn't someone he liked. I wasn't whoever he thought the letter writer was.

"Are you still hungry?" I asked, changing the subject. "There's probably more food inside."

"No, I'm good. I actually ate at my house before coming here."

"Then why did you come?" I asked.

"Because your brother invited me. He's a good kid."

I ran a flat hand over the top of the grass, letting the blades tickle my palm. "Is that the only reason?" I wanted him to talk about home. Vent, like he had in the letters. If he'd had a bad morning, I wanted him to talk about it. Maybe I wanted to prove to him that he could talk to me.

"Did you want there to be another reason?" He tilted his head and lifted one side of his mouth into a half-smile. I realized what I'd just implied without the context of the letters.

"No! Of-of course not," I stammered, willing my face not to turn red. "I just wondered why your parents didn't make you stay home. My parents don't let me leave on Thanksgiving."

His air of confidence seemed to falter. He lay back on the grass again. "Yeah . . . I'm sure my parents like me to stay home, too. My mom likes for us to spend time together."

"She does?" That's not what he'd said . . . well, written, before.

"Of course. What Mom doesn't, right?"

This boy had up the biggest wall ever. I wasn't sure what it took to get him to be real outside of his writing. "Not all moms are good moms. Or dads."

Cade didn't even flinch or squeeze his eyes shut. He just turned his head and studied me again. "Your arm is bleeding."

I looked down to see a few red drops along my arm. "Oh. Bugs got me. It's no big deal."

"You probably want to clean that. He's not exactly the most sanitary creature in the world."

I could tell our conversation was over by the way Cade draped one arm over his eyes like he was settling in for an afternoon nap. It hurt more than I wanted it to.

CHAPTER 32

It was five thirty and Cade was still at my house. I'd given him one hour and he'd lasted over three. I'd totally lost the bet I'd made with myself. Mark was long gone. He hadn't even stayed long enough for my grandparents' annual stories about Thanksgivings past, featuring my mom as a teenager who went on a hunger strike for turkeys everywhere. And he definitely hadn't stayed for the pie we were about to eat.

The pie. The event I had been pushing off for the last hour, trying to outlast Cade. He could not be here when we did the family tradition I had spelled out so perfectly in the letter. Any minute he would leave. He had to. Those were the thoughts I'd had for the last one hundred and twenty minutes. Minutes filled with my little cousins attaching themselves to Cade's ankles and not letting go while he walked around. With my dad explaining to him every step of how he built the bookcase in the living room. With my mom using his wrist as a measurement for a "man bracelet" she was making. She had said that out loud to him: "I'm going to make a man bracelet. Let me see your wrist."

I'd lost count of the number of times my face had turned red. Of how many times Cade had looked confused or amused.

I wondered how many of these stories were going to be hand-delivered to Sasha later.

"Where is Sasha, anyway?" I asked abruptly as we sat on opposite couches, Cade's wrist still being wrapped in the brown leather cording my mom wielded.

He shrugged. "Family stuff. Where's Lucas?"

"Lucas? How do you . . . Why would I know where Lucas is?"

"I saw you two at a concert the other night."

My stomach jumped. "Frequent Stops? You were there? I knew you'd—" I stopped myself before finishing with the words "love them."

Cade tilted his head. "You knew I'd what?"

"Be there. I heard Sasha say something."

"Sasha didn't go."

"Oh . . . she must've known you would be there."

"She did."

"Lucas and I . . ." Did I really need to explain my relationship with Lucas—or lack thereof—to Cade? He didn't deserve an explanation. Especially not in front of my mom. She knew I'd gone to the concert with Isabel and Gabriel and a friend from school. And thankfully, she wasn't really paying attention now. ". . . had fun," I finished quickly. "We had fun."

My mom flipped Cade's wrist over. "Don't move. I need to get the clasp." She got up and left and for the first time today, the living room seemed quiet.

A movie was playing in the other room, occupying the kids. My aunts, uncle, dad, and grandparents were in the kitchen doing dishes, and I wasn't sure where Ashley had disappeared to.

I nodded toward Cade's wrist. "I'm sorry."

"It's fun. I get a man bracelet."

I smiled. "I don't think you get to keep it. She's just using you as her model."

"Her model?"

"It's a fact, not a compliment."

"Because if you gave me a compliment you might have a stroke."

I laughed. "Probably not a stroke, but my brain would definitely revolt in some way."

He didn't laugh along with me, just looked at the cording on his wrist.

"Oh, stop, you don't need me to tell you that you're hot to know that it's true."

"Are you okay? Did that hurt your head?" Cade asked.

I kicked his foot with mine and he laughed.

"So you think I'm hot?" Cade's eyes sparkled.

"Doesn't every girl?"

It surprised me when his cheeks turned a light shade of pink. I wasn't sure why that embarrassed him in any way. I was positive he already knew it. He ran one hand through his hair. Then he said, almost too quiet for me to hear, "You're not every girl."

My eyes darted to his, not sure I'd heard him right. Was he teasing me, like he had been all day? What did he even mean by that? Was it an insult? Was our truce over?

My mom rushed back in. "Sorry, sorry. I couldn't find it. Now we have less than five minutes until the movie's over and we move on to pie." She gave me a wink.

"No!" The word sprang out of my mouth.

Mom paused where she was affixing the clasp to the cord. "What? What's wrong?"

"It's not that time of night yet."

"It is. It's getting late."

"We normally do that with family only."

"Lily," Mom scolded.

This was the moment Ashley decided to materialize, holding my notebook out in front of her. "It's time," she said with a smile.

I had completely forgotten about her vow to make me read a song. Terror raced through me. "No. Absolutely not." I stood and rushed to her, rescuing my notebook from her grip.

"You promised," Ashley said.

There was no way I could read a song now. The only one that was halfway finished was the one about Cade. And he was *here*. "I changed my mind."

"I knew you would."

"No, I was going to but . . ."

Ashley shot me a disappointed look and left the room just as the rest of the family filed in, my dad holding the blindfold.

I was trying to think quick. This would be a dead giveaway. Cade would know for sure that I was the letter writer if this happened. And then he'd be horrified. We couldn't have this huge revelation in front of my entire family where they'd get to see what the kids at school truly thought of me.

"This is a special thing," I said to my father, my voice rising in panic. "I don't think we should do this with strangers."

"Lily," my dad said, his brow dipping to disapproval level.

"I'm so sorry," my mom said to Cade, apologizing for me.

Cade stood, unwrapping the cord from his wrist and handing it to my mom. "You know what? It's fine. It's time for me to head out, anyway. It is Thanksgiving, after all. My mom wanted me home. Thank you all so much for having me. Everything was amazing."

I was a horrible person. I was sending Cade running because I was scared. I was scared that tomorrow he'd be back to his old self. That I'd be back to my old self. That he wasn't the person I thought he was. That he *was* the person I thought he was. That I wanted to find out. I was scared.

I followed him as he left, trying to think of some way to explain forcing him to leave without having to tell him the real reason. He reached the door.

"So did the truce have a time limit?" he asked without looking back. "Or is this the hour when you turn back into a . . ."

He didn't finish that sentence but I could fill in the blank. It helped solve my need to come up with an explanation.

Instead, I opened the door and said, "Three hours is just as long as I can handle being around you." I regretted saying it the second it was out of my mouth. I wanted to tell him I didn't mean it. That I'd actually had a decent time with him today.

"That's not what the other girls say, but you're not exactly a normal girl are you?" he asked with a wry smile.

"Good-bye, Cade."

"Lily." He nodded and walked down the dark path toward his car. I shut the front door and placed my forehead against it. The door felt cold which made me realize my face was hot. With shame or anger, I wasn't quite sure.

"Lily!" my mom called from the other room. "We're getting started."

"Coming!"

The pie I spent the next fifteen minutes tasting wasn't nearly as good as it normally was. Apparently guilt had a bad aftertaste.

CHAPTER 33

It was the Saturday after Thanksgiving and I sat at the sewing machine set up on the kitchen table, finishing up a skirt. My phone buzzed in my pocket. I pulled it out to see Isabel's name across my screen.

"Hi," I answered.

"You want to come over?" That's how she greeted me.

I laughed. "Can't. Babysitting." The microwave beeped. "Hold on a sec." I gathered the material hanging off the table and flung it on top of the machine. I went to the microwave as it beeped again and swung open the door to reveal four split-open hot dogs. "Wyatt, you put these in way too long."

"I'll still eat them."

I pulled them out, put them on the table in front of him and Jonah along with a bottle of ketchup. "They'll taste the same," I said to Jonah before he could argue. "Eat. And don't touch that." I pointed to the sewing stuff on the other end then turned my attention back to the phone call.

"You want to come over here?" I asked Isabel.

"Yes! I'll be right there," she said, and I grinned.

We hugged when she arrived like we hadn't seen each other in ages. It *had* felt like ages since the concert.

"How was Thanksgiving at Gabriel's?" I asked her as she came inside.

"Fun. I only got to spend a few hours over there. You know how my parents are about holidays." We walked into the living room and plopped down on the couch.

"I do," I said. "I was surprised they let you go at all. Were there a lot of people there?"

"Yes. Lots of kids. How about yours?"

"Cade came over." I felt like I had to tell her every little thing that had to do with Cade now so she didn't think I was hiding anything from her.

"What?" Her expression was as shocked as her voice. "Why?"

"Wyatt invited him." She already knew that Cade was my brother's baseball coach this season.

She gasped. "He didn't."

"He did."

"And?" she prompted, her eyes growing even bigger.

"And Cade was here for over three hours."

Her hand flew up to cover her mouth. "I'm sorry. You must've had an awful day."

I shook my head several times. "No. Quite the opposite actually. We called a truce and the day was pleasant."

She laughed. "A truce. Your idea or his? Never mind, I don't know why I'm asking. That totally sounds like you."

I shoved her arm. "What's that supposed to mean?"

"You're funny, that's all. So, wow, you and Cade are getting along now. It's a miracle. Do you think it has to do with the letters? Does he know it was you?"

"No. He has no idea. And when the clock struck midnight—well, when he left—the truce was over. We are *so* not friends. He and his girlfriend did get me sentenced to two weeks of detention, after all. I have a grudge to uphold."

"You never did explain to me exactly how that happened."

"A substitute teacher and a case of mistaken identity."

Isabel smiled. "That sounds like a mystery novel."

"It should be. Anyway, it was dumb. Sasha stole my seat and proceeded to do awful things in my name." I threw my legs over Isabel's lap on the couch. "But it doesn't matter. It's over."

"How are things with Lucas?" Isabel asked.

I frowned, realizing I hadn't thought of Lucas once today. "He hasn't called or texted at all."

"That's not a big deal."

"It's been over a week!" I protested.

"But it's Thanksgiving weekend. Maybe he went out of town or something," she said. "It'll be fine."

I picked at a loose thread on the couch cushion. "But . . . if it doesn't work out with him, I'll be fine."

"Why are you already writing him off like it won't work?"

"I'm not."

"You are. You're trying to protect yourself by pulling away before something even starts."

"I'm not. It's just . . . I don't want you to worry about me if nothing comes of it. I don't need Lucas in order to be happy. I can be happy with him or without him . . . or with someone else."

Her dark eyebrows went up. "Someone else? Who?"

Why was I blushing? "In general. I was just hypothetically speaking."

"Oh." She nodded, took a deep breath then said, "So . . . Cade."

"No, definitely not Cade!" I said over the top of her next sentence, which I couldn't hear because I was too dramatic in my protest. "What?"

She tilted her head. "I said, back to Thanksgiving."

"Oh. Yeah, Thanksgiving. What about it?" My cheeks were still red and I was trying to avoid looking at her. I swung my feet back to the floor and stacked the magazines that were spread out on the coffee table.

"What did you and Cade even talk about?" Isabel asked me.

"I don't know. The rabbit. My brother. His family." Well, that last one wasn't exactly true. I'd tried to talk to him about his family and he promptly shut down. But we had talked about his family in our letters, which reminded me of a question I had for Isabel. "When you and Cade were together . . . did he talk a lot about his parents?"

"His parents? Not really." Isabel slipped her feet out of her flip-flops and tucked them under her on the couch. "They're rich and travel a lot, but that's all I really remember. Why?"

"Was his stepdad nice to you?"

"Stepdad? That's his real dad, right? He calls him Dad. He owns Jennings Insurance? Cade's last name is Jennings."

"You're right. But . . ." Had Cade not told anyone that his parents were divorced? I guessed if his real dad never came around and he never had to go back and forth between parents, he never would have to explain anything if he didn't want to. He *had* mentioned he was pretty private in one of his letters.

"You know, now that I think about it, you're right," Isabel said, tilting her head. "He did say once it was his stepdad, but it was like a side note. So his stepdad must've adopted him? That's why he goes by his last name?"

"I'm not sure."

"I don't think he knew his real dad very well. They divorced long before he moved here."

Not that long. "Yeah . . . maybe."

"I still can't get over that the two of you got along for three hours!" Isabel exclaimed, glancing over at me. "I mean, when I was with him, you guys couldn't be in the room together for more than a couple minutes without flinging insults."

"I know." When she was with him. Isabel and Cade had been together. That had really happened. It wasn't some ancient history. Cade really dated my best friend. "Don't worry, we haven't given up insulting each other. Pigs aren't flying yet."

Isabel glanced out the window. "Are you sure? I could've sworn I saw one in the sky on my way over."

"Funny."

Isabel smiled and flung her arms around my neck. "I've missed you."

"I've missed you, too. Let me go make sure my brothers are ready for bed and we can watch a movie."

⚹ ⚹ ⚹

We were halfway through the movie when something I'd said to Isabel caught up with me. The reason I'd landed in detention. Sasha had been in my seat when Cade came in to Chemistry. He'd seen her in my seat. This was before I'd realized he was the letter writer. That's why he'd come in——not to pull a prank to get his friends out of class early——but to see who was sitting in that seat. He thought his pen pal was Sasha.

I laughed.

"What?" Isabel asked.

I couldn't believe Cade thought Sasha wrote those letters. They sounded nothing like her. Then again, Cade's letters didn't sound much like him either. I sat up with a gasp. Was that why he'd finally asked her out? Because he thought she was the letter writer? That thought brought an unexpected feeling of anger. He was probably so happy the letter writer matched a beautiful, popular girl. It was all turning out perfect for the golden boy.

"*What?*" Isabel asked again.

"I just figured something out." I explained to her about the seat exchange and the letters.

She stared at me in both awe and horror. "That's awful."

"Is it? Maybe it's better he thinks it's her."

"But then won't he get mad at Sasha when the letters stop appearing?"

I shrugged. "Maybe he'll think she stopped writing because they're together now. Maybe I'll help him think that."

She gasped. "You wouldn't."

"It won't be hard. People easily accept things that they want to be true. And he wants it to be true. He wants his letter writer to be Sasha."

Isabel's expression fell, but she didn't contradict me.

CHAPTER 34

I sat in Chemistry on Monday, mulling over my plan. Even though I knew Cade wanted the letter writer to be Sasha, it actually would be hard to convince him it was. All he had to do was ask her some details. Did she have a younger sibling? Did she like the same music we did? He'd know soon enough. He should've known already, without me having to write anything at all. Unless . . .

Sasha had seen the desk with the writing on it the day she sat in my seat. Maybe she'd figured something out. If Cade had asked her about letters, maybe she'd played it off like she knew what he meant. Went along with it.

I reached under the desk. I thought I'd cured myself of this need after a week off, after knowing the writer was Cade. But my heart still raced when I felt the new note there.

Did you listen to the Pink Floyd library in one sitting?
That's a really awesome thing. I wished I'd thought of
it. No, my thing had to do with writing my dad a letter.
I know we'd talked about me writing my stepdad. But
when I sat down to do it, I realized it was my dad I

needed to talk to. He can ignore a phone call, but it
would be harder to ignore a letter, right? Anyway, I
wrote it and sent it over the break. Now I just get to
wait. I'm used to waiting for responses now that we've
been exchanging letters. It's taught me a bit of patience.
Not really. I'm dying over here. I need a distraction.
I spent Thanksgiving with another family because I
needed to get my mind off of my life (not to mention
I told you how bad my Thanksgivings are). It was nice.
It'd been a long time since I'd seen what a real family
is like. And this family was the epitome of a real
family. It was like one of those paintings. You know
that guy who paints classic American scenes that
look too good to be true? I think he even actually did a
Thanksgiving dinner scene. This was that. It was
the best Thanksgiving I'd had in a while. How was
yours?

Mixed emotions competed inside me. So he'd had a good time at my house, and that made me melt a little. But his description of my family, the craziness that always had me on the brink of frustration, left me scoffing.

I wrote back:

Do you mean Norman Rockwell? I'm sure you didn't
spend Thanksgiving with the Norman Rockwell painting
family. No family is perfect.

I almost wrote *least of all mine,* but hesitated. Was I giving it away that he spent Thanksgiving with me by refuting his depiction of it? No, he thought he was writing Sasha right now.

> *I'm glad it was a good distraction for you. I can under-*
> *stand why you'd need one. It's hard enough to wait a day*
> *for a response to a letter, I can't imagine how you're*
> *feeling waiting this long. Your dad will write back. He*
> *has to. Is there something specific you're hoping he'll say?*
> *Or do? Or you just want an update on his life? I hope*
> *you didn't try to write a song for him or you'll never hear*
> *back. ;) No, but for real, your letters are very compelling.*
> *Almost impossible not to respond to.*

At least that was the case with me. I'd never be able to stop responding to him no matter what I knew or who he thought I was. Because he had some letter-writing spell over me.

☆ ☆ ☆

Not only did Cade's letters insist on being responded to, they also filled my mind with lyrics. It was some cruel twist of fate that the only time I thought of good lyrics was after exchanging thoughts with Cade. Today wasn't any different. Sitting in detention, I'd already written an entire verse.

> *You have me under your spell.*
> *With all the secrets you tell.*

I can't make it stop.

Please don't let it stop.

You have me under your spell.

If you knew me as well,

You would make it stop.

I can't let it stop.

I was so wrapped up in my writing that I didn't hear the teacher get up and leave the classroom until the door shut behind him. Had he said something about leaving? My eyes went to the clock on the wall. We still had thirty more minutes. I also didn't hear Sasha, who was still serving a detention sentence as well, come up behind me. So when she yanked my notebook out from under my arm, I wasn't expecting it.

"What are you writing?" she asked and began reading out loud the lyrics on the page.

My heart hammered in my chest and I wanted so badly to get up and rip my book out of her hands and possibly beat her over the head with it. But I knew that's what she wanted. I knew she wanted me to get up and chase her around the room as she read from my notebook to the sound of the other laughing students, who right now were salivating for just that show as their eyes darted back and forth between the two of us. I had learned to speak bully over the years. It was the product of secondhand clothes and crazy hair that I didn't know how to tame until freshman year. I knew their language well.

So as panicked as my insides were, I stayed in my seat, trying to keep my facial expression neutral.

Sasha had made it to the far corner of the room in anticipation of me chasing her. From there she screamed the last two lines as she laughed. "You would make it stop! I can't let it stop!"

I willed my face not to turn red. This was my worst fear. I couldn't even let the people I loved read my lyrics.

Sasha's senior friend, in the back still, laughed along with her. "What is that? A poem? A weird stalker poem?"

My mind was spinning rapidly, trying to remember what else was in that book. Had I actually used the name Cade in that last angry song I'd written after I found out he was the letter writer? I hadn't, had I?

Oh no, I had.

All she had to do was flip two pages back. There were only two design sketches between the page she was on and that page. How long was Mr. Mendoza going to be out anyway? A bathroom break should be over soon.

With a smile still on Sasha's face, she flipped back one page. My heart was going to stop. If I jumped up now and hurdled over two desks, I could possibly get to her in time. She was wearing heels, after all.

She held up my drawing of the shirt for everyone to see. "Now we know where Lily gets her awful fashion sense."

She should've been bored with this game by now. I wasn't reacting at all. And the others in the room weren't responding positively either. My notebook should've been thrown on the floor or tossed back on my desk at this point.

"I've always wondered why your nose is glued to this book," Sasha went on. "Now we know. Bad drawings and even worse poems."

I understood why my no-reaction wasn't going to work. This extended beyond just today. She'd been wondering about my book for a long time. She wasn't only doing this to humiliate me. She was doing this to satisfy her curiosity. She was going to keep looking.

My stomach was in knots. Time for a new plan.

Sasha's backpack sat on the floor by the desk she'd occupied moments ago. If her phone was in there, I was sure she'd make a trade.

She flipped back another page. Like she was reading a picture book to a classroom full of kindergartners, she held it up for all to see again. A sketch of a halfway finished skirt.

I stood. And just as I moved toward her bag, the classroom door swung open and Mr. Mendoza walked in.

"Ladies," he said, "I'm sure there is a perfectly justifiable reason why you're out of your seats. But I don't care. One more day each."

I could see on Sasha's face that she wasn't going to give me back my book. She was already walking to her seat, flipping another page.

"She stole my book," I said, whipping around to the teacher.

"This is my book," Sasha said before he responded. She was reading the lyrics now. Her eyes going back and forth along the page. She must've come to Cade's name because she stopped suddenly, her eyes jerking to mine.

"Give Lily her book back," Mr. Mendoza said sharply. "Now."

She didn't listen, but flipped back more. I saw her tilt her head, reading notes I sometimes wrote in the margins of the pages to help me with the lyrics. Was she reading the notes I'd written about Cade's dad? His home life? My skin froze.

"Sasha," Mr. Mendoza growled.

Sasha slammed the notebook shut and tossed it toward me. It landed with a smack on the floor next to me. I picked it up and opened it to one of the pages I was sure she had read. And even though there was a big X covering some of the words, most of them were still completely legible. My eyes went over the words. The words about exchanging letters. If only I hadn't added the unnecessary rant to the end of the lyrics she wouldn't know who the words were about. But I had and now she knew. And I had no idea what she'd do with that knowledge.

CHAPTER 35

Punching someone on school grounds resulted in immediate suspension. I did not want to get suspended. This was what I told myself as I walked from detention toward the parking lot.

I'd been the first to leave the room and needed to make it home without looking at Sasha or I wouldn't be able to control my actions. Making it to the parking lot didn't help because neither my sister nor my mom were there waiting for me today.

I pulled out my phone and texted Ashley. *Is someone getting me?*

"Lily," a voice from behind me said. It was Sasha.

I turned quickly to face her. Then I took a step back, but my hands curled into fists. Two very tight fists that were dying to swing. "What?"

"Does he know it's you?"

My stomach gave a jolt.

So she had pieced everything together. Now I needed to figure out how to answer that question. If I said yes, she would confront Cade. If I said no . . . what? What would happen?

Would she tell him? Keep playing it off like it was her . . . if that's what she'd been doing?

I had to make a decision.

"No. He doesn't." There was no way I was going to tell her that he thought it was her, though.

Sasha smirked. "I didn't think so. Lauren said you write and read letters in Chemistry almost every day. She didn't know who you were exchanging them with."

So Sasha hadn't pieced together all the information from *just* my lyrics. Lauren had told her about my letter-writing habits as well.

"If Cade knew it was you, he'd die," Sasha went on. "He hates you."

"I know." A lump was forming in my throat. I wasn't sure why. She hadn't said anything I didn't already know. Why had my anger turned to this sadness? Why had I gone from wanting to pummel her, to wanting to crawl into bed and never come out?

"If you heard half the stuff he said about you, you wouldn't have a thing for him," she went on cruelly.

"I do not have a thing for him. I have a . . . boyfriend." That last word came out kind of choked. Mostly because Lucas wasn't my boyfriend. But I really needed to claim him as such in this moment.

"Those poems told a different story."

"I don't have a thing for him."

"I won't tell Cade it's you but you have to stop writing him. We're together now."

"I know."

A horn beeped twice and I looked over hoping to see my sister.

I saw Cade instead.

"There's my ride," Sasha said, her smile as smug as her tone.

She must've taken one second too long to run to his car because Cade hopped out and headed our way. This was turning from bad to worse.

"Hello, ladies," he said.

"Let's go," Sasha said to him.

Cade pointed at me. "Great hair today, Lily."

I willed myself not to reach up to tame it. I could tell he was being sarcastic with that stupid smile of his. Sasha laughed.

"Are you two detention buddies?" Cade asked.

"Not at all," I assured him, trying to gather myself together. Thankfully, I no longer felt like crying. I was just mad.

"She's another one of your enemies?" he asked me, still giving me a teasing smile.

"Don't pretend like you don't know that," I snapped. "Your girlfriend was just reminding me why I don't hang out with people like the two of you."

Sasha laughed. "You don't hang out with us because you're not welcome, but nice try."

Cade looked like he was going to say something but he hesitated as though waiting for my response. I didn't give one. I was so done with them.

I turned on my heel and stormed away. I allowed myself one glance back at them and unfortunately saw that Sasha wrapped her arm around his waist. As they walked away, she threw me a wink over her shoulder as if we were now co-conspirators. As if we were anything.

Why hadn't I just punched her?

CHAPTER 36

My mom came in my room and set a small box in front of me. "Lily, I need you to do me a favor," she said.

I looked up distractedly from my notebook. I'd been trying to drown my sorrows in songwriting but it wasn't happening. I was still too distraught by what had gone down with Sasha after detention.

"Um . . . okay," I said to Mom, closing my notebook and pushing my hair out of my eyes.

"I need you to deliver that for me." Mom nodded to the box.

"What is it?"

"A piece of jewelry."

"Okay. Do you have an address?" I got to my feet. Mom had asked me to drop off some pieces to clients before. "And are they paying when I deliver or have they already paid?"

"No payment. This is an apology gift."

"I don't understand."

"From you."

"From *me*? Why?"

Mom put her hands on her hips. "Because we had a guest over the other day that you treated very poorly. We didn't talk about it that day because it was Thanksgiving. But now we are talking about it. That boy had been nothing but kind and you made him feel unwelcome."

I was too horrified to speak but finally I found my voice.

"I know. I'm sorry." I really did know and I really was sorry, but I also really didn't want to deliver this box and I was hoping with all the hope in me that if Mom saw that I was sincere in my regret she wouldn't make me. Because although our *guest* hadn't deserved my treatment of him that day, he deserved it a thousand times over for every other day.

And his awful girlfriend deserved worse.

"Good. Then this shouldn't be very hard." Mom patted the lid of the box and walked away.

"Mom! Wait!"

She stopped.

"Can't Wyatt just give it to him on Thursday at baseball practice? I don't need to take it now and tie up your car." Mom's car was run-down, messy, and very mom-like. Even though it represented the story of my life pretty well, I tried to avoid driving it at all costs, especially in super nice neighborhoods to the house of a guy who didn't need more reasons to make fun of me. "Or I could give it to him at school." *Or I could never, ever give it to him.*

"I'd like you to take it now, Lily." She nodded toward the box. "Go on. And actually use the words *I'm sorry* while you're there, too."

That would be impossible.

It had been years since I'd been to Cade Jennings's house and I'd hoped I would never have to step foot in it again. But here I was, standing in front of his large double doors.

As I rang the doorbell, I prayed that he wouldn't be home. Or maybe that some butler would answer instead. Then I could throw the box and run.

But luck wasn't my friend these days. Between the whole guitar thing and the detention thing and the Sasha thing, I shouldn't have expected this to actually go my way.

Cade answered. All six foot, slightly damp hair, sparkling smile of him. "Hey," he said, like it was perfectly normal for me to be standing on his doorstep.

"Hi," I muttered, my eyes down.

"Come in."

Had my mom warned him I was coming?

I stepped into his huge entryway, thinking my memory had exaggerated it, but if anything it was bigger than I remembered. And whiter——marble floors, large white floor vases, a huge abstract painting with nothing but white lines.

I held out the box to him. "This is from my mom."

"What for?" He opened the box and pulled out the bracelet she had been assembling on his wrist during Thanksgiving. "Ah! The man bracelet. I thought you said I was just her model."

"Well, you were until I was rude to you," I said. "This is a 'my daughter was rude to you' gift."

"If that's the case, she owes me about five hundred more." There was a smile in Cade's voice.

"Funny. Anyway, you don't have to wear it." It didn't have feathers so at least there was that. "You can give it to your mom or something."

He gave a mock gasp. "This is a man bracelet, Lily. My mom is not a man. I will wear this. And when I wear it, it will remind me that you apologized for being mean to me."

"I did *not* apologize."

"Oh." He raised one eyebrow. "So your mom is apologizing for you being mean to me?"

I gave a short laugh. "Yes."

"But not you?"

"Fine. Me too. I'll see you later."

"Wait."

I had been backing up and I stopped.

"You have to show me how to use it."

"Use it?"

"How to put it on." Cade turned and walked away. I assumed that meant I was supposed to follow him. I thought about not following him but then I'd owe him another bracelet for sure.

I met up with him in his massive kitchen. The box and bracelet were now sitting on the island and he was on the other side assembling a sandwich. I had obviously interrupted him in the middle of snack time. I kept the island between us and stopped next to the box.

Cade placed the top slice of bread on his sandwich and took a bite. "You want anything?" he asked through his mouthful.

"No. I'm good." I picked up his bracelet. "So anyway, it's just a basic clasp. You open it here and attach it to the ring."

"Wait a sec. Just let me finish eating so you can show me on my wrist."

I was not going to get annoyed because it was obvious that's what he was trying to do—annoy me. I put the bracelet back in the box, leaned against the counter, and waited. Over his right shoulder was a large set of French doors that I could see the pool through.

I thought back to his fourteenth birthday party. After we'd eaten the catered food, everyone had gone out to the pool. A lot of the guys swam and the girls sat on the side like if the water touched us, we'd melt. I'd worn my swimsuit but wasn't going to get in if Isabel didn't. Especially because my swimsuit was a hand-me-down from my sister and was a little too big on me. At one point as I talked with Isabel, I'd slipped my hand into the pocket of my shorts and felt a piece of paper there. When I pulled it out it was a five-dollar bill. It had been a long time since I'd worn the shorts and I was so surprised to see it that I'd let out a happy yelp and said, "Best day ever!" Cade, who must've been walking over to see Isabel when this happened said, "That's all it takes to make you happy? Maybe if I handed you a five every morning, you'd be more pleasant."

The barstool next to me scraped along the floor and I jumped, pulled out of my memory. Cade sat sideways on that barstool, like he'd been there all day. How long had I been staring out the window? His arm was wrist-up on the counter and he held the bracelet out for me.

I sighed and took the bracelet, wrapping it around his wrist. "It's not hard, it's just a basic clasp. You open it by pulling back this little lever and the circle end fits inside and you let go. The end."

"You did that with two hands. How am I supposed to do that with one hand?"

"I don't know. Use the counter to hold it steady." I passed the bracelet back to him and watched for several minutes as he attempted many different ways to clasp a bracelet one-handed. I bit my lip to keep from laughing.

"You think this is funny? Can you do it one-handed?"

"Yes."

"Prove it."

I draped the bracelet over my wrist, then attached the end.

"Okay. That looked easy. But this is your business, so you're trained and stuff."

I laughed. "This is not my business."

"It's the family business."

"You make us sound like mobsters or something."

He was back to trying to attach the ends on his wrist. He grunted in frustration after several more minutes.

"Give me your arm." I stepped closer to him and after one second realized I had stepped between his knees that were wide on the barstool. It would seem awkward to step back now, like he affected me in some way, so I didn't. Because he didn't. But his musky scent sure was doing a number on my breathing.

I took the bracelet, one end in each hand and tried to attach it around his wrist. Only now my hands seemed shaky.

"You smell good," he said softly.

I closed my eyes for a moment, my breath catching. "Just hold still."

"I'm not the one moving."

"Stop it."

"What am I doing?"

"You're making this hard for me."

"Can I ask you a question?"

Why did he smell so amazing? That was the question I was going to ask when he was done with his.

"Yes."

"Why do we fight so much?"

My mouth opened and shut in surprise. "We don't. I mean . . . I just . . . our history isn't so great."

"I never understood why."

"You gave me an awful nickname in the middle of a class I was already humiliated in."

"I thought I was helping. You were getting pummeled by basketballs. I thought if I made a joke about it, it would help people laugh with you instead of at you."

"It didn't work."

"I guess I can see that. So that's it? I made up a nickname and got an enemy for life?"

"You do it to everyone," I replied, looking right at him. "Humiliate them in the name of charity. Then you say rude comments and I'm never sure if you're doing it because you are trying to be funny or if you don't realize they're rude, but they are. Just today you were mocking my hair."

"What? I was not mocking your hair. You have great hair."

That made me stutter for a moment. "Yeah, well, that's, uh . . . Plus! And more importantly, you treated Isabel horribly."

"*I* treated Isabel horribly? *Me*? What about how you treated her?"

I scowled. "Me? What did I do? She was my best friend. She's still my best friend."

"You were a huge flake. She'd call to set things up with you and you'd cancel last minute because you had to babysit and I had to watch her be disappointed all the time."

I flinched at his depiction of me. "I have family obligations. She knows that."

"And then you'd snap at me like I was the one leaving her alone in the middle of a restaurant or event."

I glared at him. "No, you were the one leaving her alone even when you were standing right next to her. You were so checked out. You'd be on your phone or ignoring her in some other way."

He grimaced. "I was in the middle of . . . things at that time."

"Things? You never even told her what things, did you? You never told her anything about yourself. You don't tell anything to anyone except—" I stopped myself, surprised I had gone that far. I'd almost given myself away.

He stared at me. "Except what?"

"Your girlfriend. I'm sure you tell Sasha everything."

"Stop calling her that. She's not my girlfriend."

"Does she know that?"

His knee brushed against my hip and a jolt went through me. Why was I still standing this close? Probably because my hands were still holding both ends of the bracelet. I wasn't sure if it was the anger coursing through me now or sheer determination, but I quickly clasped his bracelet and took a step back.

"Enjoy your apology man bracelet," I snapped.

"I will love my man bracelet!"

There was something about the absurdity of that statement that made me want to laugh. I wasn't sure if Cade wanted to laugh too but a light shone in his eyes. He stood and we were suddenly even closer than before. My eyes started to water as I stared at him, and I realized I hadn't blinked. My desire to laugh was completely gone and other desires were taking over. Desires I knew he didn't share. He'd basically just spelled out why he hated me. I was angry with myself for the feelings coursing through me. I turned and fled.

When I got to the minivan, I had to wait for close to five minutes before I felt steady enough to drive.

CHAPTER 37

He was probably doing it to drive me crazy, to remind me what it stood for, but whatever the reason, Cade was wearing that bracelet, beads and all, to school the next morning. And even though winter had finally hit Arizona, bringing in lower temperatures than we'd had in months, he was wearing a three-quarter-length tee and no jacket, making the bracelet that much more visible.

I glared at him in the school parking lot.

He smiled at me, but not a real smile, a challenging one.

I decided to take him up on that challenge. "Nice bracelet," I said, falling in step beside him instead of trying to avoid him like I normally did.

"Thank you," he replied. "It was given to me by a girl who was deeply sorry for treating me unkindly."

"Deeply sorry? Is that what she said?"

"It's what she meant. I saw it in her eyes."

"You weren't just looking at your own reflection there? That sounds more like you."

He ran a hand through his hair, pushing it off his forehead, only to have it flop forward again when he dropped his hand.

"It's true. We all appreciate beauty. She recently told me I was hot."

"Huh. Well, hopefully she's had some sense knocked into her since then."

"No, just this morning when she saw me, I could tell she found me irresistible."

I laughed, trying to think of a comeback to that but for some terrifying reason, I was unable to. *What was happening to me?*

We walked by some students who called out greetings to him and he nodded back in response.

I shook my head. "You won this round." I saw Isabel up ahead, and added, "I'll win the next one." Then I picked up my pace and left him behind.

I passed Sasha, who was heading for Cade, and she gave me a look so hateful that I knew she must've seen me talking to him.

"Good morning, sunshine!" I called to her, not sure what had gotten into me.

She ignored me.

Isabel was first with our daily greeting. "Chocolate-dipped bananas."

"Yours always make me hungry. Why are you always thinking about food before you go to bed?"

"Hey, you're not allowed to respond to mine until you say yours."

"Man bracelet."

"Huh?"

"My mom made me take one to Cade yesterday after how I treated him on Thanksgiving."

I'd texted Isabel all about the Sasha-detention disaster, but I hadn't filled her in on my visit to Cade's house yet.

Isabel gaped at me. "Is your family plotting against you? First your brother invites him over and now your mom forces you to visit him?"

"I know. They must not have gotten the list of my enemies I specifically printed out for them."

"Is there more than one on that list?"

"Just Cade and Sasha for now. It's open-ended for add-ons." I paused, thinking about what Cade had accused me of the day before. "Iz?"

"Yes."

"Have I treated you badly? I'm sorry for the times I have to cancel last minute when family obligations come up."

Her hands flew to her hips. "What? Lily, come on. You don't need to apologize for that. I know you have a big family. Sometimes I'm disappointed when things get canceled, but never mad. You're an amazing sister and daughter. I'm not selfish enough to get mad about that."

My shoulders relaxed in relief.

"Did Cade say something about that?" she asked suspiciously.

I nodded.

She rolled her eyes. "Ugh. Don't let Cade put words in my mouth. Ever."

"Okay. Love you."

"You too."

The list of people I had told I wouldn't write to Cade anymore was growing by the day—Isabel, myself, and now Sasha. And after my last few interactions with Cade, that was actually my plan. This needed to be over.

Between him thinking the letter writer was Sasha, our never-ending irritation with each other, my wannabe relationship with Lucas, and Isabel's reaction when she thought there was even the tiniest possibility that I liked Cade . . . I knew it needed to end.

I sat down in Chemistry. I didn't want to leave the unread letter under the desk for someone else to find. Specifically, Sasha. Now that she knew all about the letters, I was worried she would intercept them. I didn't think she or Lauren realized *where* we hid them, just that I always had one.

Mr. Ortega held up a packet. "I'm going to pass these out and you're going to get the period to work on them alone or with a partner."

The class immediately erupted into talking and switching seats. I was glad he gave us the option to work alone. I stayed put and watched as Lauren got up and joined Sasha. In all the commotion, I snatched the letter out from under the desk.

238

I made myself keep it folded; I just tucked it in my bag. It would be easier to read at home and since I wasn't responding to it, it didn't matter when I read it.

But ten minutes in, I realized I wasn't going to get any work done until the letter was read. Using my Chemistry book as a blockade, I read it while the rest of the class studied.

You asked if there's something specific I hope my dad will say or do. That's a good question. I didn't request anything in the letter I wrote to him (which included not a single song lyric). I guess I'm hoping he'll drop everything, get on a plane, and come see me. But in the real world in which we actually live, I just want him to pick up the phone and acknowledge my existence. Acknowledge he's made mistakes. I guess I just want an apology. Well, and a commitment to try harder. I'm his son; tell me that's not too much to ask. I know that he only thinks of me when my mom remembers to remind him it's my birthday. I think my mom slowly grew tired of that chore. I don't blame her.

It's been a few letters since I whined this much. I get a free pass, right?

I always feel like I need to balance all this heavy stuff with something light but I'm kind of out of humor today. Sorry.

I set down the letter. Why did he have to break my heart like that? My irritation from earlier melted away. I was so glad I read it because I needed to respond to it now. I positioned my review packet over my new sheet of letter paper. I continually glanced at the book while writing so anyone watching would think I was writing down something I read there. I wasn't sure I was fooling Sasha, but I didn't care at the moment.

Don't apologize. You've made me laugh plenty. You're not my free entertainment or anything. You can whine as much as you want. You get at least a hundred free passes. And of course that's not too much to ask of your father. He's your father. If your dad does decide to get on a plane and fly out here, can I punch him? I really want to. That might not be good for your relationship with him, so maybe I can resist. I don't know what to say except I'm so sorry.

CHAPTER 38

I was dying to read Cade's letter the next day, hoping it would be a happier one. I'd thought about him a lot the night before, wondering if I needed to think of another excuse to go visit him, check on him. I had talked myself out of it, remembering how poorly my last visit to his house had gone. I didn't want to make him feel worse.

So when I slid into my seat in Chemistry, I let my hand immediately go to the bottom of the desk.

I found nothing there.

One strategic pencil drop later produced the same result. There was no letter today. My first thought was that Sasha had taken it. But she wasn't here yet. Lauren was looking through her review packet from the day before, and Mr. Ortega, the only other suspect, was writing on the whiteboard.

Cade must've stayed home from school. I considered several horrible reasons for his absence, but I forced myself to settle on the idea that he was probably just sick. There was nothing to worry about. People stayed home sick all the time.

I wrote him a get-well-soon note, which included a turtle soup bowl. Tomorrow, everything would be back to normal.

Only everything wasn't back to normal the next day. There was still no note—only my old letter from the day before. I was tempted to ask Sasha where Cade was, but thought better of it.

I left yet another note, telling him he was really ruining Chemistry for me by being selfishly sick and I hoped that was really all it was.

"Remember the final is tomorrow," Mr. Ortega said, just as I slipped my latest note under the desk. "Make sure you study your review packet and be ready."

Was Cade going to miss the final? Did he remember it was the final?

Sasha would tell him. He wasn't my responsibility.

After school, while Isabel and I were talking about plans for the coming weekend, I saw Cade throw his backpack in his locker and pull out a duffel bag. My heart jumped.

"He was here today?" I asked out loud.

Isabel turned to see what I saw.

"Who?" Isabel asked.

"Cade. He wasn't in Chemistry."

"He was in Chemistry."

Her statement hit me like a punch to the gut. He was in Chemistry, just apparently not writing me back. Had he figured out that his pen pal wasn't Sasha? That it was actually me?

I grabbed Isabel's elbow and hustled her out of school before Cade could see me.

＊ ＊ ＊

The noises coming from the back patio weren't unusual, but the voices accompanying those noises were. My mom and dad were out there together pounding something with a nail and hammer.

I opened the back door and saw that half of a large cage was assembled. Not just any cage, but a two story one, complete with ramps and ledges and all sorts of things a rabbit would enjoy. The kind of cage I knew my dad had specially designed, and had taken a long time designing.

Dad stood proudly by the cage. I raised my eyebrows at him.

"Really?" I said. "You've been possessed with bunny love now, too?"

My mom laughed, put down the hammer, and patted his shoulder. "He's just a really good dad."

"Apparently our family has room for all who wish to reside here," Dad said, studying the papers he held.

"And you asked the rabbit if he actually wanted to reside here?" I smiled.

"Who wouldn't?" His tone was teasing, but I knew my dad really believed that there was no one in the world who wouldn't want to be part of our family.

I laughed and looked at the rabbit, who seemed to be watching the progress in anticipation from his old small cage. I wasn't sure that little creature would ever win me over.

I waved to my parents, went back inside, and took an apple off the counter as I headed for my room. The house was quiet today. A heaviness rested on my chest and I had no idea why. Well, maybe I knew why but I was trying to convince myself that it didn't matter. That *he* didn't matter.

I pulled out my phone and scrolled until I found Lucas's phone number. I hadn't seen him at school since we'd been back from Thanksgiving break. I hadn't really been looking either.

Hey! Did you find out the name of that guitar repair girl for me? I wrote.

His response came within a few minutes.

Yes. She works at guitar center. I can meet you there tomorrow after school if you want.

I have detention. How about 4:30?

See you then.

I would see Lucas tomorrow. That would help. It had to.

I took the bottom half of my guitar out of its case. If I held the strings right below the broken section, I could pluck out a bit of a melody. It was horribly out of tune and not even close to sounding right, but it lightened my mood a little.

"I've woken up to find / that I've been Left Behind." I sang the words quietly, doing a really good job of feeling sorry for myself.

Ashley came in the room at that moment. "What are you doing?"

"Just practicing a song."

244

She looked at my guitar—my corpse of a guitar. "This is the most pathetic scene I've ever witnessed in my life."

"Thanks."

"You need a sister intervention."

"I don't. I need alone time. I just want to be alone for a while."

"In *this* house?" She laughed and pulled me up by my arms.

"A shack in the woods. A hut on a mountaintop. A submarine ten thousand leagues under the sea."

"All things you'll never have?" Ashley said. "Come on. Let's go out for pizza. I'll tell Mom and Dad."

*　 *　 *

Getting pizza with Ashley did help. I didn't confide in her about Cade and the letters, but it was nice to get out of my head for a while.

The next day, I no longer cared that there wasn't a new letter under the desk, even though I had seen Cade again in the parking lot that morning. *It's for the best,* I told myself. He was doing me a favor by cutting off the letters cold turkey.

Maybe Sasha had told him that I was writing the letters, and he'd freaked out. It was *me*, after all, with the awkwardness and the crazy family and the weird clothes. Letters were one thing, but his reputation might not survive more than the occasional parking lot conversation with Lily Abbott.

I collected my two letters that were still in place. Mr. Ortega was passing out the final and I tried to forget about letters and everything else and concentrate on the test.

The letter exchanges were really and truly over. The end.

CHAPTER 39

I stood at the counter in the music store waiting to hear the verdict on my guitar's fate. I had gone home after detention, collected its carcass, and met Lucas at the store. Now he stood in another section checking out guitar straps while I was watching the worker in front of me carefully examine the break.

"Wow. What happened to it?" she asked. She was pretty, with tattoos on her arms and black-framed glasses.

"A little brother," I explained.

"Not cool," she said with a sympathetic nod. "When the neck is broken like this, the integrity of the entire body is messed up. Too bad it didn't break up here." She pointed to the top where the headstock was. "That's much easier to repair. That said, this isn't completely lost. I can't guarantee it will ever sound like it used to, but we can try." She turned it over. "Do you have every single fragment of the splintered wood?"

"I don't know. I gathered as much as I could."

"Well, I can try."

Her words gave me hope, but . . .

"How much will it cost?" That was the magic question.

247

She studied the guitar again. "It just depends on how much time it takes. A couple hundred dollars at the most."

I swallowed the lump that immediately sprang into my throat. "Okay. I'll have to think about it then." I collected the broken pieces, laid my guitar back in its coffin, and buckled it closed.

"Here's my card if you decide you want to go ahead." She handed me a plain white business card. I shoved it in the back pocket of my jeans and headed for the door before I cried.

Lucas could meet me outside.

A few minutes later, he did, carrying a plastic bag.

"You okay?" he asked.

I shrugged because speaking wasn't an option given how tight my throat was.

"What happened?"

My guitar case felt like it weighed a thousand pounds.

Mom's minivan was parked in the front row of the parking lot so I nodded toward it and we headed there. Next door to the guitar repair was an In-N-Out and a stream of cars were waiting in the drive-through line. I opened the back of the minivan, set the guitar down, and sat in the open back myself. Lucas sat next to me. I just needed a minute before I could speak. He seemed to understand this and thankfully didn't say anything.

I watched the line of cars at the drive-through, trying to think of lyrics like I normally did when I observed things. But

I hadn't been able to think of decent lyrics in a while. And it wouldn't matter if I did, anyway. That contest was out of reach for me. I needed to accept that.

When my throat had loosened I said, "She's not sure she can fix it. And I'm not sure I can spend the money on the hope that she can."

"Bummer."

"Yes. It is." I wanted to talk the tightness out of my chest but I couldn't. As I stared at Lucas I realized how little I knew him, how little he knew me. I didn't feel comfortable sharing more than I already had.

"You want to go get something to eat?" he asked, nodding toward the In-N-Out. "Get your mind off of this?"

A few weeks ago, the idea of having burgers and shakes with Lucas would have been like a dream come true. Now, I shook my head. "Not really. I just want to go home."

"I understand. Some other time?"

I tried to digest this. Lucas had asked me out. And when I put him off, he had asked me *again*. I should've been over the moon about this, but all I felt was sadness. A sadness that had settled across my shoulders and was weighing on me.

And I was sure the sadness was about a lot more than my stupid broken guitar.

"I've done something stupid," I blurted.

Lucas frowned. "You have?"

"I asked you out for all the wrong reasons."

Both times when I'd found the courage to talk to Lucas, it was to spite Cade. For two years, I'd admired Lucas from a distance. I liked the *idea* of him but the reality was, I knew nothing about him. And I realized, right now at least, I didn't want to. Maybe when someone else that had no business being in my head was out of it, I would feel differently.

"I need some time," I added, glancing down. "I'm sorry."

"What wrong reasons?" Lucas asked.

"To get my mind off someone else."

"Ouch."

"I'm sorry." I looked up at him guiltily. "I really am."

He shrugged. "I get it. Text me when that someone is permanently out of your mind."

"I will."

Lucas left me there in the back of my van. I watched him get into his car and drive away. He didn't seem surprised or upset at all. That thought made me both relieved and sad.

I stood up and hit my head on the roof. I saw stars in my vision, my head light. I leaned against the car to keep myself upright.

A horn honked to my left followed by a chorus of shouts. I looked over to see Cade's BMW full of guys in line at the drive-through. Just what I needed. I reached up and pulled down the heavy trunk door of the van.

A car door slammed shut and then another. Cade and one of his friends were trading places, his friend taking over the driving. Then Cade jogged my way and my heart picked up speed. Why was my heart such a traitor?

"Nice ride," he said, patting the side of the minivan.

I wanted to ask him why he'd stopped writing. Why he was acting so normal when he'd left me in the cold for the last few days with not a single explanation. *I* was supposed to be the one to stop writing first. Not him.

"I don't need to see you right now," I said through gritted teeth. Cade was just another representation of something I wanted but couldn't have. And I knew that now—I wanted him. We'd been exchanging notes for weeks and I'd fallen for that guy. The one in the letters. And sometimes even the one not in the letters. But I also knew that, just like my broken guitar, it would never work right. Cade had dated my best friend. We didn't get along. He'd treated me badly. He hung with a completely different crowd. I was too odd for him. It was impossible.

"I just have one question," Cade said, "and then I'll leave you alone."

I turned to face him. "What?" I snapped.

He held up both hands. "Whoa. No need to get angry with me."

"I'm not." *I like you and that makes me angry with myself.* "What?"

"My friends want man bracelets. How much does your mom sell them for? I need like four more."

I resisted the urge to roll my eyes. Of course he'd make man bracelets cool. "I'll ask her." I pulled on the door handle but it was locked. I reached into my pocket but it was empty. Where had I put the keys? The trunk maybe?

"Hey," he said softly. "What's wrong?"

"Nothing. I'm fine."

"Is it Lucas? I saw him leave."

"Can you just not."

"Not what?"

"Not be nice right now. I need you to be mean. It helps."

"It helps with what?"

It helps me keep my feelings at bay. "Go be with your friends, Cade. They're waiting."

He left, just like I wanted him to. Just like I didn't want him to. But by the time I had opened the trunk, retrieved the keys, and unlocked the van door, he was back.

"They're not waiting anymore. Oh . . . and I'll need a ride home."

We stood face-to-face by the driver's side door, the largeness of the minivan blocking us from the view of the drive-through line. His phone rang, the ringtone a song from The Crooked Brookes, reminding me of our connection. He stopped the song after a few notes but didn't answer it. I kept my mouth shut about knowing the song. It had only been a few notes anyway; maybe it wasn't the song I thought it was.

"Three-hour truce?" he asked.

A sob crept up on me, getting out before I could stop it. "I'm not supposed to cry."

"Why not?"

That was someone's rule. I wasn't even sure whose anymore. No crying before date three. It didn't matter; we'd never have a date three. Rules were stupid anyway. They didn't work.

He stepped forward, so close I could smell his breath-stealing scent again. "Talk to me, Lily."

I leaned forward, put my forehead on his chest, and let myself be sad for a moment about what I couldn't have that was standing right in front of me. I didn't let my arms go around him like they wanted to. I didn't let the rest of my body melt into him or even my cheek find its way against his soft cotton shirt. No, just my forehead and only a few tears.

"I'll be done before they leave," I promised.

He chuckled and wrapped his arms around me. "You have three hours. No need to rush."

He pulled me closer, but my arms were still crossed over my chest, creating a very necessary barrier between us. I had once told him in a letter that hugs were magical, and they were. Hearing his breath in my ear, feeling his heart beat against me, the warmth of his body seeping into mine, sent tingles throughout my entire being. He'd bent down a little, his head filling in the space next to mine. I could swallow my objections for three hours. Live in this perfect moment for as long as possible. I didn't have to think about the past or Sasha or Isabel . . .

No, I had to think about Isabel. She was more important to me.

I pushed my arms against him and he released his hold. I wiped at my cheeks with my sleeves. "Thanks, but I'm good now."

"Too late. They already left."

I watched as his BMW pulled out of the parking lot and drove away. "You let your friends drive your car?"

"I'm not as attached to it as you might imagine."

Because it was bought with his father's money, I remembered him saying in one of the letters. I knew more about him than he realized.

"Okay. I'll take you home." I sniffled, embarrassed by the embrace we had just shared.

"Can we stop somewhere first?" He rounded the van and got in the passenger seat before I'd answered.

When I was in as well I asked, "Do I have a choice?"

"Truce. We called a truce."

I managed a small smile. "All right. Where to?"

CHAPTER 40

"I do actually have to be home at some point tonight."

"We're almost there."

We were listening to awful music on the radio. I couldn't play the kind of music I would normally be listening to without giving everything away. It was dark and I had no idea where we were, but I knew we were at least twenty minutes from my house.

"Turn right here on seventh," Cade instructed.

I turned and my guitar case in the back slid and hit the wall.

"What was that?" he asked.

"The dead body I keep back there."

"Nice." He pointed. "Okay, up ahead there on the left turn into the main drive."

"Of the Land's End? You're taking me to a hotel? I'm not that kind of girl."

He laughed. "I'm not taking you to the hotel . . . Well, I am taking you to the hotel, but not like that."

He showed me where to park and I turned off the van.

"Now, follow my lead," Cade whispered. "If anyone stops us, let me do the talking."

"Is this illegal?"

"Not really."

"That wasn't a comforting answer."

"Are you looking for comfort?"

I didn't answer, but I followed him. He must've decided at some point that I was walking too slow because he reached back and took my hand, pulling me along. The feel of his hand made my heart skip.

We went through the front doors of the hotel. There was only one attendant at the front desk who was busy on the phone and didn't even glance at us. We passed through multiple fancy rooms and halls until we were outside on the back end of the hotel.

Cade led me past a huge lit-up rock waterfall and up some stairs and down more paths until we came to a locked gate that said No Admittance After Hours. There was a slot on top of the handle to slide a card in. I was guessing that it was most definitely after hours. He must've not realized it would be closed.

I waited for him to turn around and lead us somewhere else but he looked over his shoulder, then hopped the fence and opened the gate from the inside.

"So this is what you meant by 'not really.'" I took a deep breath and walked through the gate. We followed a long cement path up a hill until we reached what I assumed was our destination—a large patio area that overlooked an enormous expanse of grass and trees and desert landscape.

"That's the golf course," Cade explained. "You can see it better during the day."

I took in the view. "Do you come here often?"

"My stepdad takes me golfing sometimes. I hate to golf, but I love to come up here and sit."

"Your stepdad's last name is Jennings, yes? The insurance company?"

"Yes."

"And your last name is Jennings?"

He rubbed his forehead. "Long story more about pissing off my dad than loving my stepdad so much that I took his last name."

"Got it." I wanted to ask him if his father had responded to his letter yet. If he'd ever asked his stepdad why he was so hard on him. But I didn't. I leaned against the railing, looking out at the lights. It really was gorgeous up here.

There were some chairs and tables stacked along the edge of the patio and Cade got two chairs and brought them over to where I stood, setting one behind me. I sat down and he did as well.

"Why are you doing this?" I asked. Why was he deciding now, when I had renewed my vow to walk away from him, when I'd reminded myself of his past with Isabel, to act more like the person in the letters?

"Why am I doing this . . ." He twisted his bracelet around his wrist several times before holding up his fist. "This."

"I don't understand."

"This bracelet. I wore it to make you angry and all it did was remind me of the conversation we had in my kitchen. The one where you spelled out my shortcomings so well. I realize that I deserve your disdain that I always thought was unjustified."

Wow. I never thought I'd hear those words from Cade. "You didn't . . . you don't," I said. "I was quick to assign you motives over the years. I'm good at that."

He shrugged. "I deserved some of it. I always told myself I was just treating you how you treated me, but that was just an excuse. I haven't been nice. Like at the fall festival. I knew you heard me talking to Mike about you, so I said what I did on purpose. I didn't mean it. I was a jerk. Anyway, I guess what this bracelet made me realize is that I owe you an apology bracelet, too. I just don't have a mom who forces me to do things like that."

I held out my hand. "Where is it then?"

He laughed. "Metaphorically speaking."

"I get a metaphorical apology bracelet and you get a real one? Totally unfair." I dropped my hand with a smile.

"I know. Words aren't quite as good as actions, are they?"

"I love words," I said too quickly, thinking about his letters and song lyrics and books and everything else that words made possible. He raised an eyebrow. "Lucas, too," I added.

His eyebrow came down. "What?"

"You were mean to me when I was talking to Lucas."

"When?"

"At the football game. You dragged him away and probably told him not to bother."

Cade shook his head several times. "No. I was trying to help. You had this frozen look on your face. I thought you were uncomfortable."

"You were saving me?"

"I thought I was. Apparently not."

"People don't always need you to save them, you know."

He looked down at his hands that he had clasped together. "But sometimes they do, right?"

When I didn't answer he went on. "It's okay to need help every once in a while . . . To ask for help."

"I don't need help. And I don't need someone who helps people to make himself feel important."

I cringed. Why did I say that? Why did I always lash out at him?

I knew why. Because I cared about him. And it was becoming obvious to me that he cared about everybody. He liked to help people, which was the real reason he was sitting in front of me right now. He thought he was helping when really he was making this so much harder for me.

"I'm sorry," I said.

"You're probably right," he said with a sigh. "Half the reason I try to help people is to make myself feel . . ." He trailed off and I had no idea how he was going to finish that sentence.

"Feel what?"

He shrugged. "I don't know. So, why were you so upset earlier?"

I swallowed hard. "I lost something important to me. And then I found out Lucas and I aren't really compatible." *Mostly because I figured out I really like you but can't have you.*

"Compatible? You seem perfect for each other."

"Is that an insult?" I normally wouldn't take it as one, but coming from Cade, it felt like one.

"No. I just mean that he's not mainstream. He's a little different. You seem to like that."

"I do."

"So then what's the problem?"

"No problem. It was just bad timing, I guess. It's not a big deal. Really."

"A big enough deal to cry over."

I had not been crying about Lucas. My guitar, yes. My never-to-be relationship with Cade, yes. But not Lucas. "It wasn't about that. I'll be fine."

"But if you like someone enough you try to work on things."

I laughed a little. "And there is the problem. We didn't like each other enough."

"Because you like someone else?"

My eyes locked on his. Had I somehow given that away? I needed to change the subject before the truth came out.

"What about you?" I asked quickly. "How have you been?"

"Since?"

"I don't know. Since Thanksgiving when a rude person kicked you out of her house."

He smiled. "Fine. Baseball keeps me busy."

I heard the static of a walkie-talkie and stood up quickly. "Someone's coming," I whispered.

Cade didn't look like he believed me at first but then there were voices coming up the walkway, talking about checking out the disturbance. Meaning us. We were the disturbance.

I jumped up and pulled Cade to the only door on the patio. We slipped inside what I thought would be a room that would lead us away from here but turned out to be a closet filled with more chairs. We wedged ourselves inside and Cade pulled the door closed behind us, instantly engulfing us in blackness.

He must've shifted to the left because his foot came down on mine. I breathed air between my teeth.

"Sorry," he whispered. "Where are you?"

I was so close to him I could feel his body heat, so I wasn't sure why he couldn't tell where I was. I put both hands up, thinking they were going to touch his back, but realized I was touching his chest instead. "Right here."

He placed his hands over mine on his chest. "Now I won't step on you."

"We could just tell them we're guests and got lost," I suggested.

"And had to jump a fence? I'm afraid they'll recognize me and take away my stepdad's golf membership. They'll know I wasn't lost."

"They'll take away his membership over something lame like that?"

"Let's just say they're most likely looking for an excuse. He's not the most pleasant person on the planet."

I nodded even though Cade couldn't see me in the darkness. Outside the door I could hear the voices. It was hard to tell what they were saying, even at full volume, so I wasn't worried about Cade and me whispering.

"Do you get along with him?" I asked.

"My stepdad?"

"Yes."

"No." And that's all he said. I assumed that meant he didn't want to talk about it.

"Did you miss any classes this week?" I asked.

"No, why?"

"Oh." I was not going to let that knowledge hurt my feelings. It didn't matter. I was happy that he hadn't written, I reminded myself.

"Why?" he asked again.

"I didn't see you much is all."

"Were you looking?" I could hear the smile in his voice.

"You wish."

He laughed softly and I felt the movement of it under my hands. I closed my eyes and willed my hands to be still, not to move or explore like they were dying to.

"Sasha told me."

That statement solved the problem of my temptation.

My breath became shallow. She told him. Why would she tell him? What was she hoping to accomplish? But of course she told him.

So that solved the mystery of why he'd stopped writing me. He had been disappointed.

"She did?" It was all I could say. My breath was gone. My face was red. I was surprised it wasn't glowing in the darkness. I tried to drop my hands but he was still holding them against his chest. "When?"

"Tuesday after the man bracelet conversation."

Right. That made sense. She'd seen us talking, she'd given me that nasty look, then she probably marched up and told him the truth. "Oh." It was all I could think of to say.

"That's why I was glad I ran into you earlier. I just wanted to clear the air."

"You've cleared it. It's nice and clear."

"Is it? Because it still feels a bit murky to me."

"Then we might as well just say it out loud, clearly. What exactly did Sasha tell you?"

"That you hate me."

"Yes . . . Wait, what?"

"It wasn't news to me, considering what we'd just talked about at my house, but I had hoped that we could get past it. Talk it out. Be friends."

"No."

"We can't be friends."

"No, yes, we can." I was in shock. "I didn't tell her that. She told me the same thing about you."

"She did? So you don't hate me?"

"No! I don't hate you. I have in the past. Not anymore." I'd said that too loud. I knew I had. It was too late to clamp my mouth shut but I did anyway. It didn't matter. The door swung open and a man holding a flashlight pointed it directly into our eyes.

"Cade Jennings?" he said.

"The one and only," Cade answered.

"Come with me."

CHAPTER 41

The night ended poorly. Cade went to hotel jail. Okay, just the security guard's office where he was forced to call his parents to come pick him up. And I was allowed to go. I didn't want to leave, but he kept telling me, "Lily, seriously, it's fine. I'm fine. Go." He was saving me again.

So I went, even though I probably should've stayed. No, I shouldn't have stayed. I needed to go before he made me like him even more. I was sacrificing him on the altar of friendship, I told myself. Isabel was more important.

I went home and finally was able to finish the rest of the lyrics for "Left Behind." A song I couldn't technically record because I didn't have my guitar. But even if I borrowed a guitar, I couldn't use this song. It was about Cade. I wasn't sure he'd take kindly to me winning a songwriting contest with a song that was based on his life that he kept very private. Like he'd want the world to know about his absent father when he had a hard time even writing about it anonymously.

As I sat on my bed with my notebook, I laughed at myself. At the idea that this song would win. That it would become world-known just because I entered it into a contest. The chances of that were slim to none. But even with those odds, I couldn't do that to Cade. I liked him too much.

☆ ☆ ☆

All Monday morning I kept my eyes out for Cade. I wanted to see him so I knew everything worked out fine with the hotel, with his stepdad. Since he was no longer writing me letters, I had to count on an actual sighting to check up on him. But I hadn't seen him at all. In Chemistry I hoped and prayed that there would be a letter. That now that finals were over, he'd write and tell me that he was sorry he'd stopped writing, he'd been too busy studying, or too busy with school responsibilities, or something. Some really good excuse as to why he'd stopped.

But as my hand searched in vain underneath the desk for a letter it never found, my heart dropped another degree. He'd either found out that I was the letter writer and was giving me a very big hint about how he felt about that, or he was just moving on—Cade always did have a short attention span.

It didn't matter. He didn't matter.

☆ ☆ ☆

"What do you want for lunch today?" Isabel asked.

I tugged on my zipper that was stuck at the bottom of my hoodie. "I don't know. Something hot. I'm cold."

"They should have a soup cart here. That would be awesome."

"In Arizona?"

"Okay, for the month of December, they should have a soup cart here."

"Agreed."

I growled as my zipper refused to budge. I was blindly following Isabel wherever she was leading us, her shoes in my peripheral vision as I messed with my zipper.

"What do you think Sasha wants?"

"Huh?" I looked up to see Sasha on a course straight for us, her face a mixture of anger and sadness. I wasn't sure what to do with that. She had a bundle of papers in her right hand and it took me a moment to place them but I knew before she reached me that they were my letters. All the letters I'd written to Cade. How had she gotten them?

"You make this impossible," Sasha grunted. "You're so weird." She shoved the letters into my arms and a few fell to the floor. "I can't be that."

Isabel helped me pick up the scattered letters as Sasha marched away.

"What was that about?" Isabel asked in surprise.

"These are my letters."

"How'd she get them? Did Cade give them to her?"

My stomach twisted into a knot. I had no idea.

I opened my backpack and started to shove my letters in with his that I kept there. I stopped, gathered both his and mine, and held them out for Isabel. "Will you just take these? Can we have a bonfire at your house after school?"

She gave me a sad smile. "If that's what you want."

"It is."

She opened her backpack and I dropped them all inside. I needed him out of my life once and for all.

☆ ☆ ☆

Cade was standing by the minivan talking to my mom through the open window when I approached. I felt like I had on the same angry/sad face that Sasha had been wearing earlier.

"Hey, Lily," Cade said when I opened the side door.

"Hey." I got in and closed it.

He looked confused. "Well, it was nice talking to you, Mrs. Abbott. Wyatt, I'll see you Thursday."

"Okay!" Wyatt said.

Then Cade looked at me. "Truce expired?"

"Yep." I could do this. I could go back to ignoring him again when all I really wanted to do was ask him if he got in trouble with his parents Friday night after the hotel incident. If his stepdad got kicked out of the golf club. If he was doing okay.

He backed slowly away from the car and my mom rolled up the window as she pulled away.

"I have no idea what you have against that young man, Lil," Mom said, "but it needs to stop."

I nodded. "It's stopped."

CHAPTER 42

I showed up at Isabel's house half an hour later. I'd thrown on a black T-shirt to symbolize what, I wasn't sure. When she opened the door though, her expression was one I didn't understand—guilt mixed with sadness mixed with something like hope.

"I'm sorry," she said.

"What? Why?" My right eye started to twitch. What was she going to confess to now?

"I read them. I shouldn't have. They were private. But I did."

I let out a breath. "Iz, I didn't know it was him when I was writing them."

"I know." She took me by the hand and led me to her room where all my letters were stacked neatly on her desk. "We can't burn these."

"What? But I wore black."

She laughed. "These letters, Lil . . . It's no wonder you fell for him."

"I didn't . . ." I started to protest, but I couldn't lie. "I know."

"But he doesn't know he's been writing you?"

"No."

"He thought *that* was Sasha?" She pointed at the letters.

"I'm pretty sure."

"Then he's an idiot. Those sound nothing like Sasha. Those letters are so you. He fell for *you*."

A lump formed in my throat. "He didn't fall for me."

"It sure seems like he did."

"Even if that were true, which it's not, it doesn't matter. I'm choosing you. I'm choosing us. I wore black."

She smiled and pulled me into a hug. "Can I tell you something?"

"Of course."

"I was always jealous of you and Cade."

I pushed away from her so I could see her face. "Jealous? Of our fighting?"

"Yes. He'd get more passionate discussing something you did than anything we'd ever done or talked about. I never told you that I always kind of thought you two had a connection you both refused to admit to."

"Iz." I could tell what she was doing and I didn't want her to feel like she had to do this.

"Hear me out." She picked up the letters and placed them gently into my hands. "I want this for you."

I smiled. "I love you for that, but he doesn't want me, he wants *her*. The girl from in here." I held up the letters. "Or at least he used to. He stopped writing and I have no idea why. Maybe because he thought she was Sasha. I don't know."

"Then tell him you're her!"

"I'm scared."

"If you don't try, you'll always wonder."

"Isabel . . ."

"Please, Lil." She looked me in the eye. "I've been selfish. I never had him. Never all the way. I tried to blame that on you, but it wasn't you. It was us. Me and Cade. We weren't right for each other. But you two . . ." She placed her hands on the outside of mine, which were still holding the letters. "You two would . . . What was that he said in one of the letters? Balance each other perfectly? Something like that? Anyway, I agree with him. You would. You do. Lily, give this a chance."

Her plea was so sincere, so heartfelt, that all I could do was say, "I'll think about it." And "Thank you."

※　※　※

When I went into my room later that night, something was on my pillow. The first thought I had was that Jonah had been in my room again messing with my stuff. But that wasn't it. On my pillow sat the newspaper clipping for the song-writing contest, flattened as best as possible.

"Don't give up," Ashley said from behind me. "I'm sorry I've been so hard on you."

I turned to see my sister in the doorway, my brothers' heads peeking out from behind her.

"Did you guys do this?" I asked.

"You're good, Lil," Ashley said. "You can do it. You just need to believe in yourself."

I picked up the newspaper clipping to reread the contest entry deadline and a glint of silver caught my eye. Beneath the clipping, there in the middle of my pillow, was money. A stack of bills and some change.

"I know it won't cover the whole cost of a new guitar," Ashely said, "but it's a start."

"I put the quarters in," Jonah said proudly.

I couldn't speak. A hot trail of tears spilled out of my eyes. My siblings came in the room and wrapped me in a group hug.

"I love you guys," I said through a sob. "Thank you."

"We've missed music around here," Ashley said.

"You guys are the best."

"We know," Wyatt said.

"What's that smell?" Ashley asked.

Jonah giggled.

"Ew!" Ashley broke free of the hug, dispersing us all, and chased Jonah out of my room to loud shrieks. I had the best family in the universe.

CHAPTER 43

I awoke the next morning immediately feeling a sense of panic. My heart raced, my lungs burned, my eyes stung. I was terrified just thinking about telling Cade I was the letter writer. I still wasn't sure why he'd stopped writing me, but it didn't seem like a good sign that right now both the letter-writing version of me and the real version of me weren't necessarily on his good side.

I wouldn't tell him.

No, I would tell him. At least if I told him it would be over and I could move on with my life.

I rolled onto my side. The pile of money my siblings had given me the night before—almost a hundred dollars worth—sat on my nightstand and gave me a boost of strength. I could do this.

🌸   🌸   🌸

If hair cooperation was any indication of how this day would go, I was in trouble. My hair refused to be tamed. When I showed up to school, my waves were a wild mess.

I searched for Isabel with an extra sense of urgency to see if she'd changed her mind, if she felt weird about me and Cade

273

potentially being together. I was trying to find a good excuse not to do this. I'd been trying to find an excuse not to admit that I liked Cade for a long time now.

But when I found Isabel, her smile was even more radiant than the night before. "You look like you're going to puke," she said, abandoning our normal greeting.

"I feel like I'm going to puke. And by the way, that's the last thing I thought before I went to bed last night, too."

She laughed. "So I take it you made a decision."

"Yes."

She didn't have to ask me what that decision was. She knew. "Just relax. I read those letters, Lil. I've never heard him talk like that to anyone. You'll be fine."

☥ ☥ ☥

I'd be fine. I'd be fine.

At first I thought I'd just march up to him and tell him who I was, but that wasn't me, that wasn't us . . . not that there was an us.

Sometime in the middle of fourth period I knew that the way to tell him was in a letter, tucked carefully beneath the Chemistry desk. Then he'd have time to process it, to think about it. He wouldn't have to give an immediate reaction. Maybe it was another way of protecting myself, but it felt right.

I wasn't going to risk Sasha seeing me write that letter though, so I pulled out my clean white sheet right there in the office where I was supposed to be sorting mail into teachers' boxes. And I began writing the letter. I started it how I had never started one of these letters before. With his name.

Cade,

   Hi. As you can see, I know who you are. A couple weeks ago, I was delivering some packets to Mr. Ortega and saw you writing to me. I was shocked, and to be honest, horrified. If you knew who I was, you'd understand why. We don't get along very well. Mostly because I hold grudges. Even if they're based off of misunderstandings, apparently. (I didn't know this about myself until recently.) I guess I want to start by saying, I'm sorry for that. I've come to know you through the letters first, which have always brought me so much joy that I should've known that the person writing them was someone who would both challenge me and understand me. And then I came to know you outside of the letters, and you surprised me. In so many good ways. I'm not sure why you stopped taking my letters or writing me back, and I hope you take this one or else I'll be forced to be brave and say this all to your face. Don't make me do that. But I hope whatever the reason you stopped writing me is that it's just another one of our misunderstandings. (There's a song in there somewhere. Do you want to try your hand at writing it?) So now is the part where I tell you who I am so that you can be horrified.

                                              Lily Abbott

275

I folded up the letter, not even wanting to reread it because that would ensure I wouldn't give it to him. I tucked it in my pocket and tried to forget about it until Chemistry.

In Chemistry, I couldn't free myself of the letter fast enough. I waited for a moment when neither Lauren nor Sasha were paying attention to me, and slipped it in place. As I pulled my hand back, I felt the edges of a new piece of paper. I sucked in a tiny breath and freed it. A letter. After a week, he'd written me a letter.

As I tried to carefully unfold it, I ripped a corner. I forced my hands to be still and finished, flattening the paper onto my desk.

> *I'm sorry I haven't been writing you. Here's the thing.*
> *I really enjoy writing you and you're great and funny*
> *and smart, but then I started liking this girl, a girl*
> *who challenges me like no one before her has, and*
> *writing you felt a little like cheating on her. Even*
> *though she and I are not together. And you and I are*
> *not together. But still. This began feeling untrue to*
> *myself, and to her. I should've told you last week*
> *instead of just dropping off like that. She's not quite*
> *convinced I'm a good guy yet, but I hope she will be*
> *soon. Wish me luck.*

The blood slowly drained from my face. This letter could mean one of two things. One, it meant that Cade liked me.

Me. The real-life version of me. We *had* been spending some time together, right?

But then there was the other possibility—that he'd fallen for someone else entirely. After all, these letters were me. And if he fell for the real me, shouldn't he have also fallen for the letter-writing me?

I was torn. Did I take my letter back and wait a few more days, see if I saw him around with another girl? Or did I leave my letter there and hope for the best either way?

I left it, much to my racing heart's objections, because if he did like some other girl, this was my best chance to win him over.

After school, I showed Isabel the latest letter and she squealed.

"So you think this is a good thing?" I asked.

"He likes you. Go talk to him."

My head whipped around, her statement making me think he was somewhere in the vicinity. He wasn't, and I breathed a sigh of relief.

"He's probably at baseball practice," Isabel said. "I think they started pre-season training today. Go find him there. Wait for him."

"I left him a letter. He'll read it tomorrow. Until then I'm going to eat an entire bucket of Rolos and slip into a food coma."

"Do Rolos cause food comas? All that sugar would produce the opposite effect, don't you think?" she asked as though I was seriously going to eat an entire bucket of Rolos.

"After the high there would surely be a crash."

"But that would take too long."

"You're right. Thank goodness you've talked some sense into me."

"Another reason you keep me around."

"One of a million."

She squeezed my hand. "Tomorrow. Big things will happen tomorrow."

CHAPTER 44

I saw Cade in the parking lot the next morning. He was walking and talking with a guy friend, his smile bright enough to stop traffic, or hearts, mine being the proof of that. How was I going to continue to see him if the day ended badly?

"There's Cade." Ashley waved but he didn't see her so she started to roll down her window.

I grabbed her shoulder. "Please don't."

"What's wrong?"

"Nothing. Can we just wait to talk to him?"

"Wait until when?" Then her eyes went wide. "Oh! Do you like Wyatt's coach? Are you in the 'being mysterious' phase?"

I groaned, thinking about that letter waiting to be read under the desk. "I am in the very opposite of the mysterious phase."

"Then you're not doing it right."

"I know. I'm sure I'm failing miserably. I've broken every rule." I got out of the car now that Cade was well past us. "See you after school."

✳ ✳ ✳

Chemistry. The desk waited in front of me like a headstone in a zombie movie. I was stuck at the door, staring at it, not sure if in my zombie metaphor that I'd be the girl to charge forward with a pickax. I'd probably be the one running the other way.

"You going to walk or block the doorway?" Sasha said from behind me, forcing her way around me, her shoulder slamming into mine. I tripped forward but didn't fall. It gave me the momentum I needed to keep walking.

I sat down, counted to three, and went for the letter. My hand only found a fresh piece of gum. So it had been option number two. He liked some other lucky girl. And now he knew it was me. At least I'd told him in a letter, where I didn't have to *watch* him be horrified. My hopes fell to my feet, crushed more than I thought they'd be.

Why had I thought a mainstream popular guy like Cade would fall for an off-the-beaten-path girl like me, anyway?

My eyes went blurry and I forced them clear again with a few hard blinks. For the first time in a while, I made myself take decent notes, even though Mr. Ortega had long ago stopped requesting them at the end of class.

When the bell mercifully sounded, putting me out of my misery, Mr. Ortega called my name. "Wait for a moment please."

Sasha gave me a satisfied look so I wondered if she had somehow gotten me in trouble again. As soon as everyone had left, Mr. Ortega held up a folded note. "Is this what you were looking for earlier?" he asked.

My heart started beating hard. He was holding hope in his hand and I wanted to charge him for it. I nodded.

"You and Cade think I'm blind?"

My shoulders tensed. Did that mean he stole my note yesterday as well? The one I'd written to Cade telling him who I was?

"No."

"I'm glad to hear that because your actions would say otherwise."

"I'm sorry."

"No more letter writing in class."

"I didn't write my last one in class," I said even though I knew it didn't matter.

"Beside the point."

"Can I have it now?" I asked, nodding toward the letter he held up like a prize I couldn't win.

"I am going to hang on to this. When you bring up your Chemistry grade, I will turn it over. Until then . . ." He opened his desk drawer and dropped it in. "It's mine."

It took all my will power not to drop to my knees and beg Mr. Ortega to have mercy on my poor overworked nerves. I grabbed my backpack and headed for the door. The halls were empty, everyone already at lunch. If Cade had written me a positive response upon finding out my identity, wouldn't he be standing in the hall right now with his amazing smile telling me he wanted to get married and have indie rock babies with me? Unless he hadn't gotten my letter at all and still didn't know who I was.

I replayed the final words Mr. Ortega said over and over. I pictured the note falling into the open desk drawer. I needed that letter. I was going to get that letter. It would tell me if Cade had gotten mine. It would tell me if I needed to avoid him forever or not.

✿ ✿ ✿

I sent my sister a text during final period telling her I was getting a ride home with Isabel. Then I sent Isabel one too, hoping she'd agree to that ride. And I added:

Want to help me steal some keys from the front office after school so I can rescue the letter??

I'd told her what had happened during lunch. She was just as horrified as I was. Her solution was for me to just tell Cade face-to-face. My solution was one that might save me a lifetime of humiliation depending on what the letter said.

Now, she texted back: *Of course I do. I'll distract, you retrieve.*

And that's where I was now. Retrieving.

I could hear Isabel's voice at the front desk talking to Mrs. Clark. I had snuck in the back door of the main office and was heading for the long desk. Isabel had a tough job. She not only had to distract Mrs. Clark while I stole the keys, but the whole time I was gone too so that I could put them back without her discovering they were missing. I'd promised Isabel I'd be as fast as possible. I'd also promised her an ice cream sundae, but that wasn't helpful to think about now.

Mr. Ortega didn't have a seventh-period class so I knew he'd be long gone. I only hoped he hadn't locked his desk like he did the door.

The keys were easy to get; I'd used them before because I was trustworthy and responsible. I was pretty sure I would single-handedly destroy that reputation with Mrs. Clark if she saw me now.

I tucked the keys into my pocket so they wouldn't jingle and rushed back outside. Once out, I picked up my pace to a run. I was not a runner. I did not like to run. But I ran like I meant it.

Maybe I should've joined the cross-country team after all because I wasn't half bad at this. For about one stretch of sidewalk. By the time I made it to the Science building, I had cursed not only the entire cross-country team, but the sport as a whole. I had a cramp that was sending a painful jolt up my side and I could barely breathe.

In front of the door to Chemistry, I bent over at the waist to gulp some air. Then I remembered Isabel talking to Mrs. Clark and I straightened up and began the process of elimination to find the key.

I had tried five on the ring of what felt like five hundred when the door at the end of the hall slammed shut. I shoved another key in and as luck would have it, the lock turned and I slipped into safety.

The room was dark, the blinds drawn, and it took a moment for my eyes to adjust. I crept forward, my hands out in front of me. I had made it to the back row of desks when the door swung open and I turned around with a gasp, frantically thinking of a way to explain myself to Mr. Ortega.

But it wasn't Mr. Ortega. It was Cade, his dazzling smile lighting up the room. The door shut behind him with a click.

"Have I started you down a pathway of crime?" he asked.

I tried to catch my breath again. "Are you trying to take credit for this?"

"I called your name outside but you were running like someone was chasing you."

"I'm practicing for cross-country."

"You are?"

"No, I'm not. Running is the worst. Why do people do that on purpose?"

He smiled. "Those aren't exactly the right shoes for it."

I looked down at my purple Docs. He was right; they were too heavy for running.

He glanced around the room. "So what are you doing?"

"Don't you have baseball practice?" I wiped at a bead of sweat on my temple.

"I was heading there when I saw you."

"Do you have to run at baseball practice?"

"Sometimes."

"I'm sorry."

Cade smiled. "I know I'm not the most observant person in the world, but I get the feeling you don't want to answer my question."

I laughed. "What gives you that idea?"

"Oh I don't know . . ."

Isabel was going to kill me if I didn't get rid of him soon and get on with the task.

"Did you change your mind?" he asked.

"Change my mind? About what?"

"You answered and now you're trying to take back whatever you said?"

My eyes, which had been avoiding his very well up until this point, now latched on to them. He knew I was the letter writer. So he had gotten my letter after all. He was at the advantage now because he knew I liked him and I had no idea how he felt. It's possible he wrote me an amazing letter about how he thought we would be great friends.

"No," I said.

"No what?"

"No, I didn't write back. I mean, I would've, probably, maybe, but I didn't get yours. Mr. Ortega stole it."

A slow smile spread across his lips. "Really?"

"Cade, please don't take joy in my panic."

He laughed. "But it's so fun."

I took a couple steps sideways, trying to get around the back row of desks and to Mr. Ortega's. "I'm just going to rescue the letter from his desk and talk to you when I'm done reading it."

I turned, passed my desk . . . our desk . . . and was almost to the aisle when he stopped me with, "Lily."

"Just wait, okay?"

"Lily." He was behind me now and placed his hands on my shoulders, turning me to face him. The heat from his hands seemed to seep into my skin, warming me. "You don't need to break into his desk. I can tell you what the letter says. I reread it a million times, I should know." That last sentence he said under his breath.

Letters were safe. They were words, easy to read if enjoyable and stop reading if hurtful. Letters didn't stare at me like Cade was now staring at me, full of fire.

"I'm scared," I said.

"Don't be." He cleared his throat. "Dear Lily," he started, and his intense gaze didn't waver. "I've known you were the letter writer since the night I picked up Wyatt for baseball practice several weeks ago. I heard the music you were playing. A song only we, and possibly up to one hundred other people, would know."

My breath stopped short in my throat. "What?" I interrupted him. "You knew before Thanksgiving? Why didn't you say anything?"

"Why didn't *you* say anything?"

"Because you hated me."

"I had the same reason. Because you hated me. I thought if you knew it was me that you'd stop writing."

My mind went back to our exchanges over the last few weeks. How he had raised his eyebrows when I mentioned us getting along because it was Thanksgiving—a reference to our letters I hadn't thought he'd put together.

Thanksgiving. He knew it was me that whole day. And then I kicked him out of my house. No wonder he thought I hated him.

There was something I still didn't understand, though. "What about Sasha?"

"What about her? I told you we're not together."

"Were you?"

"No. She asked me out. I felt I needed to give her a chance—she's a friend. I did. We weren't . . . What's that word you used? Compatible?"

I nodded. "But, how, why? She had the letters I wrote to you."

"She did?" He sighed. "I kept them in the glove box of my car. She must've found them. I'm so sorry."

"It's okay. I thought you thought she was me."

"You thought that I thought she was the letter writer?" His voice was as shocked as his expression. "Sasha?"

I laughed. "Yes."

"No. I didn't. Not for one second. Not even when I went into Chemistry and saw her sitting in our seat. I'll get the letters back from her."

"She gave them to me."

"She did? That's not like her."

"What do you mean?"

"She wasn't exactly happy when I told her she and I weren't compatible. I'm surprised she didn't use the notes against us."

I hadn't thought about it before, but that surprised me, too. "Lucky us?"

"Seriously. Now, shhh, I'm trying to read you a letter." He was still holding my shoulders. I was still warm from the inside out.

"Go on then."

"I was surprised when I found out it was you that day, but the more I thought about it the less I was surprised. Then I was frustrated, because this amazing girl I'd come to know on paper was the only girl in the whole school who wanted nothing to do with me."

"The only girl in the whole school? That might be a bit of an exaggeration."

"No interrupting letters. If you were reading this, you wouldn't be able to interrupt."

"I would've definitely stopped at that part to scoff."

He laughed and sent my heart racing. "So," he went on, "I thought maybe if you could get to know me through the letters without knowing who I was in real life that you would eventually be willing to look past my mistakes. I was again surprised to learn you had been doing the same thing. So here we are at a crossroads."

I waited for him to continue, to finish. He didn't. I spoke up. "Here we are at a crossroads? That's how you ended it? All cryptic like that?"

He took a step forward. Even though there wasn't room to take that step. My legs hit a desk.

"I think there might've been a P.S.," he said.

I couldn't breathe again, only this time it had nothing to do with running. It had to do with his closeness and his voice, which had turned quiet, and his eyes that hadn't left mine since he arrived.

My voice had lowered, too. "P.S.? We haven't written one of those before."

"It felt like it needed one."

"It did need one."

"P.S." He brushed a piece of hair off of my cheek. "I like you. A lot."

My breathing was shallow, my eyes starting to water from staring too long. "That's a great P.S."

"For our first one, I thought it was solid."

It didn't take much because he was so close. All I had to do was rise up on my tiptoes and our lips met. He tasted like mint gum and all my hopes and dreams. Well, not all of them, but a lot of them. His hands moved to my back where they pulled me against him. He deepened the kiss. My arms slid their way under his, finding his back as well. Why had we waited so long to do this? His breath was warm, his kiss as intense as his stare had been.

Something clattered onto the floor and I vaguely registered it was the keys I'd been holding. My brain was too muddled to think about that for another blissful moment in his arms. Then I remembered Isabel.

I gasped and pulled away. Too fast. The back of my legs whacked against a chair. "Ouch."

"Are you okay?"

"I'm fine. The keys. Isabel. I have to go." I somehow twisted my way out of his arms, swiped the keys off the floor, and took off.

"Lily!"

"We'll talk later! I like you, too!" I turned and walked backward for a moment, smiling his way. "In case that wasn't obvious." Then I left.

Running was fun, freeing—so easy.

CHAPTER 45

"I'll drive. You talk." That was the first thing Isabel said when we climbed into her car.

I'd managed to put the keys back in the office, thanking whatever form of luck had kept Mrs. Clark and Isabel talking the entire time. Then I went through the front door of the office.

"There you are," I'd said to Isabel, as though I'd been searching the campus over for her.

She turned around at the sound of my voice and the look in her eyes spelled murder. I tried to convey to her that I was sorry with one look as well. She'd hooked her arm in mine and said, "It was great talking to you, Mrs. Clark. Thanks for the info on dress code."

"You're welcome, hon. See you later."

We'd then walked away in silence like we were being tailed by a spy, not saying a word until in the safety of her car.

"I'm sorry," I said now, buckling my seat belt.

"Why? What happened?" She pulled out of the parking lot.

A smile spread across my face. "Nothing . . . Everything. Cade showed up. I guess he saw me running by and followed me."

"He did?"

"Yes. And he knew. He knew I was the letter writer for weeks but he thought I hated him so he didn't want to tell me."

Isabel gave a knowing laugh. "So you were both being dumb."

"Yes. How did you keep Mrs. Clark talking for that long, by the way?"

"What? No. Who cares. Why are you asking that question when you haven't finished telling me the story?"

I laughed. "Wow. I could really drag this out and make you mad."

She grabbed my hand and squeezed. "But you won't do that because you owe me big-time for what I just did."

"True. Thank you so much."

"I don't need your praise. I need the rest of the story. Tell me."

I sucked my lips in to keep from laughing again. She was portraying perfectly how I felt on the inside, all excitement and manic happiness.

"Okay, sorry, sorry. Let's see, where was I. So, he recited his letter, which he had apparently memorized, to me, not letting me get it from the desk. Basically he said that he was afraid I wouldn't like him once I found out who he was and that when he realized I was doing the same thing, he was relieved. And then he told me he liked me. So I kissed him. But then I remembered you were waiting so I ran."

"Wait, what?" Isabel cried, her eyes on the road as the car swerved a tiny bit. "You're just going to casually mention kissing him and move on like that's nothing?"

I wasn't going to casually mention kissing him. I wanted to go into detail but suddenly with Isabel sitting next to me, squeezing my hand, I remembered something I hadn't when I was kissing him—that she'd kissed him, too.

"Don't," she said as though reading my mind. "Don't think about that. We've both kissed several people since then and I'm sure it's nothing close to the same. We were young. I wasn't even thinking about that, Lil. I promise. You two are adorable. It's not even comparable to what Cade and I had. So spill it."

I let out a happy sigh. "It was perfect."

She pulled into a parking lot and I realized she was taking me up on the ice cream sundae offer right this second. "This story is going to be even better with ice cream," she said.

☆ ☆ ☆

It was seven o'clock when the doorbell rang. I was already in my pajamas and makeup free. I hardly registered the doorbell because I'd just written several lines of a new song, one that wouldn't exploit Cade's tragic life.

293

It's easy to judge not knowing the truth
Only seeing carefully built walls.
It's hard to undo years written in youth
But how amazing when the tower finally falls.
And I see you standing there
All sweet and kind of scared.
And you see me standing here.
Hope in my eyes but full of fear.

A knock at my door startled me from the lyrics. "Yeah?"

The door opened and my mom's face appeared. "Hey, you have a visitor."

"I do?"

She didn't give me a chance to ask another question, just swung my door open the rest of the way, revealing Cade. He stood, hands clasped in front of him, his posture reserved, shoulders down, head bowed slightly, like he wasn't sure how I'd receive him.

"Hey!" I jumped up, a smile instantly on my face. "Come in."

He looked to my mom to make sure that was okay.

"Keep the door open," was all she said in return, then walked away.

"I don't have your phone number," he said, looking around my room, then choosing the desk chair at the foot of my bed as his landing place. "I wanted to see you."

I sunk back down to my bed, my smile far from leaving my face. "I will give you my phone number so that I'll be better prepared for you next time." I patted my hair and tugged on my T-shirt.

"You look adorable." He rolled the desk chair around my bed so we were now knee to knee. "You *are* adorable. I want to kiss you. I can do that now, right?"

I only got one head bob of my nod in before he took my face in his hands and pulled me to him. Given the urgency in his eyes, I thought our lips would collide, but right before they did, he paused, breathed me in, then ran his lips slowly across mine. My breath was gone and I grabbed hold of the front of his shirt and tugged him toward me. The kiss didn't last long enough before he pulled away again.

"I just wanted to make sure," Cade said with a smile. "With the way you left today, I wasn't sure where we stood."

"You think I just go around kissing boys for fun?"

"I don't know what to think of you. You constantly surprise me. I honestly thought that you'd be waiting for me after baseball practice."

I made a face. "You wanted me to wait around school for over an hour?"

He laughed. "No, I did not. That would be boring."

"Oh!" I said, suddenly realizing something. "That's what other girls have done. I'm sorry. That probably would've been a good show of how much I liked you or something."

"Don't be sorry. I like that your life doesn't revolve around this." He pointed between the two of us and I grabbed his finger.

"What do you mean by *this?*"

"Us."

"Us? I like us."

He kissed my hand that was still holding his finger. "Me too."

CHAPTER 46

If I thought back over the past several weeks I could trace the days where lyrics came easy to me. Those were the days when some emotional height was reached. Days when the letter I found in Chemistry was funny or heartfelt or sad. Or the day when I discovered the letter writer was Cade. Those were the days the lyrics seemed to pour out of me in a wave of emotion.

Now, only days after kissing Cade for the first time, but with less than a week left to finish up a song for the contest, tension was definitely not an emotion that was helping at all. My sister wasn't being helpful either. She was singing pop songs she loved at the top of her lungs while telling me I should try to make my song more like whatever song she was singing.

"Please. I beg of you. Can you be quiet?" I had bought a guitar from Craigslist with the money she gave me and was feeling very ungrateful that I now wanted to kick her out of the room. I'd already come up with what I thought was a good tune, and her singing was only throwing me off. All I had to do was finish the lyrics.

"I will do your laundry for a week if you give me an hour alone."

"You'll shrink my stuff on purpose so you can wear it," Ashley said.

That wasn't a bad idea. I stood up, pulled her up by her arms, which was harder than I thought it would be, and deposited her outside of the room. "One hour."

She didn't fight it as I heard her sing her way down the hall. I sank onto my bed and picked up the guitar again. The silence was supposed to bring me inspiration but my mind went blank. I picked up my phone and shot off a text:

I need inspiration.

Cade sent me back a selfie—him making a smoldering face—and I laughed.

Yeah. That didn't work.

That's all I have to work with, he replied. *You're out of luck. You writing a song?*

Trying to. One week left.

You'll figure it out. Don't you have a whole notebook full of lyrics? Is there something you can use in there?

I stared at that notebook on my nightstand. My favorite song was the one I'd first written about him. "Left Behind." I couldn't use that. I had no right to assign emotions and words to his experience.

I'll figure something out, I wrote back. *Now leave me alone, I'm trying to write!*

He sent me another model-face selfie and I laughed and tucked my phone away.

* * *

Cade came up behind me in the school parking lot Monday morning and picked me up in a hug. I let out a surprised yelp. He kissed my cheek and put me down. My cheeks were hot as he grabbed my hand and we continued walking.

"Did that embarrass you?" he asked.

"No. Just surprised me."

He studied my face for a moment. "Are you not okay with being public about this?"

I had been more worried that he wouldn't be. I was fine. "Of course I'm okay with this."

"I'm not ruining your hipster vibe?"

I laughed. "My hipster vibe? I didn't know I had one of those."

"Oh, you do. You're casually cool. Uniquely different. And I'm totally throwing that off." He gestured to himself. His smile made it seem like a joke but I wondered if he really was worried.

I stopped, turned toward him, and kissed him in the middle of the crowded parking lot. "You're my favorite mainstream boy in the world. Don't forget it."

This time he blushed a little. "Good. Because I am pretty great. I just wanted to make sure you appreciated that." He winked at me, his confidence back.

I rolled my eyes and pulled him forward along with me. "Oh, I do."

"Did you find your inspiration over the weekend?"

I growled.

"That good, huh?"

"I wrote and erased five lines."

"When can I hear your songs?"

"When Blackout lets me write for them."

He laughed. "I have an idea for inspiration. How about you actually come to the rally today?"

"The school rally? The one they do in the gym with screaming people and chanting and school spirit? And . . . wait, how do you know I don't go to rallies?"

"I notice you, Lily Abbott."

I smiled. "I'm still not going to the rally."

"Just today. They're doing some big thing for the football team and then introducing the post–winter break sports. That's me. You want to be supportive and stuff, right? And I actually expect you to come to some of my baseball games in the spring."

"I'm super supportive. I'm going to be there. At the rally and at your games. You watch me. I will be the best girlfriend ever." I said the word before I realized I said it then quickly backtracked. "I mean, not necessarily girlfriend. Dating person. The person you go out with . . . and kiss . . . and, I'm sorry I'm still weird."

"You are adorable. And I didn't think I needed to ask. I thought it was assumed. But I'll ask." Then he did the most embarrassing thing in the world. He threw his hands in the air as we were approaching the commons and screamed, "Lily, will you be my girlfriend?"

"Not after that I won't," I said.

"Really?"

"Of course I will. Now put your hands down and stop being so . . ."

"Mainstream?"

"Loud."

He laughed and gave me a quick kiss. "See you at the rally, girlfriend."

If I smiled any more at school people might start to think I actually liked to be there. I settled into my seat in Chemistry, a new feeling of appreciation for the class coming over me. Maybe I owed Chemistry some effort for all it had done for me. I was going to get my grade up. Isabel would help me.

My hand immediately went to the underside of the desk even though Cade and I both knew Mr. Ortega was on to us and we'd said we wouldn't write anymore. My smile widened when I felt something there.

"You and Cade, huh?" Lauren said from next to me and I jumped a little. I pulled the letter onto my lap so she wouldn't see it.

"I guess," I replied. "I mean, yes. Me and Cade. Cade and I. We don't really fit but we . . ." Why was I explaining myself to Lauren? "Yes." I forced myself to stop with that.

She looked over my shoulder and nodded. I quickly glanced over as well and saw the back of Sasha heading to her seat. I was surprised she hadn't said anything. She was probably embarrassed. She'd said enough over the last few weeks. I was glad she was going to quietly lick her wounds.

I waited several minutes—until Mr. Ortega started his lesson, until Lauren was busy taking notes—to open the letter. The handwriting brought my smile back.

> *Hi. I know we're not writing anymore but I couldn't help myself. I'm thinking about you. Plus, I forgot to tell you something this morning. Remind me later. Now pay attention or Mr. Ortega will steal this.*

I grabbed my phone from my bag and sent him off a quick text.

> *You know that there is this thing that magically takes words and sends them through the air and delivers them to a recipient. It's kind of new so I didn't know if you'd heard about it. But you use it for its speed.*

He wrote back immediately.

> *Like an airplane that attaches words to its tail? I thought those only advertised sales and things. I wonder how much they charge per word.*

My cheeks hurt. He must've read my letters as much as I'd read his.

> *You're my favorite,* I replied.
> *I need your letters back, btw. They belong to me.*

The class had gone quiet and I silently cursed. I looked up to see if everyone was staring at me, but they weren't. Mr. Ortega was just writing something on the board. It was my lucky day.

A lyric came into my mind: *You're my favorite way to pass the time. But time stands still when you're on my mind.* I reached inside my backpack to write it down, but couldn't find my notebook. I must've left it on my nightstand the night before. That was new and kind of refreshing. I smiled a little and jotted the note on the corner of a scrap paper instead. The clock told me I still had thirty minutes left of class. Then it was the rally. Another thing I never thought I'd look forward to.

CHAPTER 47

I hadn't been to a rally in a while. It was loud.

Isabel leaned close as we sat in the bleachers. "The things we do for your boyfriend," she said with a smile.

"I was just thinking the same thing."

We had gotten to the point in the rally where the football team had just been congratulated for its amazing season. The sports teams we were now supposed to direct all our fan efforts toward were standing across the stage. I smiled at Cade, who had caught my eye.

One of the coaches tapped the microphone and asked, "Is this thing on?" It was definitely on.

Sasha, who must've been a tennis player or a swimmer or on some sort of spring team, walked across the stage to the coach holding the microphone. She said something too quiet for all of us to hear.

"Nobody told me about that," the coach responded back, loud and clear in the mic.

She said something else.

"A poetry contest?"

She leaned into the mic so that she could be heard, too. "This school isn't entirely about sports, right? We were supposed to announce the winner of the poetry contest."

"What is she talking about?" Isabel asked.

I shrugged. "No idea. Maybe she's the president of a poetry club." Though I couldn't quite see that.

"That's not on the agenda," the coach said. "Please take a seat, Sasha."

"Coach Davis," Sasha replied, her voice louder now. "I wouldn't want a social media blowup about how Morris High only cares about their sports teams."

The coach looked around as if expecting someone to jump to his rescue. When nobody did, he handed the microphone to Sasha. "Make it quick."

She put on a wide smile and faced the gym. "Hello, Morris High!"

This brought a loud cheer.

"As many of you know, if you read the school paper, we held a poetry contest this first semester. I'm here to read the winning entry to you. You are all going to love this." That's when she took off her backpack that I hadn't noticed before and pulled out my notebook. I recognized it from across the gym—the two-tone purple and green with my black doodles penned all over it.

My stomach fell in horror.

Noooo.

Isabel gasped. She obviously recognized my notebook, too.

"This poem was written by junior Lily Abbott, dedicated to Cade Jennings."

It seemed like the whole room let out a collective "Aww."

"What are you going to do?" Isabel asked.

I was frozen, half ready to jump up and tackle Sasha, half ready to run out of the gym. My eyes darted to Cade. He had a confused smile on.

"I know," Sasha continued, "Cute, right? Well, what many of you don't know is that Cade's dad left him and his family several years back. A tragedy really. And Lily wrote an amazing poem about it."

This was a nightmare.

I hadn't written Cade's name on any of the pages but the one she'd already read in detention. She was assuming this song was about Cade. Assuming because of the other lyrics. Assuming because of all the notes I'd written in the margins. She was assuming because she wanted to hurt me . . . and probably him.

I shook my head at Cade and mouthed the words *stop her*. He was much closer to Sasha than I was. He was on the stage with her. But he wasn't looking at me. He was looking at Sasha in horror. He seemed to be as frozen as I was. I couldn't let this happen.

I stood and began working my way down the bleachers— through students and over backpacks. But Sasha was already reading my lyrics to "Left Behind" out loud. Cade's very private life was now echoing through the suddenly completely silent gym.

By the time I was on the floor and heading toward the stage, she was reading the last two lines. My words were echoing through a gym full of people. People, I noticed, who seemed captivated by them. I stopped as Sasha finished. Now I stood in the middle of the basketball court alone, on the eye of our school mascot painted there—a bull.

"And there she is," Sasha said, in the sweetest voice. "Everyone give her a hand. Come on up and accept your award, Lily."

I did go up, because I wanted my notebook back, and I wanted to pull Cade out of there and explain everything. But it didn't happen that way. When I'd climbed the five steps to the stage to the loud applause, Cade was gone.

"You are cruel," I said to Sasha under my breath. I yanked my notebook out of her hands. "He didn't deserve that."

She smiled, pulled me into a hug and whispered. "You both did."

She wanted me to react. Wanted me to punch her or shove her and have the whole school witness that I was a jerk who treated her poorly after she'd just showered me with praise. Plus, if I acted like this was a big deal, it would turn into a big deal. People would think she'd just exposed something about Cade that she shouldn't have. I wouldn't do that to him. So I smiled, said a wobbly "thank you" into the microphone, then walked as quickly as possible off the stage and outside where I searched in vain for Cade.

Over the next thirty minutes I sent him what felt like a hundred texts that all went something like:

She stole my book

I did not enter that into a contest.

I'm sorry.

Where are you?

Can we talk about this?

This was her revenge. You know it was. Please know I did not want this to happen.

He didn't respond. Not to a single one. It was over. We were over before we'd ever begun.

I rounded the baseball field a second time, hoping he had shown up there sometime between me searching the boys' locker room and the cafeteria kitchen. Then my phone buzzed. Hope shot through me until I saw the text was from Isabel.

Where are you?

Home plate, I responded, dejected.

She was there in minutes. "Should we beat her up now or later?" Isabel asked, her eyes flashing.

I pressed my palms to my temples. "I'm worried about him."

"Don't worry about him. He'll be fine. It was a really good song, by the way. Everyone was talking about it."

A small surge of pride went through me, the same one I had felt for a split second while standing in the middle of that gym, my words filling it. I pushed the feeling back down.

"Isabel," I said, my voice breaking. "He's kept this a huge secret and now the entire school knows because of me and my stupid lyrics."

"Not because of you. Because of Sasha."

"I should've never written about his life in the first place."

"He stuck those notes all about his life under a desk!" Isabel pointed out. "Anybody could've gotten ahold of them. You could've been anyone, Lily, not you. Not kind, loyal, trustworthy you. He got lucky. This could've happened to him weeks ago because of his own doing."

"But it didn't. It happened now because of me."

"Well, go explain that to him."

I looked at my phone again. "He won't answer me."

"Then go find him." She dug her keys out of her pocket and held them out for me. "I'll have Gabriel pick me up."

I didn't hesitate. I grabbed the keys, hugged Isabel, and took off running.

CHAPTER 48

I had been everywhere. Cade's house, the kids' baseball field at the park, In-N-Out, along with every other fast food restaurant I had ever seen him at in the past, as well as the ones where I hadn't . . . he wasn't anywhere. I was now just driving, looking around. Because he was obviously some-where and it killed me that apparently I didn't know him well enough to know where that somewhere was.

School was long out by now. I'd texted my sister earlier not to pick me up. Had he gone back to school for practice? Did he go somewhere to think? I drove home. Maybe he'd gone to my house. He liked my house.

His car wasn't in front when I pulled up, but I checked all the rooms and backyard anyway. He wasn't here. I didn't know why I thought he'd come running to me when I was the person he was quite obviously running *from* right now.

I dropped Isabel's car keys on the floor in my bedroom and collapsed onto my bed, not sure what to do at this point. Just wait for him to text me? I felt like there'd been too much waiting when it came to the two of us and I wasn't sure we'd survive another session of it.

Wyatt's head appeared around my partially open door. "Hi."

"Hey."

"Can I talk to you?" He inched his way into my room, but lingered by the door.

"Sure, come in." I scooted over on the bed, still on my back, and patted the space next to me. My brother joined me there, lying next to me, staring at the ceiling. When he didn't say anything I asked, "What's going on?"

"I hope you don't hate me."

I propped myself up on my elbows, worried now. "I don't hate you. What happened?"

He couldn't look at me. He stared hard at the ceiling like it wasn't just an empty white expanse. Like it might actually be telling him something. Judging him. Finally, he spit out, "I was the one who broke your guitar. I'm sorry."

I sighed and let myself fall back again.

"You hate me now."

"No, I don't hate you. I could never hate you. I'm tired. I've just had a long day."

"You're not mad?"

I was mad and sad and frustrated and feeling very guilty for having blamed Jonah all this time for something he hadn't done.

"We need to apologize to Jonah, don't you think?"

"Yes."

"Together?" I held up my hand and Wyatt put his against it. His fingers were nearly as long as mine. When had that happened? "How did you break it, anyway?" Maybe I shouldn't have asked. The story might only ignite the anger that I didn't have the energy for right now.

"I fell on it."

"What? Why was it out of the case?"

Wyatt looked embarrassed. "I wanted to learn how to play . . . like you."

I smiled and tousled his hair. "Who taught you the flattery rule?"

"Dad."

I grabbed him by the arm and helped him off my bed. "Come on. Before you learn how to play, you need to listen to all the music in the world."

"All of it? That's a lot."

"Well, you need to figure out what you like best. First, let's go talk to Jonah and then I'll give you a few tracks to start with."

Wyatt's foot connected with the keys on the carpet and they flew into the wall with a clunk. He picked them up and held them out for me. "Why do you have Isabel's car?"

"I had to do something important."

"Oh. Do you need to go do it?"

I pocketed the keys. "Later. This is important, too."

✿   ✿   ✿

I was in the car again. Wyatt and I had apologized to Jonah. I'd found a few perfect songs for Wyatt. And I'd written Cade a letter. It was all I could think of to do. Now I was going to drop the letter off at his house.

It was a letter that talked about how sorry I was and how all these years I'd misjudged him. How I understood why he'd acted like he had at his birthday party—he'd been waiting for his dad to call and was hurt when he hadn't. I understood why he tried to help other people when he thought they were hurting by diverting attention, by making people laugh, because that's how he dealt with his problems. I ended the letter by telling him that I wasn't going to walk away from him. He couldn't get rid of me this easily.

I gripped the steering wheel, the letter sitting on the passenger seat, waiting to be read. I wished Cade were sitting in the passenger seat instead.

I was halfway to his house when I realized there was one place I hadn't looked. The one and only place he had ever taken me—the hotel with the golf course.

I crossed three lanes of traffic to make a U-turn, eliciting a long honk from a black Suburban. I waved but didn't make eye contact.

Cade was going to be there. He had to be.

I got to the hotel, parked, and followed the path he had led me on that night. I got turned around a few times, but eventually I found the gate. The one he had climbed. It was locked, like it had been that night. The moon was bright tonight and lit the path beyond the gate better than it had when we had been here.

I leaned against the gate and pulled out my phone again.

Are you at the hotel? I texted. *If you are, I'm here and in 5 minutes I'm going to climb this gate even though I'll totally get caught . . . and I'm not sure I can actually climb a gate. And I'm wearing a skirt. Please don't make me climb this gate.*

I stood on my tiptoes and tried to see even a glimpse of the patio where we had sat. I could only see some colorful tips of a potted plant. I tugged on the bars. The gate wasn't going to open. The top was flat, without pointy spikes like I'd seen on many gates. The kind of points that could impale a person. This was a good thing. But the bars that led up to the top had no horizontal connections. How had Cade climbed it that night?

"I can do this," I muttered. "After all, I'm the world's greatest runner now; this should be easy." I shoved my foot in between a couple of bars to give me my first boost up.

"Are you talking to yourself?"

Relief poured through me as I heard his voice on the other side of the fence. I not so gracefully unwedged my foot from the bars and peered through them at his familiar face. I wanted to throw my arms around him but the fence separated us.

"I'm so sorry."

"Why?" he asked, his normal Cade smile bright on his face. "I talk to myself frequently."

"No. You know why." I wrapped both hands around the bars, using them for support.

He shook his head. "Don't be. It was Sasha." He didn't sound angry but he also hadn't moved to let me in.

"Are you going to open this? I need to hug you. I can hug you, right?"

"If you can climb that fence, you can do anything you want, baby." He winked, his flirt voice on. I knew what he was doing—putting up his wall—and I hated it. I hated he felt the need to do that for me.

"Don't."

"Don't what?"

"Don't treat me like you treat everyone. Don't hide from me."

"And you haven't been hiding from me?" Now his voice had an angry edge to it.

"What do you mean?"

"That song. When were you going to show it to me? When it won the competition?"

"No! Of course not. I wasn't going to enter that into the competition."

"Why not? It was really good."

"It wasn't meant for anyone to hear. Especially not the entire school."

"I think you mean, especially not me."

I started to shake my head, but he was right. I was never going to show him that song.

"You still don't trust me?"

"I do."

"You still think of me as the guy who treated Isabel badly. As the guy who's going to hurt you one day, too. You aren't willing to be completely open with me."

"No. That's not true. Cade, I tell you more than I've ever told anyone." My throat was tight. "You've actually helped me find my words. My voice. But I didn't feel like the words to that song belonged to me. I didn't feel like I had the right to them." I retrieved the letter I had written him out of the waistband of my skirt and slid it through the bars.

He gave a breathy laugh. "Another letter?"

"You haven't gotten one in a while."

He picked it up from where it had landed in front of him. "Not from you."

I raised my eyebrows. "Someone else has been writing you letters?" When he didn't say no right away, I gasped. "Wait. Your dad?"

His eyes snapped to mine and all the pain he'd been hiding since I'd arrived was burning there.

I lowered my voice. "Will you let me in, Cade? Please?"

He stepped forward and opened the gate. I rushed through and flung my arms around him.

"I was just about to read a letter," he said, close to my ear. "You're so clingy."

I smiled. "Stop making jokes and let me be here for you."

We sat on the patio overlooking the golf course. We each held a letter. I held one addressed to Cade from his dad, and he held the one I'd written earlier.

"I don't have to read this," I said again. "If it's too personal."

"I want you to. I need objective eyes on it."

"Okay." I took a breath, and opened the envelope.

I removed the single sheet of paper that was folded in thirds and carefully opened it. The handwriting looked hurried but I wasn't familiar with his dad's handwriting, so it could've been his best effort for all I knew.

> *Cade,*
> *My son, good to hear from you. Life has been busy for*
> *both of us, I'm sure.*

Already, it felt like his dad was diffusing the blame. I paused and moved one of my hands to Cade's knee. He didn't look up. His eyes were on the letter I had written. I continued to read.

> *A new job where I have to relearn an entire computer*
> *system is keeping my mind occupied and between that*
> *and family obligations, time seems to get away from me*
> *every day.*

317

Ouch. As if Cade wasn't one of those family obligations.

I'm sure you know how that goes seeing as how you're
basically a grown man already. How's school? Baseball?
Any prospects for college? I'll have to see if I can get out
your way sometime in the next year so we can catch up
properly. In the meantime, I'm sure we can both be
better about keeping each other updated. Love
you.——Dad

I closed my eyes for a moment, then waited for Cade to be done reading my letter. When he was, he gave me a smile and a kiss.

"I needed this," he told me.

I refolded his dad's letter and shoved it in the envelope before I gave into the impulse to rip it to shreds.

"I'm sorry," I whispered, handing it back.

"No. Don't be. He's right. I could've tried harder."

"Don't give him permission to pass the blame to you."

"What do I do?" Cade asked with a sigh.

"Either call him out or let him go."

Cade pulled me over to his chair and buried his face in my neck. He held on tight to me. I wished I'd been here for him earlier, hadn't pushed him away for so long. But I was here now and there was nothing wrong with needing someone else to hold on to.

"Did you pull me over here so we could make out?" I asked.

"Yes, I did."

He kissed me and I kissed him back.

"I think I might call him out," he said between kisses.

I smiled. "Can I be there for that?"

CHAPTER 49

I walked into the kitchen to see Cade staring intently at two necklaces on the counter. My dad sat at the table pretending not to be interested.

"Dad, no." I grabbed Cade's hand and pulled him away.

"He's an impartial third party," my dad called after us.

Cade yelled back, "Sorry, Mr. Abbott, I've been abducted."

"More like saved," I said under my breath.

"Your parents are so funny."

"Yes, they are." I pushed open the door to my bedroom and picked up my guitar. "Now, I need your help. You *are* the lyricist for our band, right? I need to finish this song in two days and my inspiration has run out."

Cade grinned. "I thought you said that I inspired you."

"I'm counting on it. Now sit there where I can see your cute face and help me think of words."

He sat in the chair, his gorgeous smile in place.

"Okay. Let's get to work."

☆　☆　☆

One hour later I put down the guitar.

"You're as bad as my sister," I groaned. "Your lyrics aren't any better in person than they were in letters."

"That's a good lyric: You're no better in person than you were on paper."

I laughed. "Just stop. Come on. I know you can help me for real here. I just need the chorus to flow better."

My notebook sat next to me on the bed. I'd been using scratch paper to try to work out the song instead of writing down words only to cross them out in the book.

Cade leaned forward and picked up my notebook. "Can I look?"

My heart raced. I could do this. The worst had already happened. Sasha had read my lyrics to the entire school and people had actually liked them. Little did she know that her attempt to hurt me had actually ended up giving me a confidence boost. "Yes."

Cade smiled, like he knew how hard that was for me. "Thank you."

"No mocking me."

"But I'm so good at that."

"Oh and there's a mean song in there about you. I was mad."

He laughed and sat down on the floor, his back against Ashley's bed across from me. "Of course there is." He flipped through the pages as I continued to write. "Monsters in trees?"

I moved to the floor, sitting against my bed, letting my legs stretch out in front of me and intertwine with his. "I said no mocking."

He chuckled and my breath caught at the sound. I watched him as he read, the line of his jaw relaxed, his hair flopped onto his forehead, his fingers poised to turn another page. And I started to write. My pencil flew across the paper beside me.

> *Words brought us together though they almost kept*
> *us apart.*
> *You trusted me with your secrets and then you stole*
> *my heart.*
> *They say that love is rare, like . . .*

"What's rare?" I asked.

"What?" His eyes lifted from the page and met mine.

"What are some things that are rare?"

"Meat?"

I laughed. "We're more alike than you know."

His gaze softened as he stared at me. "Love?"

I smiled and pressed my knee against his. "I already used love, I was trying to compare it to something else." I tapped my pencil on the page, biting my lip.

His eyes went back to my notebook. "This is really good."

"Which one?"

"You know which one. You need to use it for the competition."

"I can't, Cade. It's yours."

"It's raw. It's real. It's perfect. Do you have music for it?"

I nodded, the melody immediately coming into my head.

"Will you play it for me?"

I blushed. "I don't really perform. I just write. These words were always meant for someone else to perform them."

"Will you play it for me?" he asked again.

I held my hand out for the notebook and he placed it there. "I actually have a second verse for it that's not in here." I pulled a page out of my nightstand drawer, immediately nervous to share.

"I won't look at you if that will help," Cade said as though reading my mind.

I pulled my guitar off the bed. "Yes. That will help."

But when I started to play, I couldn't help but look at him and when his gaze found mine, it only proved to calm me. I sang the lyrics by heart.

> "*I've turned waiting into a form of art*
> *Tied twisted lines around my broken heart*
> *To keep me hanging on for one more day*
> *I've painted on a crooked smile*
> *Hung the tears to dry awhile*
> *Because I knew that you'd come back to stay*
> *But my . . . arms are empty*
> *And my . . . heart's in pieces*
> *And my . . . soul is twisting*
> *And my . . . throat is aching*

Because I've finally woken up to find:
That I've been Left Behind."

As I started in on the second verse, my emotions closed my throat a little, making my voice husky.

"I'm done with this waiting game
My heart may never be the same
But it's time to live my life and move on.
This may have made me stronger now.
Even though I'm not quite sure how
I think it may be good that you are gone.
So my . . . arms are reaching
And my . . . heart is healing
And my . . . soul is hoping
And my . . . throat is screaming
Because I've finally woken up to find:
I can't be Left Behind."

I transitioned into the bridge, his soft stare encouraging me.

"I needed you. I wanted you. I tried to please you, but
that's no way to live. It's all up to me now, and if I see
you again soon, maybe you'll stay . . . "

I stopped playing, letting silence hang for a moment before singing the end.

324

"Now my . . . arms are stronger
And my . . . heart is beating
And my . . . soul is soaring
And my . . . throat is speaking
Because I've finally woken up to find:
I won't be Left Behind."

The last notes rang in the air for a moment before everything went still. My throat closed up even more now, with nerves.

Cade still hadn't looked away, but his playful glimmer had come into his eyes. "I think I love you."

My heart soared. "We—we need to save important admissions like that for letters," I stammered.

"Or songs."

"Yes, that would be good in a song."

"I'll write that one," he said. "It'll be a good one."

I laughed.

"No, but seriously. Who told you that you weren't meant to perform? You are amazing."

My cheeks went red.

"And that song, Lily. Please enter it. It is perfect. Will you enter the song in the contest?"

I took a deep breath. Before I could answer him, though, Jonah burst into the room.

"Wyatt stole my tooth fairy money!" he cried.

"I did not!" Wyatt said, running in after him. "He lost it."

Ashley appeared then. "Can I come in my own bedroom yet?"

I smiled at Cade in the chaos.

"Will you enter the contest?" he mouthed at me through the noise.

I nodded. I would. I couldn't wait. It didn't even matter if my song won, just knowing that I could, I would, was a huge step for me.

And then I mouthed, "I think I love you too."

ACKNOWLEDGMENTS

You'd think this would get easier the more books you have out, but in my opinion, it actually gets harder. Maybe because now I recognize more fully just how many people have helped me along this journey. Maybe because the further I get the more and more people there are involved in this process. I don't know, maybe it's because I feel very lucky to still be writing and to still have people reading what I write. Whatever the reason, I'm feeling very sentimental and thankful and terrified that I'm not feeling either of those things nearly as much as I should. Regardless, I will try to express the appropriate amount of gratitude in the couple pages that I have to do that.

First, I want to thank my family. You'd think they'd get tired of my deadlines and crazy late nights and sometimes weeks of shutting myself away from life to finish a draft. But they don't. They are very understanding and supportive and help me make the most of the times I'm not on deadline and don't have to shut myself away. So to my husband, Jared, and my kids, Hannah, Autumn, Abby, and Donavan, I love you dearly. You are my everything.

Next, I'd like to thank my agent, Michelle Wolfson. She is truly a rock star. She reads my drafts at the speed of light and as many times as I need her to, she has excellent advice, and she keeps me sane. Thanks, Michelle, you are the best.

I got to work with Aimee Friedman for this book and she is an amazing editor. It was like she had direct access to my brain. We had the same vision. That makes for a fun and easy working relationship. I'm so happy to have her. Thanks, Aimee, for making this book better than it would've been without you. You are amazing. And thanks to the rest of the Scholastic team—David Levithan, Emily Rader, Yaffa Jaskoll, Ingrid Ostby, Janelle DeLuise, Anna Swenson, Ann Marie Wong, Tracy van Straaten, Monica Palenzuela, Bess Braswell, Lauren Festa, and so many others—for all you did: a fun cover, a great copy edit, marketing, and on and on.

I got lucky in life to have some of the best friends. It helps to have friends both in and out of the writing industry. As a writer, it's nice to be able to unload some stresses on people who understand. Also, it's nice to have friends who help with reading and editing and all that other stuff that sometimes comes up at the last minute. Knowing I can count on people I love and trust to help me with these things is invaluable. Those people in my life are Candi Kennington, Jenn Johansson, Renee Collins, Natalie Whipple, Michelle Argyle, Bree Despain, and Julie Nelson. Love you ladies, so much. On the other side, having nonwriter friends keeps me balanced. My lovely ladies who get me outside my own head are Stephanie Ryan, Rachel

Whiting, Elizabeth Minnick, Brittney Swift, Mandy Hillman, Jamie Lawrence, Emily Freeman, Misti Hamel, and Claudia Wadsworth.

I also want to thank you, my readers. It means so much to me to have people from all around the world interested in reading what I write. It still feels very surreal. I make things up and people want to read them. How awesome is that? It's the coolest job in the universe (aside from colonizing Mars) and it's mine. I love it. And I love you for making it possible for me. Thank you!

And last but not least (mostly because there are too many of them for them to be "least" in anything), my huge family. People often ask me how (and why) I can write such big, crazy families in my books. It's because I have a big, crazy family. So here goes, a long list of the names that make up my family (people I see often, by the way; they aren't just family in name): Chris DeWoody, Heather Garza, Jared DeWoody, Spencer DeWoody, Stephanie Ryan, Dave Garza, Rachel DeWoody, Zita Konik, Kevin Ryan, Vance West, Karen West, Eric West, Michelle West, Sharlynn West, Rachel Braithwaite, Brian Braithwaite, Angie Stettler, Jim Stettler, Emily Hill, Rick Hill, and the twenty-five children who exist between all these people. Love you all, so much.

READ ON FOR A SNEAK PEEK AT KASIE WEST'
NEXT BOOK, *LUCKY IN LOVE!*

I pulled up Google and stared at the blank bar, wondering wh
I should enter. I typed in "Powerball numbers." A list dating bac
years came up. I entered last night's date, followed by "Powerball
The site came up in the results and I clicked on it. Then I was starir
at the numbers drawn the night before.

The first number was 2. My ticket said 2 first as well. My heart was pounding in my throat now. The next number matched as well—15. My eyes went blurry for a moment and I blinked hard, clearing them. 23. 75. 33. All matched. There was one number left on the site. A red ball. The Powerball, it was called. It was a 7. Lucky number seven. I took a deep breath and looked at my ticket. 7. All six numbers matched.

I checked them again and then a third time, just to make sure. Was this really happening? Had I just won fifty million dollars? This felt like some sort of joke. I checked the heading of the site again—Powerball. And my ticket heading, same.

I won the lottery. I just won fifty million dollars.

A scream that started in my belly and traveled up my throat burst from my mouth. I almost didn't recognize it as my own. It was a scream of pure joy.

"Maddie?" My mom was at my door, her shoes now on but untied. "What's wrong? Are you okay?"

I jumped up and down, happy yelps coming out of my mouth.

She must've realized this was a celebration of sorts because her worried look disappeared, replaced by a smile. "What's gotten into you? Oh!" She clasped her hands together. "Did you get into UCLA?" She jumped a couple times before I shook my head no. Then her jumping stopped. "This isn't about college?"

"I won!" I managed to get out even though I was now breathless.

"You won?"

My dad appeared in the doorway behind her. "Is everything okay?" he asked.

"I won!"

My brother came wandering into my room looking like he ha
just rolled out of bed. "What's going on?"

"She won something," Dad said.

"You won what?" Mom asked.

"Powerball! I just won fifty million dollars!"

My mom's smile slipped off her face and confusion took ove
"What?"

My dad crossed his arms over his chest and his expression wer
hard, like I was playing some sort of unfunny joke on him. "Bu
you've never played the lottery."

"I've never been eighteen."

Beau tilted his head and was the first to step forward. "Yo
won? Really?"

"Yes!" I held up the ticket for him to see.

He grabbed it from me and went straight to my still-open lap
top. It didn't take him nearly as long as it took me to match th
numbers. He whirled around and yelled, "She did! She won!"

Now my parents were crowded around my desk, checking ou
the site as well. Soon we were all in a tight circle jumping around.

"How did this happen?" Dad asked, and we stopped jumping fo
a minute. "When did you buy the ticket?"

"Last night. I thought it would be a fun rite of passage int
adulthood." I hadn't really thought anything of the sort. I wa
actually trying to prove a point to the insulting cashier. No, th
amazing cashier. I loved that cashier now. She was my favorite per
son ever. "I didn't think I'd win."